THE LYRIC HOTEL

THE LYRIC HOTEL

A NOVEL

SUSAN SISKO CARTER

atmosphere press

En ce moment j'ai une chambre jolie.

(At the moment I have a pretty room.)

– Arthur Rimbaud

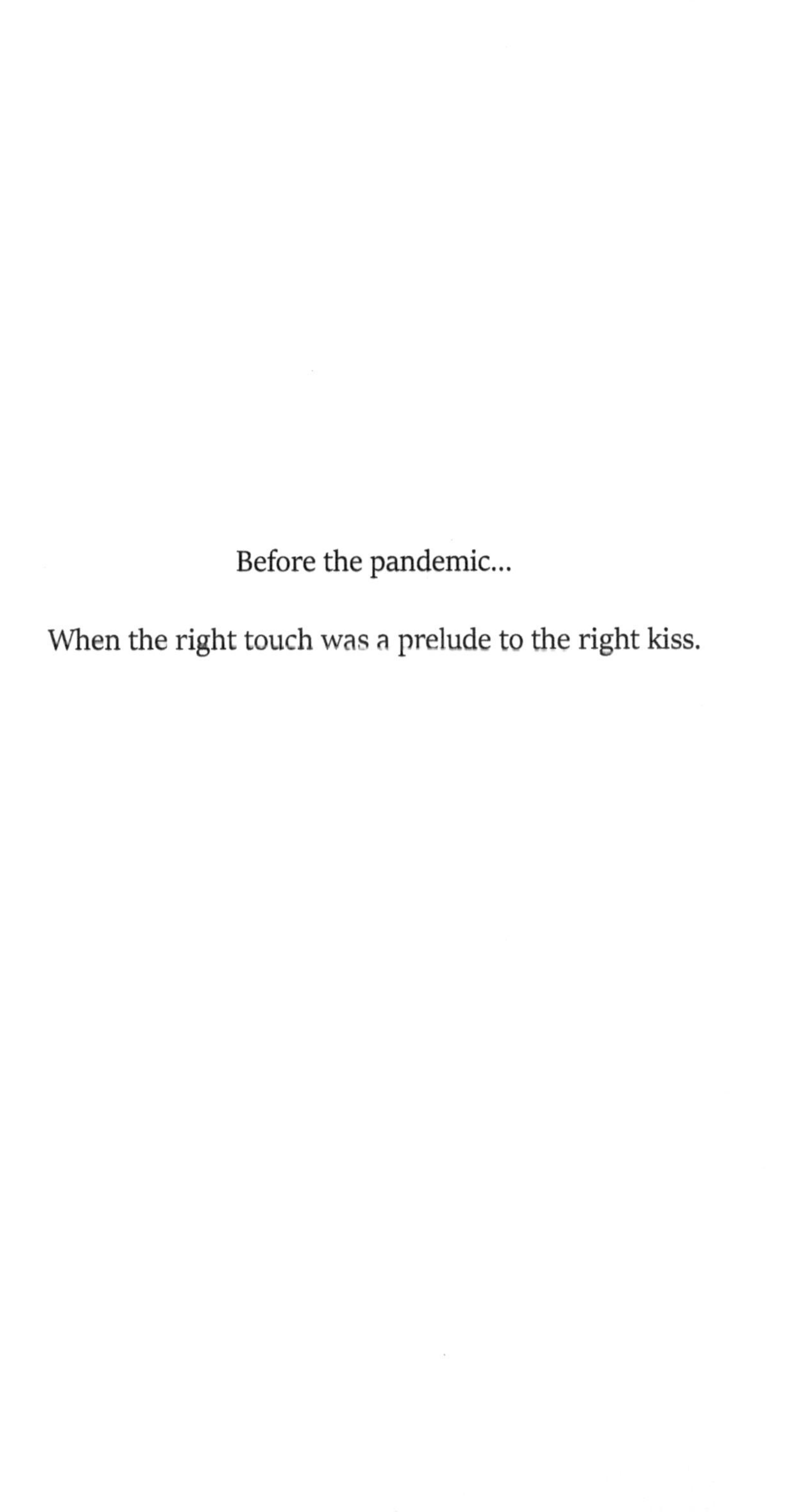

Before the pandemic...

When the right touch was a prelude to the right kiss.

1

TIMELESS

She was no Edith Piaf. At the end of Pont Notre-Dame, the second oldest bridge in Paris, an accordionist, possibly the second oldest busker in Paris, played and sang a sloppy "La Vie en Rose." But who can resist "La Vie en Rose" in Paris? Not the tourists who videoed the busker, without paying for the privilege, on iPhones sticky from Berthillon ice-cream cones. The first time Jeanette saw the accordionist was twenty-six years ago; another bridge. Same tune. She'd taken a black-and-white photo of the busker with her trusty old Canon AE-1 camera: an evocation of Paris. For years, Jeanette had displayed the photo on a shelf that was packed with LPs, beside the Miles Davis soundtrack to *Ascenseur pour l'échafaud,* its black-and-white cover featuring a sultry, French-noir-cool Jeanne Moreau. Today, Jeanette barely paid attention to the busker. But she placed a euro and her last Metro ticket inside the open accordion case.

Only six more hours and Jeanette would be on a plane, wishing she were arriving in Paris instead of leaving. It was a quick trip, three days, long enough to see her mother. And to meet with an expat ad exec about directing a commercial for a new feminine hygiene spray. Could she in sixty seconds persuade women that their vaginas would be more appealing if they smelled like room deodorizer? The ad exec would be meeting with two other candidates, both men, before he made his decision. Jeanette was the only woman being considered for the job.

She'd purchased a postcard on the rue de Rivoli: a nineteenth-century painting of a nude woman, leaning over an unmade bed, her left breast sloping toward crumpled sheets; the beige-red of her nipple the same color as her lips. Her brown hair was fastened in a loose bun and thick strands that looked damp curved her cheekbone.

Jeanette leaned against the railing of the bridge as she studied the postcard. Was the nineteenth-century woman warm from the heat of her small Paris apartment? Or because she'd just had sex? Or maybe she was simply longing for it; longing for *someone*. Perhaps, some nineteenth-century, brooding, bohemian dreamboat, she'd met while sipping absinthe at Café de Flore. One thing Jeanette was certain of: No way that woman's vagina smelled like room deodorizer.

She decided she would frame the postcard. Hang it on the wall back home in San Francisco as a reminder—longing is timeless.

2

DID I DO THAT?

Jeanette sat with her mother, outside the Café de la Paix, sharing a millefeuille and mousse cheesecake—infused with tea, mandarin, curry, and ginger—an au-revoir-Paris indulgence that Jeanette had insisted this morning she would not have time for. "Oh, darling," her mother said. "You don't have time *not* to enjoy a millefeuille on the terrace where Oscar Wilde used to dine." And how could Jeanette argue with Tess's delicious logic?

Tess was seventy-one and beautiful. Not beautiful for seventy-one. Beautiful. Period. She'd been vibrant at every age, mistaken for younger even as a teenager, radiating a luminosity, an energy that made people—who knew her age—wonder: What was her secret? "So you think you got the job?" Tess said.

"Don't think I did," Jeanette said, taking in all that she could of Place de l'Opéra and the glorious Opéra Garnier (a binge of its own kind). "I failed to convey the requisite enthusiasm for the product."

"And why *should* you have?" Tess said.

"Because I wanted the job?"

"It's good to have standards," Tess said. "Something else

will come along where you won't have to fake enthusiasm."

"That'd be refreshing," Jeanette said, smiling at the custard that oozed from the millefeuille as she cut it in half.

"I remember when you got your first job directing," Tess said. "A Tampax commercial. I asked how you felt and you said, 'Super Plus.'"

Jeanette laughed. "Sounds like me."

"You were excited. But you thought the only reason you got the job was because of Michael."

"Well...it was true."

"He never would have gone out on a limb for you, if he thought you would have made him look bad."

"This is also true. *C'est vrai*, Madame Mom." Jeanette turned from her mother's gaze to the mousse cheesecake on her plate. "Michael prefers being the one who makes himself look bad."

Tess smiled as she watched Jeanette take a forkful of cake from the side of the slice. "It tickles me...that you still eat cake from the side instead of the front."

"I've always liked narrowing it. Keeping the shape of the slice intact," Jeanette said, "for as long as I can."

"This cake *is* divine, isn't it."

"It's dreamy."

"How are things with you and Michael?"

"Not so dreamy."

A waiter approached their table, balancing a tray containing two espressos, a Campari, and two éclairs, en route to another table. "*Espresso? Café au lait, une allongé?*"

Jeanette told the waiter, *en français*: It was hard to resist an espresso at Café de la Paix...but she didn't want to arrive late at the airport and miss her plane, her voice conveying earnestness rather than pressure, her French vocabulary superior to her French grammar. "*Normalement je parle comme un femme intelligente*," she said. "Normally, I speak like an intelligent woman."

"*Vous parlez **bien** le français*," the waiter said. "*Deux espressos. Très vite.*" And off he went, hurrying past a flamboyant fashion designer who was holding up his almost-empty glass of Bordeaux, requesting another.

"On this very terrace, Jeanette...Oscar Wilde saw a golden angel floating above the opera house. Didn't matter that his angel was just the sun reflected through the mist off a golden allegorical figure," Tess said. "People around him believed his hallucinatory reverie...convincing themselves—what he saw must be." Tess brought a delectable forkful of millefeuille to her mouth as she said, "They could only see what *he* was seeing."

"Colorful Paris folklore? Or sneaky metaphor for me and Michael?"

Tess laughed. "Sneaky metaphors are in the eye of the beholder."

Jeanette smiled. "Well, you *do* have your own style of making a point."

"Colorful Paris folklore. That's all it was, dear."

The waiter returned, setting two espressos on the table.

"*Très **très** vite*," Jeanette said, surprised.

"I told the other table these were for *you*," the waiter said, his French accent thick as the crema on the espresso.

"*Je l'apprécie*," Jeanette said, delighted.

"They are Parisian," the waiter said. "They have no plane to catch."

"*Merci beaucoup*," Tess said.

"*Vous êst très gentil*," Jeanette said.

"*De rien, ma belle*," the waiter said with a wink, already on his way to another table.

"Bravo, Jeanette!" Tess said. "Not only did a French waiter bring us two espressos intended for Parisians...he enjoyed doing it."

Jeanette beamed. "Did I do that?"

"You and only you," Tess said, like the proud mother that she was. She stirred sugar into her espresso. Then, oh so casually, said: "A lot of women think of marriage as an endurance test." She sipped espresso. "I never did."

Jeanette loaded her fork with mousse cheesecake, carefully whittling the side of her narrowing slice. "I don't want to think about my marriage while I'm in Paris," she said. "I'll be home soon enough."

Tess brushed a wave of hair from her daughter's face, like she used to, when Jeanette was a little girl who had inherited her energy and spark; a little girl gifted with imagination, curiosity and wonder.

Jeannette gazed at the gilded bronze busts of Rossini, Beethoven, Mozart, and the other revered composers that adorned the top of the opera house. She saw no angels.

3

THE COLOR OF A GOOD NIGHT

Evan was dreaming. She was licking him. And she was kissing the wet trail of her tongue along his thigh.

"Happy anniversary," she said. But it wasn't *her* voice.

It was his *wife's* voice, waking him from the best part of the dream. Evan opened his eyes and saw his wife looking at his dream-induced hard-on.

"Happy anniversary, sweetie," he said, sleep in his voice, secrets in his head. He kissed his wife and tasted Listerine.

"Brush your teeth," she said. "Then come back to bed." It was a mother's advice given in the soft tone of a lover.

He got out of bed, disappointing his penis. On the way to the bathroom, his penis disappointed him, sulking and shrinking inside his paisley pj's.

He stood at the sink, squeezed toothpaste on his toothbrush, and thought: I cannot think of her. Not today; not on my anniversary. Seven years, he'd been married to Nancy. One-two-three-four-five-six-seven years.

The Seven Year Itch—he thought of that movie. With Marilyn Monroe and the famous white dress and that horny, middle-aged, married guy, all fantasy and false hope; all desperate for sex with a woman who sought relief from the summer heat by cooling her underpants in the freezer. And could you blame the married schnook? Of course you couldn't. Oh, what was the actor's name? Just last week he read about the movie in the *New York Times,* an article on Billy Wilder.

The Seven Year Itch. Is that what he had?

Tom Ewell! The actor was Tom Ewell. Well, Evan wasn't like Tom Ewell. And Jeanette wasn't like Marilyn Monroe. Jeanette didn't keep her underpants in the freezer. Although, she did wash her lace thong in the hotel ice bucket.

Yes, he'd been married to Nancy for seven years, but they lived together, first, for two. Which means, technically, today was their ninth anniversary not their seventh. Anyway, *The Seven Year Itch* was fiction.

Jeanette was real.

He was sitting on a bench outside a hotel in West Hollywood, his cello in its case on the sidewalk beside him, a Winston cigarette between his gifted fingers; blowing smoke rings toward a sad, skinny palm tree; thinking how, later, when he called his wife, she would ask if he'd been good about not smoking, and he would say, yes, he'd been very good. Perfect, in fact.

And that's when he saw her.

She was wearing a black tank top, black low-cut jeans, and Saucony running shoes, bounding up the steps of the hotel with a black mutt on a green leash, a Lab-golden retriever mix, loaded with canine charisma. Evan was immediately struck by their similarities—the dog and the woman—energetic with dark, shiny hair and smart, brown eyes, alert for play.

Evan dropped his cigarette into an empty Perrier bottle. The ember sizzled as it hit bottom, and he said: "Great dog."

"If you find me I'm lost," she said, walking toward him. "It was scribbled on his collar when I rescued this beauty-boy from the freeway."

The dog offered his paw. Evan felt the warmth of the rough paw pad against his palm.

"Al doesn't trust most men."

"Did you tell her she could call you, Al?" he said to the dog.

"Al knows you're a dog person."

"My golden. Golden retriever," he said. "Fifteen years he was my best friend. Yesterday, he..." Evan relinquished the dog's paw. "He died."

Jeanette sat on the bench beside him.

"When my dog died I..."

She put her arms around him.

"I wasn't *with* him."

Evan—he tried not to—cried into her shoulder, a shoulder that smelled of lavender and suntan lotion, and sweat at its absolute best; a shoulder soft against his mouth.

"Just let it out," she whispered.

"You call taxi?" A harsh, male voice with a Russian accent collided into her tenderness; a miserable slob, driving a Beverly Hills Cab, pulled up in front of them.

"Me," he said to the Russian, feeling like he'd just emerged from anesthesia. "I called." Evan ran his fingers through his hair, which was brown and full of untamed waves, suggesting an equally restless mind.

"You okay?" she said.

"This is"—Evan rose from the bench, clearing his throat of tears—"it's not something I do every day."

"You don't lose a best friend every day," she said, looking up at him with those smart eyes; and he could see they were wet with empathy. He figured she was thirty-nine, forty, maybe. Maybe older; probably. Evan was forty-three.

"You're sweet," he said. "Both of you." He kissed the dog's head, picked up his cello, then got into the cab.

"If you need to talk," she said, "I'm in room 144."

As the Russian pulled away from the curb, Evan leaned out the window and heard himself say, "I'm in 219."

It was later, at the recording studio, while playing cello for a rapper who was awaiting trial for murder—and who was boasting "cellos and oboes and shit" would show the world he was "sensitive as that died-deaf-motherfucker Beethoven"—that Evan realized two things: He didn't know her name; and he couldn't wait to call her.

He arrived back at the hotel at nine. Midnight in Connecticut. Still time to call his wife. He picked up the phone, dialed room 144, instead. He listened to five long rings as he paced the deodorized carpet of his junior suite.

"Hello," she said, sounding confident that whoever was calling would say something she wanted to hear.

"Hey...I met your dog, Al. Al and you. This morning outside the..."

"Hey! I'm dripping wet from the shower," she said, like it was good news. "Hold on while I put on a robe."

Evan had just enough time to picture her naked and wet, when she came back to the phone and said, "So how are you feeling?"

He picked up the complimentary In-Room-Care-Package from the kitchenette counter, peered through the cellophane envelope: four Tylenol, four adhesive bandages, two Sudafed, two Alka-Seltzer tablets, and one latex condom. "I'm okay," he said. "I'm thinking about having a drink at the bar."

"Unproductive thinking. Bar's closed," she said. "Private party."

"Well, that's hardly fair." He stepped outside onto the terrace. "Don't feel like walking to the liquor store. And the lock on my minibar's busted, so they won't stock it until it's fixed."

"My minibar's jam-packed. Come down to my room in fifteen minutes."

She hung up.

Evan felt a rush of energy...like every vitamin he'd ever taken in his life was finally working. In the distance, he could see klieg lights raking the sky over the Hollywood hills—a movie premiere, maybe, or a nightclub opening—the beginning of something new for someone out there. Evan made a decision: He would call his wife in the morning. Why take the chance of waking her?

Jeanette's black leather jacket was beside her red silk scarf on the iron post of a stand that contained a TV and the hotel's definition of a sound system. She'd only been in the junior suite for two days, but her presence enveloped it: dog on the terrace, Murakami book on the coffee table, flowers on the kitchenette counter. Her sheer satchel of dried lavender was on her pillow—massage oil on the night table. Evan noticed the bottle was two-thirds empty before he saw the small, framed needlepoint beside it. "'A place is a piece of the environment claimed by feelings'...I like that," he said.

"I try to bring a little bit of home with me wherever I am," she said, catching his gaze shifting to the bathroom—and her black lace thong, hanging on the shower rod. "If I were really home," she said, "I'd have more underpants hanging on the shower rod."

"In what city would those underpants be hanging?" he said.

"Those underpants would be hanging in San Francisco," she said, as she led the way to the minibar.

Jeanette liked living in San Francisco, although she often thought she should be living in Paris. Sometimes she felt Paris was the real home of her heart. That's what she told Evan. "Me and Jerry Lewis," she said, "we're both appreciated more in Paris."

Evan laughed. And when he told her he lived in Connecticut, she right away asked, "Is there someone in Connecticut waiting for you to come home?"

"My wife," he said. "And you?"

"No. Nobody's waiting." She unlocked the minibar, peered inside, and said to the booze bottles, "You don't wear a ring."

"Don't like anything on my fingers. I'm a cellist," Evan said, as he thought, *she has an incredible body and she's wearing a dress so I'll notice.* The last time his wife wore a dress, it was for a school function, their seven-year-old daughter's music recital—Evan couldn't remember the last time his wife wore a dress just for him.

Jeanette was wearing a violet-colored dress that clung to her curves and accentuated her breasts, which were full and bounced a little as she walked, like only real breasts can; and he was trying not to look at her nipples, which were hard as those pastel candy buttons he used to eat off paper when he was his daughter's age.

"Right. Your cello...on the sidewalk this morning," Jeanette said. "Is that why you're in L.A.?"

Evan told her about the recording session with the rapper, and that, today, he'd finished his last track so, tomorrow, he'd be going home. "You..." Evan said, as he removed two one-shot bottles of J&B from the minibar. "Why are *you* here?"

"Maybe I'm here to make you feel better."

But there was nothing overtly sexual in her voice, so Evan just said, "Well, you certainly did that this morning."

"Actually, I'm here to direct a TV commercial."

Evan noticed a long, black, dog hair on her dress. He considered brushing it off, imagining, if he did, feeling the hollow of her belly button through that clinging violet jersey.

"For Prozac," she said.

Evan laughed. "The antidepressant?"

She told him she'd been scouting locations and had found the perfect carousel in Santa Monica. "Just right for a Prozac-popping mommy and her twin daughters who Mommy no longer wants to sell to the highest bidder. Because Mommy has lost her edge—and the world is a better place without it."

"Boy, you're here to make everyone feel good, aren't you?"

"I'm on a mission," she said. "But unlike Prozac...I'll never give you constipation, yawn, or tremors."

"You're funny. A funny woman."

"My side effects are only pleasant ones."

Jeanette took his hand, studying his fingers like she was about to read his palm. She inserted his middle finger into her mouth, sucked the length of it; slowly; sliding it in and out between her lips. Evan moaned softly; she released his finger. "I just wanted to see what the fingers of a cellist tasted like."

"And how do they taste?"

"I detect notes of caramel *and* Camille Saint-Saëns."

He laughed. So did she.

"I'm married... I have certain boundaries," he said. Although, he'd never allowed himself to be in a situation where he'd had to define them.

"I can respect that," she said, opening a mini bottle of J&B. "So we'll just drink and talk. How does that sound?"

"Sounds good," he said. "Tell me something about you that you think I should know."

"My black lace thong...hanging on the shower rod?"

"Uh huh," he said, excited by her words and how she said them.

"This morning, I washed my black lace thong in the ice bucket. Can I trust you with that information?"

"Your secret's safe with me," he said. "That's quite a dress you have off."

She laughed.

"Did I say off? I meant on...I think."

"The French have a phrase for this color," she said. "*La couleur d'une bonne nuit.*"

"*La couleur d'une bonne nuit?*"

"The color of a good night."

Evan accidentally stepped on a dog toy, a plastic hamburger; it squeaked.

"Squeaks happen," she said.

"They do," he said. His hands moved gently down the sides of her clinging dress to her waist, and the curves of her hips. "A man designed the cello...so he made it in the shape of a woman."

"You know, the tone of a cello always gets to me," she said. "No matter how closed down I'm feeling."

"The tone is in the fingers." He kissed her; a tender kiss that lingered long enough to build. The kiss led to another. And another kiss led to the king bed.

Ten minutes later, Jeanette's dress was still on, but it was above her thighs, and Evan's gifted fingers were inside her.

She moaned, then said, "I know what you're doing."

"What am I doing?" he said, barely above a whisper, his finger tracing her nipple.

"You're playing me. Aren't you?"

His fingers induced a tone of ecstasy from her.

"I am your rare and valuable instrument," she said.

＊

What they did was sexual. Extremely sexual. But it did not constitute an affair. True, Evan made Jeanette moan like she didn't care if she woke every guest in the hotel. "I want you inside me," she said. "I am inside you...fingers and tongue *count*," he said, Jeanette laughing and climaxing simultaneously. Evan had denied himself the pleasure of fucking a fantastic woman, for Chrissake. And why? Because the only woman he'd give that much of himself to was his wife. By denying himself he had remained loyal—hadn't he? *I did not have sex with that director of Prozac commercials*—and suddenly he understood Bill Clinton's rationalization for Lewinsky-head...like comprehending the lyrics of a complex song years after the initial listening (kind of like that, yeah).

Evan had defined his boundaries, and now he was defining his right to define them. He had no regrets. Except, maybe one:

"How far is Connecticut from Manhattan?" Jeanette asked, as she zipped Evan's jeans. If he took the train from Greenwich, he told her, he could get there in forty-three minutes. "That quick, huh? Because I'll be in New York," she said, tucking her phone number inside his hip pocket. "Soon."

Evan wrote on a hotel dry-cleaning form. Beside the warning: SHIRTS WITH POLYESTER WILL NOT HOLD STARCH, he wrote his cellphone number.

Maybe he shouldn't have done that.

✳✳✳

"I don't say every vacation should be separate."

Aldo, the Sicilian owner of Evan and Nancy's favorite Italian restaurant in Greenwich, was still in love with his wife after thirty-two years, which is why he was divulging the secret of marital bliss as he poured champagne into their flutes. "The more you miss..." he advised with a conspiratorial wink, "the more you kiss."

Evan leaned across the linen tablecloth, past a lit candle and a red rose; he kissed his wife. Their tongues met in their mouths like old friends at a familiar hangout.

Nancy broke the kiss.

"Evan spent more time on the road this year than he did at home," she told Aldo.

"And look at you two lovebirds," Aldo said, placing the champagne bottle into a silver ice bucket. "You are more in love than ever."

"I love my pearls," Nancy said to Evan. She was wearing the pearl necklace that Evan had given her in the morning after pancakes.

Evan flicked a crumb of focaccia from the navy-blue turtleneck that Nancy had finished knitting just hours ago—it was too small—so he could wear it to dinner. He looked into her eyes, same blue as his eyes. So identical, Evan and Nancy were often mistaken for brother and sister. "I love my sweater," he said.

He shouldn't have eaten dessert, but he'd ordered the soufflé during the main course, when he was hungry, which is why at ten past midnight—ten past his anniversary—Evan was walking in his beautiful and silent neighborhood; he was stuffed. And he was dialing his cell, stopping in front of a large, overgrown lawn that sloped gracefully toward, what used to be, a charming home. The old couple, who'd built it in 1949, had sold their dream house to a young couple who'd torn it down. The young couple divorced. Now, all that existed of either couple's dream was the frame, baseboards, front door, and, in the space that used to be a living room, the one surviving relic of the old couple's home: a brick fireplace with an oak mantle.

No matter how many times Evan passed it, he felt sad; sad for a house that had been destroyed by a marriage that had been destroyed. Except, tonight, he wasn't thinking about the house; he was thinking about the woman whose voice he was hearing on his phone.

"Hello," Jeanette said.

He'd been certain she would call. *Worried* she would call. But she hadn't. Now here he was, watching his breath drift like smoke toward a full moon, heart pounding against his too-small sweater, as he said, "Hey, Jeanette! It's your...your hotel friend."

His voice was loud in the night's stillness, so he spoke softer, "It's Evan...calling from Connecticut."

"Hey...I was just thinking about you," she said, sounding even better than the woman who'd been living inside his head for the past two months. "Thinking how good you made me feel."

Evan laughed. "Then we were thinking the same thing."

His cell beeped.

"My phone's dying," he said. "So this'll have to be quick."

"I'm leaving my husband," she said.

"What?" he asked, even though he'd heard what she said.

"We've been together since I was twenty-three."

"You didn't tell me...tell me you were married."

"I'm a private person."

Evan didn't know what to say, so he said nothing.

"Hello?" Jeanette said. "You still there?"

"I'm here."

"You stirred everything up."

"I hope I, I hope you're not saying I had anything to do with—"

"I'm coming to New York next week. Be great to see you."

"I'll be on the road," he said, sounding oddly flat and distant. "I'm starting a tour...tomorrow."

"Any chance you'll be playing San Francisco?"

"I don't have all the dates yet," he said, lying, knowing that's why he'd called her: to tell her he was coming to San Francisco, tell her he wanted to see her. "Why didn't you tell me you were married?"

"You made me feel like I wasn't."

His cell beeped.

"Evan?"

His cell beeped again.

"You were my *detonator*."

His cell died.

Evan the Detonator walked, crunching parched maple leaves beneath his boots. He walked past cherry trees, ancient oaks, and silver maples; past long driveways leading to expensive homes, dark inside with families sleeping. He walked through a small apple orchard to a lovely farmhouse that Evan and Nancy couldn't afford to buy but lived in, the house that Nancy had inherited from her mother; the house where Nancy grew up, with logs in the fireplace and photographs on the mantle.

"Someday," Nancy had assured Evan, "the memories in this house will be *our* memories."

Evan the Detonator opened the door. Nancy was lying on the sofa, wearing a flannel nightshirt patterned with breakfast food: bacon, eggs, toast, a stack of pancakes on the breast pocket.

"You look awful," she said, muting the TV with the remote.

"Too much of a good thing," he said. "I shouldn't have had the soufflé."

A commercial was on for Prozac. A blissed-out mommy, riding a carousel with her twin daughters. Evan watched the mommy's soundless mouth laugh.

He watched his wife's mouth. He thought she was saying something about the soufflé being too heavy. But he wasn't sure. He was listening to Jeanette—inside his head—and she was saying:

"Unlike Prozac, I'll never give you constipation, yawn, or tremors...my side effects are only pleasant ones."

He checked his gifted fingers to see if they were shaking. They weren't.

4

MESSAGE IN A FIFTH

Michael's arm dangled from the hammock, an empty tumbler in his hand, a half-empty fifth of Ballantine's Finest, within reaching distance, on the brick patio of a house that was dark on the sunniest of days. The house in San Francisco was an oddball home of charm and quirk, built in 1920, with a treacherous staircase spiraling down to the bedroom.

Jeanette watched her husband from the kitchen window. She looked past the magenta impatiens that bloomed in the planter box in optimistic defiance of the gray day. The hammock swayed slowly toward the herb garden, then back to the marigolds and geraniums. Michael's fingers felt for the bottle; the fifth of Ballantine rolled across the brick into the dirt, among the Borinda bamboo shoots, like a bottle washed to shore—a bottle containing a message.

***

She'd wanted to tell him yesterday, but decided it would be better to tell him when he wasn't drunk. This morning, he was battling a merciless hangover, drinking black coffee while engrossed in the sports section of the *San Francisco Chronicle*. Jeanette sat across from Michael at the circular, scarred, wooden dining table that they had bought twenty-five years ago for their first apartment—before they were married, but living together because they couldn't stand being apart.

Jeanette stared at her untouched oatmeal; Michael had finished his. They sat in silence...long enough for Al to slurp his entire bowl of water.

"Michael."

"Two more paragraphs," Michael said, his bloodshot eyes fixed on the newspaper.

"I can't wait two more paragraphs."

But he could. She finished her coffee, watching him read like she wanted to swat the newspaper from his hand.

"I can't do it anymore," she said.

Michael put down the paper. "I'm all yours."

The irony of his words at this moment was not lost on her.

"I can't keep thinking we'll somehow be happy in the future. Because we used to be happy in the past."

Michael padded into the kitchen, arms stretched out in front of him, imitating a sleepwalker. "Must...have...more...caffeine." She followed him, as he headed straight for the espresso machine—she bought it for him five years ago—a present for a year of sobriety.

"I can't keep deluding myself," she said.

"If this is about my drinking in the afternoon, yesterday"— he spooned coffee beans into the grinder—"I drank because I'm stopping for good on Monday."

"So many Mondays, Michael."

"I mean it. You'll see."

She gave him a skeptical look worthy of Kamala Harris.

"*Believe* in me, Jen." His need for her to believe in him segued seamlessly into his need to charm her: "How about I make you another cappuccino?" he said, a smile with a motive sneaking onto his tired face. "If you're not happy with it, I won't charge you."

She almost smiled. "Yeah...sure," she said. "Do you know how long it's been?" She raised her voice over the shrillness of coffee beans being pulverized. "Since I felt any **passion** from you?"

He stopped the grinder. Spooned the ground beans into the machine. "You're the one who encouraged me to go on antidepressants."

"What?"

"Antidepressants. I did it for you. I ruined our sex life for *you.*"

"You ruined our sex life for *me*?"

"Love means never having to have a hard-on."

"Ah, Michael...Jesus. I'm not just talking about your disinterest in sex. I'm talking about your disinterest in *life.*"

"You know..." he said, as he steamed milk. "You haven't exactly been a woman lately who oozes sexual allure."

Yeah? Well, tell that to the musician who gave me two orgasms in my hotel room before I even took off my dress. That's what she wanted to say.

What she said was: "The last time I wore a sexy dress for you...you didn't even look at me long enough to pause Netflix."

"Do you remember what I was watching?"

His answer was so *him.* It pissed her off yet, somehow, reminded her of something that she loved about him.

"All I know is..." she said, "you weren't watching me."

"Well, this is a great strategy to help me stop drinking."

He handed her the cappuccino he'd made for her. "Thanks," she said, as they sat back down at the table. Jeanette stared into his failed attempt at latte art, a steamed-milk heart that looked like a kite missing its string. "I want—"

"November 27, 1993," Michael said, gazing at a date that was faintly carved into the wooden tabletop. "Remember how mad I was at myself for writing a check for the table *on* the table... damaging it before it even left the shop? But you thought it was hilarious."

Was he trying to make it harder for her than it already was?

"I'll never forget what you said, Jen. You said, 'It's like notarizing a memory. But the fingerprints come later.'"

"I want a divorce," Jeanette said.

Whatever bravado Michael's hangover had allowed him, evaporated.

"You knew this day was coming," she said. "Didn't you know, Michael?"

She waited for him to speak. But he took a sip of the cappuccino that he'd made for her; set the cup back down in front of her.

"I was young when we met," she said. "One day I'll be old." She ran her hand along the date carved into the table. "I'm afraid there'll be nothing of me in between."

Michael just leaned his head into his hands.

It was too cold a night to be standing beneath a starless sky, wearing a thin sweater and no coat. Jeanette shivered as she leaned into the open passenger window of Michael's SUV. "I'll be here when you get home," she said. "Here to help you pack."

Michael's hands gripped the wheel like he was already driving and focusing on traffic. He looked at her as if he was about to say something. He didn't.

"We're not going to be like those couples who stop talking to one another," she said. She watched her husband drive away.

5

CHECKING IN

If this were a movie, she thought, there would be a *TIME DISSOLVE:* a black screen to show that time had passed, maybe the amount of time in white letters over the black. Time passed from what? From which jolt? Which altering of sameness? Which reshaping of the person she'd become as if she had nothing to do with the design of her own being?

Jeanette and Al stood outside the hotel. The exact spot where she'd met Evan eight months ago—could it be eight months already? (Her sense of time was way out of whack.) She would have figured him for a musician even without his cello, staring into space with a tranquil focus, looking like he'd just woken up and had combed his restless hair with his fingers.

She counted the rooms that had lights on at midnight. Nine; three with the drapes open. On the first floor, a man wearing only a towel clicked a remote at the TV, bringing Jeanette back to the present like he'd changed a channel of her life. In the room next door, a long-haired, pale guy rolled a joint on a round, glass table while another long-haired, pale guy smoked one. And on the third floor...a man kissed the shoulder of a woman who was wearing only a black bra.

The woman closed the drapes.

"Here you go, sir," the Graveyard Guy said, offering a guest a roll of adhesive tape.

The rapper reached across the front desk, a tattoo so fresh on his buffed arm it was wet, shielded by Saran. "Just had it done," he told Jeanette as she approached the desk.

"What's it say?" She tried to decipher the tat: words—plenty of them—from his shoulder to his wrist.

"Letter my father wrote me," the rapper said. "Just before he passed."

"A loving tribute," Jeanette said.

The rapper nodded in agreement as he removed a white cloth from the hip pocket of his sagging jeans. He placed it over the Saran, struggling with the adhesive tape. "Tat got to be protected so it don't smear."

"Let me help you with that," Jeanette said, knowing that if she saw this man at midnight on a San Francisco sidewalk, she would not be doing what she was doing now: taping cloth around his tat like she was bandaging a wound.

"Bless your rare and beautiful soul," the rapper said. He sauntered to the elevator.

"I'm checking in," Jeanette said to the Graveyard Guy. "Jeanette Coles."

"Welcome back, Ms. Coles." The Graveyard Guy entered her arrival on the computer. "Room 144 is available as per your request," he said. "Just let us know when you have a departure date."

A musician dashed past her, his red hair streaming down the encased guitar strapped to his back. She watched him hurry out the door to an idling cherry-colored, chrome-trimmed, Provost tour bus.

"Departure?" Jeanette said, as she turned to the Graveyard Guy. "I don't know when I'll be checking out."

She only knew why she was checking in.

LYRIC HOTEL

GUEST FOLIO

MS. JEANETTE COLES ARRIVAL: August 25, 2019

DEPARTURE: OPEN

She listened to the soft, steady hoot of the owl until she realized it wasn't an owl. It was a woman. Woman moaning.

"Oooh....Oooh."

Jeanette heard a man's voice. He said something to the
woman that made her laugh. Then he did something to the
woman that made her moan again. On the other side of the
wall—the other side of the wrought iron headboard—a man
and a woman were having sex; sex at three in the morning.

And here was Jeanette, naked in the dark, alone on a king
bed, listening to the urgency of another woman's yearning;
the rhythm of another woman's pleasure, her soft moans es-
calating, then fading; subsiding...commencing again; a slow
crescendo like a DJ was mixing a track of her passion.

Not fair. Not on her first night back at the hotel. Not fair at
all—that she was anticipating another woman's moans...their
duration lengthening, the silences between them lessening, until there were no silences, just one sustained moan that spilled
into a word—"God."

"Woman Finds God in Hotel Room," Jeanette said in the
dark. She listened for more sex; the hum of the refrigerator
in her kitchenette underscored the post-coital quiet next door.
She put her hand between her legs.

Nope.

Jeanette had her standards. She would not feed off the scraps
of another woman's passion—let herself be fucked by her own
imagination—not when the woman on the other side of the wall
was spent from the real thing.

She reached across the night table for the light, knocked
over a prescription bottle of lorazepam, the anti-anxiety tablets she rarely took but kept close by—just in case.

Al opened his eyes.

"It's okay," she assured her best friend who would make a
fine, young, handsome man for some lucky woman, if only he
were a man instead of a dog. "Everything's okay, Al."

Al looked at Jeanette from his bed like he didn't believe her—

he saw right through her.

Jeanette removed the plastic cap from the prescription bottle, shook out a tablet. She stared at the pill in the palm of her hand. Did she really need a sedative, tonight? Anxiety was encroaching. But just because someone you don't want to see knocks on your door, that doesn't mean you have to open it. After all, she was the doorman of her own mind. Doorman and bouncer. She could control which thoughts got in; kick out the ill-behaved ones. Right? She put the pill back into the bottle. Snapped on the cap. Shut off the light.

"*Some* things are okay," she told the dog in the dark.

6

DO NOT TRUST YOUR JUDGMENT

The counselor sat beneath a water-stained, cottage-cheese ceiling. Jeanette wasn't looking at the counselor; her gaze was fixed on the lone stab at cheer in the small dim room: a purple orchid in a green, cracked, plastic pot, perched on an ashtray stand. Two blossoms had survived, but the other two had fallen from their stems—or had made a suicide pact, preferring to leap to the carpet rather than live in this gloom, Jeanette thought, just before she said, "I want to sell the house."

"You need to give it at least a year before you make any important decisions," the counselor said, her drab hair, parted down the middle, exposing gray roots, clusters of them, inching their way south to the ends where it was dry. Lifeless.

The four other women in the group nodded agreement like they were about to cry—cry for Jeanette, cry for themselves; pain embedded in their faces.

"Well, I'm not living in the house right now," Jeanette said. "I'll rent it out." Jeanette saw unanimous disapproval on the women's faces, so she added: "Furnished."

"It's only been six months," the counselor said. "Six months since your husband died."

Jeanette's mother had talked her into this. "A bereavement group might be cathartic, darling," her mother had urged. "Just try it...try it once."

Well, she was trying it. And she wanted to beeline for the door—race into sunlight. The despair in this room was contagious, a defeated energy that threatened her emotional immune system.

Get me outta here.

"Do not trust your judgment," a widow, whose husband had drowned eighteen months ago, cautioned.

Well, that's some messed up advice. Who knows what I need more than me?

"Being a sudden widow...it's treacherous," a widow for eight months, said.

And Jeanette noticed that the woman had a—widow's peak. "My situation, it's, it's different than yours."

"Every loss is different, Jeanette," the counselor said.

"How did your husband die?" said the young widow, whose husband died on their honeymoon.

"How?" Jeanette said. "Why is it when someone tells us a person that they loved died... we immediately ask *how*?"

They all looked at her, waiting for her to tell them...how.

She didn't want to talk about—how Michael's SUV (the SUV he'd refused to sell) had flipped over. She didn't want to talk about—how, maybe, if she hadn't told him, the day before: she wanted a divorce...maybe, he wouldn't have crashed into a phone pole to avoid an oncoming truck so he could get home. Home to her, where she was waiting to help him pack.

She didn't want to talk about—how in all her imagined scenarios of separation, she never imagined Michael disappearing from her life so completely.

And she didn't want to talk about—how her husband had deprived her of being single on her terms...which didn't include the concept: widow.

So, she simply answered, "Car accident."

"I'm finally beginning to forgive my husband for the love letters I found in his bowling bag," a widow told the counselor.

*Love letters in a bowling bag. Now that **is** sad.*

"A man wrote me a love letter once," the widow said, "but I didn't sleep with him. I was faithful."

I was faithful too, Jeanette thought. Except for her night with Evan, when she'd wanted—needed—the musician to fuck her...but he didn't.

Michael had been a faithful husband; she believed that. She even believed it three years ago.

When he was sprawled on the Art Deco sofa, watching a bum sprawled on a park bench—the movie, *The Conversation*—as Jeanette entered the den, which was dark at two in the afternoon. And Michael was speaking her favorite line along with the actress, Cindy Williams, "He was once somebody's baby boy."

"Chlamydia," Jeanette said.

Michael freeze-framed the bum. "What?"

"Chlamydia. The gyno said I've got it." Jeanette tossed her purse onto the Stickley rocker. A lipstick fell out, rolling across the hardwood floor, careening into a dusty clump of dog hair. "Just be honest with me—have you had sex with another woman?"

Their ancient springer spaniel, Etta, gnawed at her paw, her teeth click-clacking like castanets.

"No," he said, nudging the spaniel's paw with his slipper.

"Are you saying no to Etta? Or no to me?"

"I'm saying no to you." His voice was calm, certain; the voice that had assured clients: his ad agency could seduce consumers into buying products they didn't need or want. "Now *you* be honest with *me*."

"Have *I*? Have I had *sex* with a man...man besides *you*?" She was aware that her voice had escalated a notch in volume and pitch, sounding as if she were lying. "No," she said, in her normal timbre. "Of course, course I haven't."

They were locked in a staredown, knowing an averted glance might be construed as a guilty plea.

"Maybe you can get chlamydia without having sex," Michael said.

"How can you get a sexually transmitted disease without having sex?"

"Call your gyno, ask her. Call her now."

But the gyno was delivering a baby—*somebody's baby boy?* A nurse took Jeanette's call: "Have you been in a swimming pool or hot tub lately?"

"A hot tub! Yes!" Jeanette said, like she'd just won a day at a spa during an NPR pledge drive.

"Because sometimes chlamydia can be transmitted in a hot tub, if it's improperly chlorinated."

"Then it's possible? Possible to get chlamydia without having sex?"

"It's possible," the nurse said. "Sometimes."

So, they blamed the chlamydia on a slutty hot tub; they took antibiotics, and the sexually transmitted disease that wasn't transmitted by sex became history. She believed he'd been faithful because she'd trusted him. And because the antidepressant he'd been taking for two years had wiped out his sex drive.

"My husband's hair…it's still in his brush," the honeymoon widow was saying, summoning Jeanette back to the purple orchid in the green, cracked plastic pot. "I should throw out his brush. But I can't."

Michael's hairbrush—suddenly it was in her mind, vivid as a photograph—strands of his hair tangled in his brush on the bathroom sink, beside her hairbrush. How long had it taken her to throw out his brush? Two weeks?

"When you're ready to say goodbye to his hairbrush," the counselor said, "you'll know."

The widows nodded.

"I feel for you. Really, I do," Jeanette said. "But I don't belong here."

"Everyone here is in the same boat," the counselor said.

"No, no. My boat is very different. I'm the only person here who wanted a life separate from her husband *before* he died."

The widows looked at Jeanette like she'd betrayed them.

"Where are you living, now, Jeanette?" the counselor said.

"A hotel."

"A hotel?" the counselor said. "That can be very lonely."

"It's the last place I felt truly alive."

Jeanette wasn't looking at the counselor as she answered her. She was transfixed on an orchid blossom...falling from its stem, leaving one lone blossom. "This blossom left on the stem," she said. "It's a metaphor. A beautiful fucking metaphor."

They all looked at the orchid blossom, confused.

"A survivor left to bloom on its own. Like me. I want to *bloom*," Jeanette told the group. "I want to bloom like this determined blossom!"

She wondered if it needed plant vitamins. Maybe it was thirsty. She removed her water bottle from her bag. She looked back at the surviving blossom...just as it fell to the carpet.

Jeanette bolted from the chair. All eyes were on her as she hurried out the door.

7

RUBBERS

Oversized tip intensifies sensation for both partners. Reservoir end for added comfort.

The last time Jeanette had sex with a guy who used a condom she was a teenager.

A sensuous extra of ribs and dots. Much like skin itself.

At eighteen, she went on the pill; at twenty-four, she traded the risks of the pill for an IUD.

Contoured shape for a better fit. Orange, banana, and strawberry add flair to your sexual experience.

At twenty-six, she had the IUD removed because she couldn't endure the cramps and heavy periods that barely ended before beginning again.

Over 300 passion xxx's designed to stimulate both partners' most sensitive areas.

Jeanette and Michael were both anti-diaphragm, spontaneity difficult enough to muster, what with the routine of marriage and work and Michael more strategist than in-the-moment guy.

Ultra frictional sensation.

Michael refused to wear condoms. All those years they had sex as husband and wife, Michael pulled out early.

An unmatched exquisite sliding. Jelly-like water-soluble lubricant for a natural feeling.

Now here she was, three months shy of forty-nine—how did *that* happen?—perusing the "Family Planning" aisle of CVS Pharmacy, shopping for condoms, dizzied by her choices.

Heads up every time so there's no fumbling around. Ultra sensitive with spermicide.

"Enhanced pleasure...can't reach it," the bland, sparkless girl said, as she halted her cart beside Jeanette. She was twenty-one, if that, the drawstring of her navy-blue exercise pants dangling, untied, beneath a T-shirt featuring a litter of kittens. "Condoms," she said, pointing to a package that promised *Enhanced Pleasure.*

Jeanette noticed the girl's breath smelled like Reese's Peanut Butter Cups.

"The word—condom...it's so clinical," Jeanette told the girl with peanut-butter-cup breath. "I prefer the word 'rubber.'" She handed the girl the package.

"Thanks," the girl said.

"What about you? You ever call them rubbers?"

"My mother does," the girl said.

"'Alternating rows of raised bumps and ridges for her. Roomy at the tip for him.'" Jeanette mulled the pledge on another package. "So many choices," she said. "How do you decide which kind?"

The girl shrugged. "Figure I might as well try 'em all." She tossed into her cart: *High Sensation...Natural Feeling...Ultra Texture.*

"Your boyfriend," Jeanette said, "does he have a favorite?"

"He likes *Extra Thin Lubricated,*" she said with zero enthusiasm. She threw a pack of her boyfriend's favorite into her cart, along with a box that boasted 45 CONDOMS FOR THE PRICE OF 26! Then embellished the collection: *America's Favorite Condom, Assorted Lubricated,* and—why not?—*Pleasure Mesh.*

Jeanette wondered if the girl had a special cupboard just for condoms and Reese's Peanut Butter Cups. She grabbed a package from the shelf. "'Thin and ribbed for mutual sensation.' Something to strive for," she said, imitating the girl's nonchalance, as she tossed the rubbers into her empty cart.

The Persian clerk was tired and bored as he rang up Jeanette's purchases on the register. He couldn't care less that she was spending forty-two dollars on condoms.

✳✳✳

"Hello! You've reached the hotel message center," a woman's digitalized voice, reeking of professional cheer, greeted Jeanette. "You have one new message. The message is..."

"My legs are lonely." It was a young woman's voice—sleepy; needy.

Jeanette put the woman with lonely legs on the speakerphone.

"Where *are* you, Keith? It's me...Nessa."

Jeanette folded the pink flowered bedspread, careful not to look at the quilted lining where stains immune to dry-cleaning often lurked; souvenirs of more than one guest's pleasure, or pain; or both.

"When I left your room you said you'd call, call tomorrow. And now tomorrow...tomorrow is *yesterday*."

Jeanette stripped the hotel sheets from the bed.

"Call me, call. You said it was you know...special. You said we—"

BEEP! The machine aborted Nessa's need.

"The woman with lonely legs was connected to the wrong room," Jeanette told Al. The dog was curled up like a furry cashew on an easy chair. "Or worse...Keith checked out and didn't even say goodbye." Jeanette put the ivory-colored sateen sheets

38

she'd brought from home on the bed. "You'd never check out of the hotel without saying goodbye to me, would you, Al?"

Al looked at her like he understood every word. She kissed his canine cheek. Saw her framed needlepoint on the table beside the lorazepam: *A place is a piece of the environment claimed by feelings.*

Talk about a piece of the environment claimed by feelings. She could almost smell the desire in her junior suite—if it weren't for the artificial scent of deodorizer that Housekeeping so generously sprayed to rid the rooms of olfactory-ghosts—scent of vagina and penis; sweat and cum: the funky bouquet of lust.

Jeanette emptied her CVS bag of rubbers into the drawer of the night table. Then she wrote on a hotel pad with a hotel pen: MY LEGS ARE LONELY.

8

DISCOUNTED CUPIDS

Evan's breath smelled like Listerine; just like his wife's breath. He tossed his pj's onto the oak rocker—where Nancy's mother used to breastfeed her—then slipped into bed, beneath the summer comforter.

"I should shave my legs," Nancy said, smoothing her shins below the cotton nightshirt, which was patterned with cupids. "They're so hair—"

Evan muted his wife's admittance of hairy legs with a kiss. He looked into her blue eyes and said, "When was the last time I made you moan?"

"Where did *that* come from?"

"I was just trying to remember the last time I made you moan."

"I moan."

"I mean *really moan*?"

"You expect me to *really moan* with our seven-year-old daughter in the next room?"

"I'm not talking about when Sarah's in her room. You know what I mean."

Their daughter was spending the night at a friend's house so Evan and Nancy could be alone—just the two of them—since he was leaving in the morning for a short road trip.

"This is so not the time for us to be having this conversation," Nancy said.

Evan propped his pillow against the oak headboard. He stared at the drawn, white curtains, thick enough for privacy, thin enough to let the light in. That's what Nancy said when she'd arrived home with the fabric it had taken her a year to find, and Evan was too busy packing for his summer tour with Bjork to care.

Nancy moistened her fingertip with saliva, dabbed at a stain of strawberry jam on her pajamas right on the tip of a cupid's arrow. "Brand new," she said. "I hope this comes out in the wash."

"If it doesn't it's in the perfect spot."

"Expensive nightshirt."

"Cupids are overrated," Evan said.

"I didn't buy it because of the cupids. I bought it because it's beautiful cotton. On sale, 25 percent off."

"You just said it was expensive."

"It was expensive, even at 25 percent off."

"Discounted cupids," Evan said with a laugh. But he was thinking: discounted romance.

Nancy peered at the strawberry stain like she was still wondering if it would come out in the wash as she said, "Want me to rub your back?"

"Only if you *want* to rub my back."

She scratched the stain with the nail of her pinky. "Why would I ask if I didn't want to rub it?"

Nancy massaged Evan's back for five minutes.

They had sex.

Neither of them moaned.

They slept facing opposite walls, enough space between their hips for a dog to lie between them, if they still had one.

9

WATCHING THE DETECTIVE

The tour manager gulped vodka and tonic at the bar. "Barely out of their teens on their first tour," he said. "I'm too old for this." He was hovering around forty-eight.

"What's it like?" the doughy man beside him said. "Being a tour manager for a rock group?"

"My last gig was more my style...Lyle Lovett."

"Lyle Lovett, huh?" The doughy man wiped his horn-rimmed glasses with a cocktail napkin. "Heard through the grapevine he's interested in antique money. That true?"

"I wouldn't know."

"Reason I'm asking is that's a sideline of mine—old money...buy and sell it."

The third man at the bar chimed in, "And when you're not buying and selling old money?"

"I'm a market research manager. For Michelin Tires."

"So you're the Michelin Man," Jeanette said, as she took a seat at the end of the bar.

"Michelin Man has a more defined chin," the doughy man said.

Jeanette couldn't argue with him; not much chin beneath his crooked teeth. She ordered a glass of Cab.

"Your favorite seat has been waiting for you," the Filipino bartender said, a welcome-back smile on her pleasant, round face.

"You remember?" Jeanette said, pleased.

"I remember you like to watch the hallway...see the people."

"Nothing slips by Angie," the tour manager said.

"Been at this hotel nineteen years is why. I see a lotta people come back."

"I remember this place when it was the LeeRick apartments," the tour manager said. "Lee and Rick...the original owner's sons."

"He kept the name when it became a hotel," Angie said. "Until his divorce...terrible. His wife turned Lee and Rick against him." Angie set a glass of Cabernet on the bar for Jeanette. "Reason he changed it from *LeeRick* to *Lyric*."

"That a fact?" the Michelin Man said. "Name sure seems to attract musicians."

"Musicians don't care about the name," Jeanette said, crossing her legs, exposing a hint of thigh through threadbare jeans—not $200 jeans that *looked* worn—jeans that had aged, naturally, right along with her. "They care about price and vibe."

"Why are *you* at the hotel?" the third man at the bar said to Jeanette, shifting his chair for a better view of her.

She got up from the bar with her wine. "Now that I'm not at liberty to say."

"Mysterious," he said.

She walked through the small restaurant: just ten tables, coffee table wedged between a gas fireplace and a love seat, easy chair at either end. Jeanette sat on the love seat.

Sip.

Sip.

Sip.

Three sips of Cabernet.

And the man who'd pronounced her mysterious was standing at the love seat with a martini, telling her he was a photographer, shooting pictures for a book, the reason he was staying at the hotel until tomorrow night. "Now it's *your* turn," he said. He flicked a switch on the wall and—presto!—blue flames hissed beneath fake logs. "Why are you here?"

Her eyes met his stare. "I'm a private investigator," she said, surprising herself more than the photographer.

"Really?" he said, intrigued.

Before she could say, "I'm kidding," he said, "I've never met a real-life private investigator before."

"We keep a low profile," she said. "Nature of the beast."

He sat on the adjacent cushion of the love seat. "Can I ask what you're working on?"

"Maybe I'm here *tailing* you."

Jeanette watched him considering that possibility.

He laughed, dismissing it.

She was about to reveal something that *was* true: Her father had been a photographer; he'd shot a couple of classic album covers while art director for a major label. But that would encourage questions. And she didn't want to give answers. So, she rattled off some of her favorite photographers—Herman Leonard, Ruth Orkin, Guy Le Querrec, Lynn Goldsmith—deciding if she was attracted to him, tallying her observations: Greek...or Italian? Brown eyes, dark brown, watching her watch him. Probably her age, although he looked older (most people her age looked older—to her, anyway); spiky hair, salt and pepper; height five feet seven, max; expensive black jacket, black shirt, black pants; thin lips; bump on the bridge of his nose (possible souvenir from a fight); short fingers, clean nails, bitten; especially the nail of the finger that sported a wedding ring.

He mentioned the French photographer, Robert Doisneau, talked about passion—capturing it—through a lens.

"Ever see the Truffaut film, *The Woman Next Door*?" Jeanette said. "*La Femme d'à côté*. Best film about passion—ever."

"Who's in it?"

"Fanny Ardant and Gérard Depardieu...back when Gérard Depardieu used to be Gérard Depardieu."

The photographer laughed.

"They play former lovers," Jeanette said. "Fanny and her husband move next door to Gérard and his wife, creating quite a lust storm!"

"Lust storm," the photographer said, as Jeanette caught him glimpsing her thigh through the tear in her jeans. "Describe your favorite scene."

She didn't have to think about it.

"Fanny puts her groceries in the car...Gérard kisses her—and she faints. *Faints.* Sinks to the pavement from his kiss."

"Can't get more French than that," he said, noticing Jeanette's lips were tinged with Cabernet. "You'd probably like my photos."

"I saw a surreal image you'll appreciate, you being a photographer," she said. "A few minutes ago. A tiny white feather drifting in the air...in the ladies' room. Who knows how it got there?"

"The feather. Did it ever land?"

"Yes, it did," she said, marveling at the occurrence, nothing coy in her voice, just relating the facts: "I watched the feather slowly descend into my underpants."

"Wait—a feather just happened to be drifting in the air in the ladies' room...and just happened to drift into your underpants?"

"Like I said...surreal."

"Know what I think?" He fished the olive from his martini, ate it. "I think you're a sexy private investigator messing with my mind."

Jeanette stood in front of the fireplace, gas flames hissing behind her as she reached into the pocket of her jeans. She held out her hand. Right there in the center of her palm—the tiny white feather. "Evidence," she said, in a voice that could belong to a private investigator. She placed the feather on a cocktail napkin beside her wineglass.

He stared at the feather like maybe she was a private investigator *and* a magician.

"Evidence of the unexpected," she said.

"Some photos I shot for my book," he said, "they're on my computer in my room. Would you like to see them?"

Let's go to my room and have sex. Her mind translated his words like there was a website in her head: Unlimited Free Translation for Men's Words and Phrases.

Sex. She wanted sex. And she knew she was exuding her want.

The feather. Drifting into my underpants—like some kind of sign. Sign of what? I should let this man inside my thong?

There were two problems with that theory: 1) She didn't believe in signs. 2) She felt no pull toward the guy. She wished she did. What she felt was the power of *her* sexuality—not his.

So, she said, "I've got an early day tomorrow. I should get some sleep."

"You, you mean you're not going to finish your glass of wine with me?"

"Case I'm working on...it's a motherfucker."

Angie was on the phone, taking a room service order, "One poached salmon, one salad, dressing on the side, one vodka and tonic with lime. Very good, Mr. Millburn." She muted the receiver with her hand as Jeanette approached the bar. "Gentleman paid for your wine," Angie whispered, nodding toward the photographer.

He was staring at the almost-empty glass of wine, he had paid for—and the feather that had drifted into the underpants of a private detective.

10

A FEATHER TICKLED BY A WOMAN

The tattoo needle didn't hurt like she thought it would.

"I want to see it," Jeanette said.

"It suits you," the tattooist said.

"I want to know what it is."

"You know what it is."

"I don't. I don't know," Jeanette insisted.

Why had she trusted a stranger to tattoo her...and surprise her with a tattoo of his choosing? What happened to her judgment? Where did it go?

The needle stopped.

"It's finished," he said.

"What's finished?"

"The tat. It's a part of you."

Jeanette looked at the tattoo—just above her groin—letters: W...I...D...O...W.

"I don't want this tattoo," Jeanette said, trying to rub the word *widow* from the skin that bordered her pussy.

The tattooist covered the tat with gauze. "Widow needs to

be protected," he said.

Jeanette tried to scream, but her throat could not produce a sound. What she heard was...

The dog barking.

Al was barking in the dark.

Jeanette turned on the light, tossed aside the sheet. She looked at the skin that edged her pussy...where the word *widow* would be tattooed—if she hadn't just been dreaming.

Al's barking escalated, clearing the dream from her mind, making room for lucid thought: *I just got to sleep, now I'm awake.*

"Go to your bed, Al."

The dog voiced his own opinion with an irritable bark, connoting his ability to think for himself.

Jeanette switched on the light as someone in the hallway slipped a hotel envelope beneath her door.

Al pounced on the envelope. Jeanette rescued it from his soggy mouth. She peered through the peephole of the door: no one in the hallway. She got back into bed.

The return address in the corner of the envelope was a room number. She removed a folded page of hotel stationery from the envelope. At the top of the page, three words were scripted in black ballpoint pen and underlined: *A Drifting Feather*.

It was 2:42 A.M. on the clock radio as Jeanette read to the dog:

"A Drifting Feather
Drifting from who knows where
Descending magically through air
From heaven? no – to heaven
From space to lace underwear
Magical flight – feather in
the night
Guided by wordless lips
wet invite...'"

She read the rest of the poem, silently, until the last line, which she read aloud:

"A feather—tickled by a woman."'

She doubted the photographer could have written the poem from scratch so quickly. But there was enough tailor-made to constitute a poem for *her*. No one had ever written Jeanette an erotic poem. No one had written her a poem of any kind.

She'd done the right thing, returning to this hotel. Arousal—even the corridors were charged with it—a force, a palpable energy. If only she could bottle it. And direct the thirty-second spot for the product. She affected a Heidi Klum-esque voice:

"Take two capsules for temporary relief of feelings of undesirability. Avoid contact with married men in sunlight."

A car alarm blared from the parking garage. Horns. Sirens. Everything but kazoo, as Jeanette read the poem, again: "'Drifting from who knows where...'"

***

The maid knocked on the door of room 315. "Housekeeping."

The guest opened the door.

The maid handed the guest a freshly laundered, terry cloth robe.

"Thank you," Evan said. He tossed the robe onto the bed.

11

MOOD INDUCERS

The photographer stood in the doorway of his junior suite, tying the drawstring of his pajama bottoms. "I'm sorry if my poem woke you," he said, as if the poem had slid itself beneath her door.

"Your poem was quiet," Jeanette said.

She entered his room; he closed the door.

"My dog woke me. Couldn't get back to sleep," she said. "Figured I might as well accept your invitation to see your photographs."

"They allow dogs in this hotel?"

"Wouldn't stay here if they didn't," she said. "You like dogs?"

"I might, if they liked me."

He sat on the sofa. Jeanette settled into the easy chair, the two of them, once again, at a coffee table, staring into a gas fireplace.

"I haven't written poetry in a long time," he said. "You inspired me."

"You don't write poetry to your wife?"

"You asked me that question without judgment," he said, reflexively glancing at his gold wedding ring. "You're probably a good detective."

"There are those who would say I'm a damn good one."

"I used to write poetry to my wife," he said.

"Why'd you stop?"

He dimmed the lamp on the end table beside her.

"We've been married seventeen years," he said, explaining his marital-poetry drought.

"So, when was the last time you wrote a poem to a woman who *wasn't* your wife?"

"Six years ago," he said. "Woman I was having an affair with."

"How long did your affair last?"

"Two years."

He stretched out on the sofa, feet crisscrossed in black socks, resting his head on an upholstered pillow, same two-toned green as the chair Jeanette was seated on.

"I moved in with her," he said. "For ten months."

"What happened after ten months?"

"The woman I left my wife for...she kicked me out."

Jeanette removed her slingback shoes. She rested her feet on the seat cushion, hugged her knees to her chest. "Must have been rough."

"I would have gone back to my wife eventually," he said. I *love* my wife."

That may be true. But there it was, on the coffee table, beside a complimentary *Los Angeles Magazine*—the feather that had drifted into Jeanette's underpants and into a poem.

"Why'd your wife take you back?" Jeanette said.

"I lied, told her I ended the affair."

He dimmed the lamp on the end table beside him.

"Plus," he said, "my wife was married when I *met* her." He smiled sheepishly. "I was irresistible."

He looked sexier here on the sofa—in his pajama bottoms and Fruit of the Loom T-shirt—than in his straining-for-edgy black ensemble.

"Was it difficult for you...to trust your wife?"

"Sometimes, yeah...after we were married awhile, yeah. I'd think some guy will take my wife from me—like I took my wife from her husband."

"You don't worry now?"

"Past few years she's all about being a mom. External beauty, it's not important to her anymore."

Translation: *She let her looks go and he can't imagine another man wanting her.*

Jeanette walked, barefoot, to the round glass-topped dining table (like the table in her room, all the rooms, a few feet from the terrace). The photographer's laptop was open, black screen, except for the silver Apple logo and silver words: DAVID'S MAC PRO.

She didn't know his name until now, and he still didn't know her name.

"So, you came to see my photographs," he said, his pajama bottoms scraping the carpet as he joined her at the table.

He pressed some keys on the laptop, and—*voilà*—a photograph of a naked woman on the beach, naked and beautiful, lying on her stomach. Another naked beauty knelt in the sand, squeezing tanning oil onto her probably twenty-two-year-old breasts...as oil dripped from her nipples onto the small of the other woman's back. Erotic but tame.

The photo surprised Jeanette, and she wondered why. What kind of photos did she think he'd invited her to his room to see? Photos of architecturally splendid churches?

"What do you think?" he said.

"What time of day did you shoot this?"

Really, that's what she said.

Jeanette's question threw him—he'd anticipated a more visceral response—and she knew it.

"Dawn," he said.

"Gorgeous lighting," she said.

He clicked on a new photo of a nude woman reclining dreamily on a red velvet divan, one leg raised at the knee, red grapes on her white belly.

"Reminds me of a Modigliani I saw in Paris, minus the grapes," Jeanette said. "'*Nu Couché.*'"

"When was the last time you were in Paris?" he said, trying to duplicate her coolness.

"November," she said.

"And did you sink to the pavement from some Frenchman's kiss?"

"No sinking to the pavement...not yet."

Four photographs later, each impressively shot, each of a woman, totally or partially undressed, he shut the computer. "So, you get the idea."

He has no confidence in his own ability to excite me—he needs props.

"Mood inducers," she said, as she opened the sliding glass door to the terrace. The apartments in the pale-pink building across the street were dark except for one: a solitary light on in the living room, towel over a birdcage.

"Mood inducers," the photographer said, his mouth sampling Jeanette's words as he stood behind her. "I might borrow that."

He placed his hand on the back of her black cashmere tank top. His palm pressed against the clasp of her bra, a hand waiting for instructions. From her? Or from himself? The hand moved along her tank top to her right shoulder blade, then her left shoulder blade; right, then left again.

It felt like he was wiping his hand on her cashmere.

Heavy touch.

Clumsy.

Not a mood inducer.

The hand tried a new location: beneath her tank top. The hand moved in fast circles along her lower back. His tempo was way off—like he was in a hurry to get this part over with, the part where he was supposed to make *her* feel good, so they could get to the part where she would make *him* feel good.

She'd come to his room hoping for more than he could

give. Oh, why didn't she go with her original instinct? The poem. That's why. An erotic poem only *partially* written for her.

Sexual attraction—if it's not there in those first few seconds she's looking into a guy's eyes, it's never there later. She's known this since high school. Grade school. *Kindergarten...* when she allowed five-year-old Marty Fleischer a glimpse up her purple velvet skirt, straddling his face on a chalked hopscotch court: left foot on the nine square; right foot on the eight.

If she had been in kindergarten with the photographer, she never would have straddled his five-year-old face on a hopscotch court.

"I believe in being in the moment," the photographer said. "I want to kiss you like they kiss in the *movies*."

He leaned toward her lips for his version of a movie kiss. "No hickeys," he said.

No hickeys, as if he were ordering a margarita without salt.

She could not have sex with a man who did not know how to touch her.... *or* kiss her. "Like I told you," Jeanette said. "I'm a private investigator."

He stepped back from her.

"I could wallpaper this junior suite with the photos I've taken of cheating husbands," she said. "We can't allow ourselves to get swept up in a moment." She put on her slingbacks.

He looked at her shoes like there might be a camera hidden inside one of the heels, or a microphone.

"You've had enough complications in your marriage," she said, because she believed it. "You don't need another one, David."

"You're probably right," he said, trying to remember when he'd told her his name. "You're probably right."

He opened the door for her.

"Thanks for the poem," she said. "I'll keep it as a souvenir of our meeting."

She walked down the short hallway that led from his room,

and the room beside it, to the main hallway. He called softly after her:

"In the restaurant...you said maybe you were tailing me."

She looked back at him.

"You were *kidding*," he said. "Right?"

He stood outside his room, in his too-long pajama bottoms, afraid of her answer.

"You're not tailing me," he said. "*Are* you?"

"This wasn't business," she said. "It was strictly pleasure."

"Can I believe you?"

"That part's up to you," she said.

He entered his room. Closed the door.

***

Evan reached for a bottle of Heineken, trying to wind down from a gig that ended hours ago—Diana Krall at the Greek Theatre—first of two sold-out nights, only there was no more Heineken, so he took a Stella Artois from the minibar, thinking: the last time he stayed at this hotel, it was because of an empty minibar he'd ended up in *her* room.

No, it wasn't.

The minibar had just facilitated an invitation. He was certain they would have ended up together that night, if not in her room, then his. He swigged beer, tightened the sash of his terry cloth robe, *Lyric Hotel* stitched in red on the pocket. He didn't have to be in this hotel to be reminded of her. At home or on the road, she'd appear in his imagination, invited or not. A few months ago, he'd called her from the road in Detroit, hanging up after the first ring. And from a Greenwich car wash, snapping his cell shut halfway through dialing. What would he say? "Hey, Jeanette. It's me...your detonator? The Man Who Stirred Everything Up?"

If her marriage was disintegrating—she lit the fuse, not him—he wasn't going to be in earshot of the demolition. She'd assigned him too pivotal a role for a one-night encounter that hadn't even amounted to a full-fledged fuck. He'd asked himself (more than once), if she'd told him she was married, would he have gone to her room?

Probably...yes.

Would he have called her after their night together?

Definitely...no.

It was a complication he wasn't suited for. He'd been tormented enough, contemplating the repercussions to his own marriage if his wife found out. He didn't need Jeanette's potentially devastated and/or enraged husband in the guilt-fear bouillabaisse.

At first, he'd felt deceived by Jeanette. But she hadn't lied exactly. She'd merely withheld information, which was her right. And what did it matter if she had deceived him? A night with an attractive woman at a hotel, that's all it was. All it was ever meant to be.

A night.

Evan stood at the kitchenette counter. He watched the leaves of a eucalyptus tree fluttering against the railing of the terrace. He set the beer down beside the ice bucket. And he wondered: Had some woman-guest washed her underpants in the bucket?

He stared at his phone book on the counter, her number inside it—*J* for Jeanette—he didn't even know her last name. He was afraid to open the book, as if opening it could, well... detonate the place.

Dial her number—hear her voice. Don't, he told himself.

He opened the book. Looked at the clock on the microwave, 3:47 A.M. Way too late to call. But he picked up the room phone, hit 8 for long distance, dialed. His heart hammered his chest. He didn't stick around for the first ring. He hung up, feeling worse from having almost called her.

Evan stepped outside onto the terrace. He sat on the green Adirondack chair in his hotel robe, listening to the rustling of the eucalyptus long enough to define a rhythmic pattern. If he'd stayed inside his room, he would have heard a man in the hallway, talking to a woman. And maybe, if Evan had been close enough to the door, he would have heard that the woman was Jeanette.

∗∗∗

The dog was talking in his sleep. Jeanette respected Al's soft, staccato yelps—his dreamland adventure—as she removed two *Ultimate Pleasure* rubbers from the pocket of her jeans. She quietly returned them to the drawer of the night table and the rest of her unopened collection. Then she wrote with a hotel pen on a hotel pad:

MY WIFE WAS MARRIED WHEN I MET HER.

12

SMALL HOTEL

Charles Millburn had made her cry. And laugh. And wonder—what men could teach her that boys couldn't—when she was barely a teenager, in a dark movie theater, watching his face on screen exuding a wounded sensuality that Jeanette knew had emanated from some deep, private place. The last time she saw the actor was ten years ago, on TV, starring in a canceled-after-three-episodes series: retired detective who'd won the lottery, but continued solving crimes no employed cop had the savvy to tackle. She couldn't get past the teaser; he'd deserved better.

Jeanette looked up from the *New York Times*—and there he was, the one and only Charles Millburn, stepping out of the elevator. (She had a bird's-eye view of him from the restaurant.) The actor's face had always been craggy enough to offset his handsomeness. This morning, his face was *all* craggy. Tired. Maybe because of the way he was walking, head down, stooped over, trying not to be noticed. Or maybe that's how he walked when he thought no one was looking, and he could just be himself: wounded minus the sensuality.

"Mind if we steal one a your itty-bitty bottles?" a tall, skinny old dude sporting a black string tie, said. He stood at her table, gesturing to two small, unopened bottles of maple syrup.

Steal 'em both," Jeanette said, wondering if he was the same age or older than Charles Millburn. She looked back at the elevator; the actor was gone.

The skinny old dude sat beside a big hungover redhead half his age. She spread syrup on her waffle in the shape of a heart; he got a real charge out of that. He leaned back into the claret-velvet banquette like it was the headboard of a bed as he massaged her wide neck and said to Jeanette:

"I told her she's so sweet...when that waffle touches her tongue it won't need syrup."

Jeanette turned to the woman whose tongue could sweeten a waffle. The big redhead flaunted massive cleavage in an off-the-shoulder black dress, patterned with last night's creases. "We met on the internet," she said. "We've known each other seventeen-and-a half hours."

"My wife has Alzheimer's," the skinny old dude said. "She thinks I'm her former boss, keeps askin' for a raise."

"Tell her you're doubling her salary *and* her vacation time," Jeanette said, en route to the maître d' stand (always minus a maître d').

She had hoped to see a waiter, maybe folding green linen napkins like pleated party hats. No waiter. Just a cute guy kneeling at a low shelf of newspapers, sorting through them.

The cute guy looked up at Jeanette. "You're a hazard to my health," he said, his back-East accent a perfect match with the boyish intensity of his face. "Now I gotta walk around the corner to the newsstand before my first shot of caffeine—no telling *how* my body's gonna react." He stood, a few inches taller than her, more than a few years younger. "All because you took the last *New York Times.*"

"I have enough on my conscience." She handed him the newspaper, as the big, wide redhead yelled to her:

"I used to have a figure like yours. Before my marriage went bad. My husband tried to kill me—twice."

"I can see where that could lead to bingeing," Jeanette said.

Back East Guy laughed. "I take it your marriage is pretty good?" he said as Jeanette walked to the bar.

"I'm not married," Jeanette said.

"Why not?"

Her check was on the bar beside a stack of cocktail napkins. She signed it, then stepped into the corridor.

Back East Guy persisted. "How come you're not married?"

She looked at the mirror on the wall. Her reflection included a man and a woman behind her, in the elevator, kissing.

"It's complicated," Jeanette said.

Back East Guy had another question for her. But Jeanette rounded the corner before he could ask it.

***

A porno movie played on a huge TV screen inside an empty tour bus—for no one. Except a cluster of Japanese tourists on the sidewalk, videoing the unlikely sight through the front window of the gold-and-black bus.

Jeanette ran up the hotel steps to the sidewalk with Al, leash in one hand, cell in the other, sudden witness to the porno movie—two women and a man in the throes of a three-way—as she listened to the first of five messages on her San Francisco landline:

"Darling, it's your mother."

On the word "mother," Jeanette turned away from the porno movie so quickly, she dropped her cell. She retrieved it, missing a sentence or two but getting the gist of the update: Mom was in Italy with Massimo—her small-but-elegant boyfriend who owned a small-but-elegant movie theater *and* a small-but-elegant house in Penna San Giovanni (view of hills and sea)—sweltering from a heat wave.

"Massimo closed the theater, it's so hot. So be happy you're in San Francisco, where it's cool. Ciao...I love you."

BEEP!

"They *love* you at Lunesta." Her rep, Helena Lutz—voice plowing through static. "They'll want a meeting. So we'll hook up, have lunch when you're in L.A." Helena yelled to her assistant as if she weren't still on the phone. "Tell him I can't talk...I have laryngitis."

BEEP!

"Jeanette, it's Pete!" Former friend of Michael, inviting her to join him and his wife to see Mike Birbiglia in Berkeley. "So give me a call. Bye...hope you're okay," he added, a hesitant afterthought—as if she might not be.

BEEP!

"Jen! It's me. Sophie! Taking a break between bikini waxes." Her oldest friend calling from her salon (eight miles away in Venice). "Let me know how you're doing...and when you'll be in L.A. Humungous hugs and kisses."

BEEP!

"I'm outside your house, late for Caravan as usual." The Coldwell Banker Realtor never had time for pleasantries. "I found the perfect tenants for you—if you'll do a short-term rental."

BEEP! BEEP! BEEP!

Jeanette turned toward the porno movie—two bad actresses were climaxing, simultaneously. It was then that she realized the messages on her cell had a common theme: No one knew she was here in Los Angeles. Here, looking at a porno movie through the window of a tour bus. Here—living in a hotel.

The actresses flashed dim-witted, post-orgasmic smiles as Jeanette made a decision: People who knew her (or thought they knew her) would not infiltrate her insulated hotel world— no interfering with her new unfurling life. They could continue to leave messages on her cell, or her landline in San Francisco, even when she rents out the house.

Inside the hotel, she could be Jeanette Unfettered. Unfettered by preexisting conditions of who she was—or wasn't. She could be the brilliant architect of her evolving self.

Right?

***

The black guy with the shaven head glistened beads of sweat as Jeanette looked up from the exercise mat—seven feet up. He was lean, muscular without the bulk, a work of art, like his mother hadn't given birth to him; she'd sculpted him: a bronze statue of a man, naked except for blue nylon shorts and rubber flip-flops.

"Forgot to wipe my sweat," he said.

The Sculpted Man padded past Jeanette—the gym was narrow, just enough room for a mat between the weight machines and the mirrored wall—to the elliptical bike. "I'm *used* to sweating," he said, wiping his perspiration from the bike. "I played basketball." He stepped onto a Stairmaster, which made him look even taller. "Professionally."

He kept an even rhythm on the Stairmaster, offering bio-tidbits: four years with the Nets, two with Detroit. Bad knees; early retirement. But he'd made some wise investments, wise enough to be shopping for property in L.A. That's why he was at the hotel.

"Rooting for the Lakers...habit I can't shake," Jeanette said, settling into the lotus position. "My mom dated Elgin Baylor."

"Elgin Baylor? He was one of the all-time-all-time great shooters. Your mom must have been *fine*."

"My mom *is* fine."

"I've got a date tonight," he said, stepping off the Stairmaster. "I've been thinking about canceling." He sat on the seat of the pec machine, above and behind Jeanette, spoke to her reflection in the mirror. "But it's not right to do that to a woman—not at the last minute."

"How come you want to cancel?"

"I already took her out once. She liked me too much...too fast."

He was talking to her as if she was some matchmaker on TV who finds malleable women for loathsome millionaires. He couldn't possibly know that Jeanette was exercising the muscle inside her vagina—tightening and releasing—as he said: "I'm Keith."

Keith extended his long fingers toward her. He shook her hand.

"Large hand," she said. "Small hotel."

Keith's large hand helped her up from the mat.

"I look at you, and you know what I see?" she said.

"What do you see?" he said, thinking she's seeing a fine-looking man gazing back at her.

"I see a man who stayed"—she slid down the mirrored wall into a leg-squat position—"in room 144."

"You a psychic?"

"Matter of fact, I'm an *internationally known* psychic," she said.

He squinted at her. "You really a psychic?"

"I'm a psychic who happens to be staying in room 144," she said. "There was a message for you on my machine from"—she held the leg-squat until she couldn't, then slid up the mirrored wall—"Nessa."

Keith winced, like hearing Nessa's name gave him a migraine. "She's the reason I changed rooms...girl won't let me *be*," he said. "What's the message?"

"She was sad you didn't call her—like you said you would."

"I treat women too good."

"How can you treat a woman *too* good?"

"I'm not saying they don't deserve it."

He walked toward the door, mopping his brow.

"I treat them too good...considering I'm not looking to take it past a certain point."

He ducked beneath the doorframe so as not to hit his head, leaned back into the gym. "If you asked a man to call you... would you want him to tell you the *truth?*" he said. "Tell you that he wasn't going to call?"

"I don't ask men to call me."

A memory pushed its way to the forefront of Jeanette's mind, brazenly cutting in line. *Excuse me—but you did tuck your number inside the pocket of Evan's jeans...after you zipped them.*

"I'm almost thirty-seven," Keith said. "She's twenty-one. Still in school."

"Nessa?"

"Girl I'm seeing tonight," he said. "Maybe my problem is they're too young."

"That's why my mom stopped seeing Elgin Baylor. He was too old for her."

Keith's brows furrowed at the thought of being too old for a woman, which (in his mind) was different than a woman being too young for him. "I want to show her a good time," he said. "I show her *too* good a time...she'll just want more of the same from me."

Keith tossed his sweaty towel into the hamper. "You're a good listener," he said.

Well, that was a first: a man telling her she's a good listener.

"I guess you have to be a good listener," he said. He opened the door to the sauna. "To be a good psychic."

***

"Now this is what I like about a small hotel," a familiar voice said. "I get to run into *you* again."

Back East Guy stood at the front desk, carrying a guitar in its case, looking even younger than he did in the restaurant, as Jeanette walked toward him with Al. "I'm checking out tomorrow," he told her.

She wondered if he played guitar with a group or an artist or if *he* was an artist: a singer/songwriter she'd never heard of or didn't recognize.

"If we don't see each other again...stay awesome," he said. Then he told Al, "You're a lucky dog."

"He knows it," Jeanette said.

Back East Guy walked to the door. He walked back to Jeanette. "You like Diana Krall?"

He's playing with Diana Krall, she thought. "I like her," Jeanette said. "I do."

"Gonna see her tonight at the Greek," he said. "Got two tickets. Great seats."

He's not playing with Diana Krall.

"How 'bout we meet at the bar first...at five-thirty?" he said. "Sound like a plan?"

"Sounds so much like a plan, it's got to be one."

"Genius," he said, rushing toward the door with his guitar like if he stuck around, she'd change her mind.

A young rapper, high on weed and low on giving-a-fuck, sported a durag beneath a backwards baseball cap as he plunked three bracelets and a watch on the counter of the front desk.

Laurie, a fresh-faced, perky, corn-belt blonde, new enough to the job and L.A. not to be worn out by either, looked like she should have a Miss Hospitality sash draped across her hotel blazer. "Your copy of the incidentals paid in full," she told a smartly dressed black woman as the rapper started for the door.

"Sinsation!" the woman yelled at the rapper. She brandished the bracelets. "What's *this*?"

"Someone's gonna pick 'em up," Sinsation said.

"*Who's* going to pick them up?"

With the least possible energy he could expend and still be awake, Sinsation strolled back to the desk. "Girl I was with last night."

"What's her name?"

"Don't know."

"You don't know her last name?"

"Don't know her first or last."

"You spent the night with a girl...and you never even bothered to find out her name?"

"Didn't care about her *name*."

"Well, you can't just leave her jewelry here."

Sinsation shrugged. "You the manager. You suppose to take care of shit like this."

"This is not the shit you boys hired me to take care of."

"Why don't you write *your* name on the envelope?" Jeanette said. "If she comes by, she'll probably ask if you left something for her."

Sinsation looked warily at Al. "That a drug dog?"

Jeanette laughed. "Al? He's a *rug* dog."

Sinsation smiled, offering her a glimpse of dental bling.

"Get on the bus, Sinsation," the manager said, pushing him with both hands toward the door, then letting go, watching him like he was a kid on his first two-wheeler, hoping he wouldn't fall off.

A bellman stood at the elevator, scratching his head with the antenna of a walkie-talkie; a man's voice, muffled by static, blared into his skull: "Engineering to front desk." The bellman pushed the elevator button for Jeanette. "Going to your room?" he said.

"Thanks," she said. "But I'll take the stairs."

Jeanette and Al waited as a musician (she was pretty sure he was singer/songwriter, Ron Sexsmith) descended the stairs, followed by a masseuse, carrying a massage table. Al climbed the first few steps ahead of Jeanette. As Jeanette's Saucony shoe hit the second carpeted stair...

The elevator doors opened—and Evan stepped into the lobby, combing his hair with his fingers.

✳✳✳

There were sound problems at The Greek last night. Diana Krall's mic went out for most of the second number. And again at the end of the show, forcing her to close with an instrumental version of "The Night We Called It a Day." So, the mood was tense now at this afternoon's sound check.

Evan had his own reason for being tense. He didn't get to sleep till four-thirty in the morning, having requested a wake-up call for ten-thirty. When the phone rang, he'd picked it up without speaking, expecting to hear a digitalized voice wishing him good morning.

"Good morning, sweetie."

It was his wife.

Evan sighed and grunted simultaneously.

"I woke you. I'm sorry," Nancy said.

He yawned: "What time is it?"

"Eleven-thirty at home."

"It's eight-thirty in L.A.," he said, his voice a raspy whisper. "I'll call you in a couple hours."

"Evan—"

"If I talk anymore, I won't be able to get back to sleep."

"I'm pregnant."

"Nance..." He switched on the light above the night table; the brightness hurt his eyes, so he closed them. "How, how do you—"

"The doctor confirmed it, Ev."

He gulped Arrowhead water from the bottle. Before he could ask, she told him:

"My new diaphragm...it wasn't fitting right."

"You knew this?"

"No. That's the doctor's theory."

Evan set the water on the night table, noticing the card from Housekeeping: YES, WE DO CHECK UNDER THE BED.

"You think I did it on purpose, don't you? You think I knew my diaphragm didn't fit."

"I don't know what I think, Nance. My brain's asleep."

"Evan...I want you to want this baby."

"I need to absorb this, Nancy...when I'm awake."

"I love you."

"I love you too."

The production manager yelled at the sound man as Evan sat on the stage of the Greek Theatre with the rest of the orchestra, gazing out at the seats that were empty except for sun and shade, thinking: *My wife is pregnant.*

Nancy had been campaigning for another child for the past two years...all the while bemoaning his absences from their daughter. Evan had been on the road for Sarah's birthday—three years in a row he'd missed it—Fourth of Julys, Labor Day Weekends, New Year's Eves, school plays, recitals, soccer practice; he'd missed his daughter's first baby steps.

He felt a deep love for his daughter, a protectiveness he'd never known until she was born. Yet, when he returned home from the road, Daddy-responsibility was never a seamless blend with Daddy-capability. There was always a lag time, like a voice track in a movie too fast for the actor who was speaking. Evan needed to wind down, needed energy for the next rehearsal, next session, next gig. He needed to compose. Needed to breathe— needed to lie beside his daughter's mother and feel like he'd come home to his lover.

Way back when...when living together was just a concept they discussed, after making love and falling asleep and making love again and eating breakfast in the bed they'd fucked and slept in—her bed, not their bed yet—he told her who he was:

"I'm a musician. *Playing*...it's what I *love*. What I *do*."

"Doing what you love," she said. "What a great way to live."

"It's who I am, Nance." Then he told her who he wasn't: "I'm not a man you'll find around the house a lot."

"I love the man you are. That's who I love," she said, almost ten years ago—five years before the *New York Times* dubbed him "the most sought-after cellist in so-called alternative music." When Nancy read him the quote over the phone, he was in Amsterdam with David Byrne. "I wish I were reading this to you across the kitchen table. I wish you were here in your pajamas, eating pancakes with Sarah and me," she said. "But I guess that's the trade-off when you're sought after."

Just last month, Evan had called from London, after a gig with Janelle Monáe, and Nancy told him, "While you've been making music, basking in British adulation, I've been cleaning up Sarah's vomit. She has the stomach flu."

"Tell her I love her," he said.

"I know you love your daughter," Nancy said. "And I know you love to have fun with her...but sometimes I need you to be here for her when it isn't fun."

Now another child was on the way that Nancy would want him to be there for when it wasn't fun.

The orchestra was rehearsing. Evan looked at the chart on the music stand, saw that it was time for him to play. So he did.

13

THE HEART OF A GUITAR

Treating a woman too good.

She contemplated the concept as she outlined her pussy with shaving cream, showering in the same tub that Keith had showered in when this was his room. Jeanette imagined the former basketball player leaning under the shower nozzle, the water's long-distance journey from his face to his toes.

Treating a woman too good.

She picked up the razor from the soap ledge. The basketball player fled the little theater in her mind—the cellist entered. She didn't know Evan was married when she manicured her pubic hair, in this very shower, eight months ago, prepping for sex with him. And he didn't know *she* was married. Not until she'd blurted on the phone, *I'm leaving my husband.*

Husband he didn't know existed while he was going down on her. Husband he didn't know existed while he was giving her four orgasms.

Husband who, now, *doesn't* exist.

Fear—she'd heard it in Evan's voice. Fear—the mess of her

marriage would spill into his. Fear—their one night...a pleasurable diversion for him, had been life altering for her.

She'd called him a few weeks ago, got as far as the first ring. What would she say? "Hey, it's Jeanette, just calling to say my husband left *me*...made me a widow instead of a divorcee?"

No. If Evan wanted to talk to her, he had her number.

She washed her pubic hair with Clarins shower gel (which softened and tightened the curl).

And if he didn't have her number, he didn't want her number.

She spread the lips of her vagina, allowing shower water to trickle down her clitoris. She stuck her finger inside her, gave it a whiff—clean. And thought: *He treated me too good.*

✷✷✷

"Please don't think I'm a *total* fuckup." That's how Back East Guy greeted her.

He sat at the bar, wearing jeans and a forest-green T-shirt featuring an illustration of an acoustic guitar, beneath the guitar, scripted in white: *COPELAND.*

"How do you define fuckup?" Jeanette said.

"We're not seeing Diana Krall—I tried. Tried to get tickets."

"I know I didn't dream you said you had tickets because I never nap."

He held up two tickets. "Check out the date."

"These are for *last* night."

"I thought they were for tonight. I swear," he said, raising his right hand like a witness about to testify. "I've been running nonstop since my plane landed."

"When did you realize this fuck up?"

"Couple hours ago."

"Couple *hours* ago?"

"I couldn't contact you. I, I don't know even know your *name.* And even if I did, I would've been afraid if I told you...

you wouldn't see me, tonight. For*give* me—at least let me buy you dinner."

Jeanette removed her thin, crushed-velvet coat, revealing a white blouse, delicately threaded with lavender that sparkled. She caught him glancing at the hint of nipple beneath her blouse that dotted the center of a sparkling lavender flower stitched on the pocket.

"How 'bout we see how we do over a drink first," she said.

***

Here's what she knew about him after a glass of Cabernet and most of her grilled salmon. The name on the T-shirt was his: Copeland. Matt Copeland was twenty-eight. "I'm a luthier... guitar maker," he'd told her. "Second generation." He was in L.A. to deliver a guitar he'd made for Elvis Costello—which is why he had the Diana Krall tickets he'd assumed were for tonight but weren't. (Elvis was married to Diana.)

And what did Copeland know about Jeanette? She looked like a rock star in that velvet coat. He pictured her playing one of his guitars, all earthy sass and attitude. That edgy feminine thing like Chrissie Hynde (whom his Dad had made two guitars for and whom Jeanette kind of reminded him of), and her slammin' body was younger looking than her face, which had its own definition of prettiness, and the combo excited him and made him nervous because she was older (he wasn't sure how much older), old enough to have had experiences he hadn't had. He couldn't believe he was sitting with her, here in this hotel, just a pink tulip, white candle, and basket of bread between them.

He also knew she was an architect who lived in Italy but consulted frequently in Los Angeles—and wasn't in the mood to discuss her work.

"Can I tell you something?" he said. "First time I saw you I thought...this woman rocks."

"First time I saw you I thought, this guy would be looking up my skirt if I were wearing one."

He laughed. "I was kneeling, looking for the paper. I couldn't help it if your legs walked into my peripheral vision."

He told her he was born in New York, grew up in Jersey, moved to Austin three years ago. "Sold my first guitar in Austin."

Jeanette peered into the vase, saw it was low on water, told him where she grew up because he'd asked. "Los Angeles," she said, sharing her Pellegrino water with the thirsty tulip. "Laurel Canyon."

"People in Los Angeles have an agenda when they smile," he said, dipping a forkful of steak into mashed potatoes. "'Please like me, so you can do something for me.'"

"You think I want you to like me, Copeland...so you can do something for me before you check out?"

"I hope so," he said, laughing.

"Mashed potato," she said. "On your lip."

He ran his finger along his upper lip.

"Lower," she said.

He licked his lip. "Still there?"

She dabbed her finger along his lip where his tongue had been. "Now it's just a mashed-potato memory."

"I don't get an L.A. vibe from you," he said.

"Been a while since I've lived here," she said, thinking the alcohol had softened the Jersey in him. "Ever miss Jersey?"

"I miss making guitars with my dad in the house I grew up in. But he was all for my moving to Austin. Good for business."

She looked past Copeland...and saw Keith stepping out of the elevator. The former basketball player's large hand was on the shoulder of a barefoot ingenue who carried a high heel in each hand instead of a pom-pom; she looked like a cheerleader. Jeanette imagined her cartwheeling down the hall to Keith's room.

"When I was a little boy," Copeland said, "I watched my

dad make a guitar for Bruce Springsteen."

"How old were you?"

"Ten."

She did some speedy math: 10 + 20 = 30. *When he was ten...I was thirty.*

"My dad took me to see him in concert," Copeland said. "Know what I remember most?"

"Tell me."

"The tech guy came out on stage, handed Springsteen the guitar that my dad made for him. He played "Nebraska." And Springsteen sounded awesome because my dad made him an awesome guitar."

There was a sweetness to Copeland that Jeanette hadn't anticipated. A lovely surprise. Like biting into a dark chocolate-pistachio truffle and discovering its taste was exactly what you were in the mood for.

"Can I interest you in dessert?" Angie said from the empty bar.

"I would love a glass of port," Jeanette said.

Copeland had never tasted port. "We'll each have a glass," he told Angie. "Glass of your best."

"Very good then," Angie said.

"I'm open to trying new things," he told Jeanette.

She stared at his name, scripted on his T-shirt, beneath the guitar. "Copeland," she said, "I am in no way a cougar."

"Of course you're not," he said. "I've never met one. What exactly *is* a cougar?"

"A cougar is a cartoonish concept of a woman who desires younger men," she said. "Sells products and bad TV shows. And unfortunately..." she said, feeling a sudden urge to stroke his forearm. "Real-life women have bought into it."

"I asked *you* to see Diana Krall. I asked *you* to dinner. You didn't ask *me*."

"This is true," she said.

"And I'm still trying to figure out if you even *like* me."

"Me too," she said with a smile.

"You know something?" he said, leaning toward her across the table. "You've got some awesome lines on you when you smile."

Jeanette laughed.

"And when you laugh too," he said. "It's a *compliment*."

"You think?"

"You're experiential…you're enriching my life," he said. "You are so not a cartoon."

"Copeland," she said. "What do you say we have our port on the roof?"

Flags from eighteen countries flapped above the rooftop tennis court, lit only by a moon sliver in a starless sky. A chain-link fence covered with green mesh, except for a few small, rectangular openings, allowed a letterbox view: Hollywood Hills in the distance to the right, Century City to the left, Design Center, all blue and green and shiny, beyond phone poles and palm trees.

Jeanette and Copeland shared a slatted, wooden patio chair in the center of the court as Rihanna played on the tinny speakers.

"I can't believe I'm looking at the Hollywood Hills," Copeland said, "while an architect is giving me a lap dance."

"Me neither," Jeanette said, as she slid down the illustrated guitar on his T-shirt, settling onto his lap.

Copeland downed the last drops of port. He tossed the glass recklessly onto the court. "I've always wanted to do that."

But it was plastic, lacking the impact of shattering glass as it rolled to a sluggish halt. He took Jeanette's face in his hands. She felt urgency in his kiss. He slid one hand beneath the back of her blouse, his other hand cupping her ass, repositioning her on his lap, all the while kissing her, kissing her as Rihanna faded and St. Vincent began. Somewhere in the song "Los Ageless"—after the lyrics: *how can anybody have you and lose you and not lose their minds too?*—Copeland withdrew his tongue from Jeanette's mouth, and said, "We are *so* making out."

He placed his hands against hers like they were about to play patty-cake, peered into her eyes, searching for a clue to who this woman was that he'd been so making out with.

"You're pretty," he said. "Pretty in your own groovy way. Pretty without trying."

He said that like he absolutely meant it, and the sincere specifics of his compliment allowed her to not doubt it. This, for her, was a big deal.

How sweet is this guy? She put her arms around him. His T-shirt smelled of Tide (the only detergent available in the laundry room).

"I'm learning," he said.

Jeanette watched his twenty-eight-year-old face in the midst of an epiphany: "Learning that if a pretty architect invites me up to the roof—I'll go with her."

Jeanette laughed. She got up from his lap.

"Hey. You. Lady—C'*mere.*" He pulled her into his embrace, kissed her head, spoke into her hair, "Wanna see the guitar I made for Elvis Costello?"

✳✳✳

The guitar sat on an easy chair like a woman who had been waiting up for him to come home. "Isn't she a beauty?" Copeland said.

"She is," Jeanette said. "And just think...you're the one who made her beautiful."

Copeland beamed. "Small body," he said.

"You like a small body?"

"For a subtle finger style of playing."

"I appreciate a subtle finger style."

He sat down with the guitar: a rich, espresso-brown, accented with a beige bridge, abalone on the fret marker dots, grapevine motif on the fingerboard. "I used cedar for the top," he said. "Feel."

She placed her palm on the guitar; he put his hand on hers, gliding it gently along the even-grained wood.

"The top," he said. "That's the *heart* of a guitar." He picked out a melody on his creation, Elvis Costello's "Alison."

"Pretty tone," Jeanette said.

"The softer the wood, the more it vibrates." On the word "vibrates," his eyes met hers. He stroked the guitar's long, smooth neck. "I gave her the attention she deserves."

Jeanette's fingers traced the letters at the top of the neck: C O P E L A N D.

"Wanna hold it?" he said.

"Yeah...I do."

He handed her the guitar. She stood in her black velvet boots, feet wide apart, holding the guitar, feeling an edgy excitement—like she should plunge into a PJ Harvey song. PJ Harvey recently widowed, hanging out in a hotel room with a guy twenty years younger, inspired to write her next album.

"Comfortable against your body?" he said.

"Very."

"Claro Walnut," he said. "I used a light wood for the back— that's the part you feel against your body."

He put his arms around Jeanette, hugging her *and* the guitar. He stepped back, eyed her from her boots to her direct gaze. "You rock, holding a guitar," he said. "I *knew* you'd rock." He kissed her, not a long kiss, but a good kiss. "How's it feel?" he said.

"Your kiss or the guitar?"

"Both," he said.

"I feel the craftsmanship in your guitar *and* your kiss."

He took the guitar from her, set it on the easy chair.

They were smack dab in the middle of some crazy-delicious foreplay—foreplay that *rocked*.

"A guitar's a living thing," he said. "The more you play it... the more you *touch* it. The more you touch it, the more it sings—

'cause it's been *loved*."

And the more Copeland talked about his guitar, the more he sounded like he was talking about a woman. She didn't wait for him to kiss her again; she kissed him. Kissed him like she was embossing his lips with an imprint of hers. His tongue welcomed her into his mouth, which was warm and tasted like port—she'd forgotten how much she liked the combo of port and sex...even better than port and chocolate—as they kissed with eyes closed. Although their eyes must have opened for a second or two, because she was walking up the stair with him that led to the king bed.

He unsnapped her blouse...all the snaps at once, revealing her French lace bra. "*Look* at you," he said. He unzipped her jeans; she lay on the bed (palming an *Ultra Pleasure* condom from her hip pocket). He slid her jeans down, but arrived at a sexual roadblock, her boots. He tried to remove them. He couldn't; she did. Then she let him finish what he'd started. She watched as he took off her jeans, lowered her lace thong to her thighs...her calves...her ankles. Copeland tossed her thong onto the carpet. He hurriedly got out of his jeans and jockey shorts, as if they were sewn together for easy removal. He kissed and sucked her where she liked to be kissed and sucked. She tore open the *Ultra Pleasure* packet, removed the rubber. (She'd seen a woman "instructor," years ago, on that old HBO show, *Real Sex*, teaching women the best way to put a condom on a penis, demonstrating on a banana.) There was no Chiquita sticker on Copeland's cock, and the task of clothing it was awkward. She managed to get the rubber on halfway when he said:

"My wife's *first* husband really hurt her."

"Wife?" This sweet guitar maker?

The luthier had thrown her for a loop.

"You're *married*?"

"Almost two years," he said. "Now I'm close to being as awful as my wife's first husband."

"Why didn't you tell me you were married?"

"I couldn't imagine having sex with anyone but my wife until a few *minutes* ago," he said. "I'm sure this is probably a first for you and me both."

"What?"

"I mean you probably..." He removed the *Ultra Pleasure* condom that half-covered his softening erection. "You probably never got this close to having sex with a married man before, right?"

"You're a guy who misses making guitars with your *daddy* in the house you grew up in. It never occurred to me that you were married."

"I'm sorry and I know this is the second time tonight I said I'm sorry—but this is a *different sorry.*"

She sighed. "Hand me my thong, please."

He picked up her lace thong from the deodorized carpet, handed it to her. "I don't think the part that's against your, you know, the pussy-part of your panties. I don't think it touched the carpet."

She slid her thong up over her thighs.

"We don't wear rings," he said. "My wife doesn't believe in them."

Jeanette got into her jeans as Copeland said, "This is kinda like seeing a movie of our last few minutes, together, while it's rewinding. I mean I was just watching you take *off* your jeans. Now I'm watching you putting them back on."

"Actually," she said, "*you* took my jeans *and* my thong off *me.*"

"Right, right. I did, didn't I? Oh, fuck me!" he said. "Not you, no. I'm not telling *you* to fuck me...I'm telling *me* to fuck me. I can't believe how close I came to having sex with another woman. I never even *thought* about cheating on my wife until tonight."

She was actually starting to feel sorry for him.

"I know me," he said. I *know* me."

"Maybe I should call room service, order you some soothing chamomile tea?"

"If we *did* it tonight," he said, "when I got home, I'd end up confessing to my wife. And that first husband of hers—he *SO hurt* her."

"How? How did he so hurt her?"

"He left her for a younger woman. And my wife was only twenty-five."

"The ex...younger or older than your wife?"

"Eight years older."

"What a louse." Jeanette put on her boots.

"I *like* older women," Copeland said. "My wife's older than me—five years older."

"Five, huh." Jeanette smoothed the cuffs of her jeans over her boots. "How'd you meet the older woman who doesn't believe in rings?"

"I had a toothache in Austin. When I sold my first guitar to Britt Daniel, from Spoon?"

Jeanette nodded recognition.

"Brit recommended a dentist who wasn't in the office that day. So I saw the dentist's daughter, instead." Copeland ran his tongue along his rear molar that had ached. "That was the first thing we had in common. We both worked for our fathers," he said. "Plus we have the same *birthday*."

Copeland got into his jeans as he followed Jeanette into the living room. "My wife and I share a birthday cake."

"Who blows out the candles?"

"She blows out one half. I blow out the other."

"Cute."

"She had her breasts enlarged," he said. "I told her they looked great the way they were."

"She's insecure because of her ex-husband."

"No sensation in her nipples anymore. She can't feel a thing there, no matter *what* I do to them."

"Messed up trade-off," Jeanette said.

He stood within kissing distance of Jeanette and said, "I *hate* that first husband of hers for hurting her."

Jeanette walked to the door.

"You going?" he said.

"I think I should. Don't you?"

"I think we should hug goodbye."

They hugged.

"You smell great with your clothes on *or* off," he said.

"You're doing the right thing tonight, Copeland."

He slid his hands up the front of her blouse, stroked her nipples beneath the sparkling lavender. "Does this feel good?" he said, wanting to hear her say: yes.

"Yes," she said. "And you're the husband who's *not* going to hurt your wife."

"Yeah...that's exactly who I am."

She stepped into the hallway; he did too.

"Hey. You. Lady—C'mere." He pulled her toward him. Kissed her like he wanted her to remember him. "You should be an Elvis Costello song."

"I should?"

"A song about a woman that a guy doesn't expect to meet and when he does he—he meets a part of himself he didn't expect to meet."

Jeanette smiled. "Deep."

"If we were both single," he said, "it would have been *ferocious*."

"Ferocious," she said.

"Stay *awesome*."

"All I can do is try."

She headed down the hallway, past a room-service tray containing an empty bottle of Rosé; and a puddle of chocolate ice cream in a glass goblet.

✳✳✳

"Goodnight, Beauty Boy," Jeanette said to Al, who was already asleep in his wicker bed, as she shut off the light. Someone on the second floor was listening to Brandi Carlile singing "The Joke," the emotional range of her voice reaching Jeanette through the ceiling.

She turned on the light, picked up a hotel pad and pen from the night table. She wrote: I NEVER EVEN THOUGHT ABOUT CHEATING ON MY WIFE UNTIL TONIGHT.

14

OUT OF YOUR CONTROL

Curtis Ames held down graveyard at a hotel, in Westwood, three nights a week. Today, he was at the Lyric, faking energy, image being important to him. Handsome enough to be a model, which he didn't want to be, or an actor, which he did want to be (merely because he resembled a young Idris), the trajectory of his vague dreams was on hold. Like his call to Housekeeping, as he worked the front desk with Laurie.

"Did you enjoy your stay, Mr. Copeland?" Laurie said.

"Enjoyed it a lot." Copeland slipped his Visa card into his wallet. "Listen, have you got a piece of paper I can write a note to, to...somebody. A guest?"

Laurie placed a sheet of stationery on the counter along with an envelope and a pen.

"Great," he said.

"No problem, sir."

Copeland wrote on the stationery:

Sunday, 11:45.
Dear Jea

"Outta ink," he said.

"Pen?"

He turned to the guest who rolled a hotel pen down the counter. "Thanks," Copeland said.

"Sure," Evan said.

Copeland resumed writing.

"I'm sorry, sir," Curtis told Evan as he hung up the phone with Housekeeping. "Your cigarette case has not turned up as of yet."

"It's Art Deco. Has a built-in lighter," Evan said. "Has special meaning. Lou Reed gave it to me. So if it turns up…"

"We can always send it to you," Curtis said. "No worries."

"If it looks expensive…forget about it," Copeland said to Evan.

"There are still some decent people in this world," Laurie said.

"Hope I'm wrong," Copeland said as he slipped his note inside the envelope. "Hope your gift from Lou hasn't taken a walk on the wild side," he told Evan, as he wrote on the envelope: *Jeanette—Room 144.*

"I'll put her message light on right now," Laurie said as Copeland handed her the envelope.

"Well," Evan said, "so long."

"We'll see you again, sir," Laurie told Evan. "You know what they say…when you leave something somewhere, it means you want to come back."

"Maybe so," Evan said, clasping his hands on top of his head. "Or maybe I'm just navigating too much mental traffic."

He lit up a Winston (striking a match three times against a coffee-stained matchbook) before he reached the sidewalk and the musicians who were boarding an idling silver tour bus. He exhaled a slow stream of cigarette smoke, watching it drift toward the terrace of a first-floor room; and a woman's bikini-top and bottom drying on the railing…drip, drip, dripping, as he stood there, think, think, thinking, ready to board the bus that would take him to his next gig. Next city. Next hotel.

At the entrance to this hotel, a Beverly Hills cabbie tossed a suitcase into the trunk of his taxi. The cabbie got into the car, a Tic Tac and a Boston accent in his mouth as he boasted, "I speak English *and* I take showers. Today's your lucky day."

Copeland laughed from the backseat, holding the guitar that, in half an hour, would belong to Elvis Costello. "I've been feeling lucky since last night," he said.

"I just got a message in 144," Jeanette told Curtis as she approached the front desk with Al. "Something at the desk for me?"

"Let me see what we have." He entered the small mailroom.

Jeanette leaned across the desk as she watched Curtis remove an envelope from a wooden mail slot.

She read her name, precisely written across the envelope, as she hurried out of the hotel with Al, thinking: *Open it now or after my first sip of coffee at Urth Caffé?*

If Jeanette hadn't been looking at the envelope, at that exact moment, she might have seen Evan down the sidewalk, boarding the silver tour bus. She glanced up at the bus as it rolled down the street.

Jeanette walked past the wet bikini that was drying on the terrace railing, outside the first-floor room. On the terrace of the room above it, a short maid gathered last night's beer bottles as she sang a song in Spanish. It had to be a love song: pretty melody, and Jeanette recognized the word "*amor*"—as she broke into a run.

She ran with Al, who held the envelope (that was so neatly addressed to her) between his dog lips, his freshly washed green leash in Jeanette's hand. They caught up with the silver tour bus. As it turned left on Melrose, Jeanette and Al turned right.

"Sit," she said. Al sat on the sidewalk in front of a gallery.

Jeanette removed the envelope from his mouth—she couldn't wait until she got to the cafe. She tore open the envelope, removed a single sheet of stationery:

Sunday, 11:45.
Dear Jeanette,
A bottle of port is waiting for you in the
restaurant. I was right. You enrich.
You rock, Lady.
    Copeland

Jeanette caught a glimpse of herself in the window of the gallery. She spoke like she was introducing herself to her reflection.

"I *rock*," she said. "Sometimes."

✷✷✷

The first time Michael and Jeanette had a problem with sex, they'd been living together for two years. Up until then, they'd enjoyed enough sex to fly first class—round trip—to Singapore on Frequent Fucker Miles, if Frequent Fucker Miles existed. That's what they were doing on vacation in Maui—fucking—when the homicide detective called to say: Michael's best friend, Bobby, had been killed in Berkeley. At home.

Their home.

The night Jeanette met Michael, she met Bobby, too.

She was stranded in a San Francisco parking lot after a Lucinda Williams concert. (Her date had been busted, selling shitty weed, outside the box office during the opening act.) Bobby offered her a ride home. But Michael drove, eyeing her in the rearview mirror of his Thunderbird while Bobby defined their friendship: a mutual obsession with music that dated back to Cub Scouts in Chicago.

"We're *promoters*," Michael said. "But only artists we're into—like Lucinda. This was *our* concert, tonight. We did it all,

86

me and Bobby," he said, with an energetic confidence that Jeanette found sexy.

By the time Michael pulled up to Jeanette's apartment, Bobby had asked for her number. But Michael walked her to her door, gave her *his* number. Six months later, she moved into a rented house with him in Berkeley; Bobby helped them move.

The homicide cop said Bobby had come home to a burglary in progress—shot through the heart—in Michael and Jeanette's living room.

"Dying in a *living* room. Is that some kind of tragic oxymoron?" Michael asked Jeanette, sobbing before he'd even told her the news. She had to ask three times:

"What? What happened? Michael. Honey. *Tell* me."

They couldn't bear to be in the living room or even walk by it. Sex was out of the question in any room—not in the house where Bobby was killed.

They rented another house in Berkeley two months later. Jeanette wanted to make love, wanted sex to transport them back to where they were before the tragedy. But guilt consumed Michael; the ifs and whys tormented him. "If I didn't ask Bobby to house-sit. If I didn't tell him, it would *lift his spirits.*"

Bobby's girlfriend had left him. Her things were still in his apartment. "Her scent...it lingers," Bobby said. "It'll do you good," Michael said, "to be where you *can't* smell her scent."

Three-and-a-half months went by before Jeanette and Michael had sex again. She didn't realize until years later that Michael had lost another desire—one that would never return—his need to succeed at something he loved, *music.* It died with Bobby.

Jeanette's mother had offered advice as they sat outside Tess's then-boyfriend's restaurant, in Santa Barbara, mother and daughter sharing flourless chocolate cake à la mode:

"When you live with a man, what you have to remember is he's not just living with you. He's trying to live with himself too. And if he doesn't like who he is. Or was. Or who he thinks he will be, well, you're not going to change that, sweetheart. Doesn't matter how smart you are, how beautiful. Whether you wear heels or flats...it's out of your control."

15

THE ANTIDOTE TO GRIEF

"Only reason you won is I got laid last night and you didn't."

The gate to the tennis court opened, revealing a thin wax bean of a guy with a bony, bare chest; pierced silver studs hung from the corners of his lower lip over a scraggly beard, suggesting he'd, perhaps, been a walrus in another life or was due to become one in the next.

The Man Who Didn't Get Laid pantomimed a backswing, displaying emerald-green fingernails. His racket whooshed the air...inches from The Walrus's head, as they walked across the patio past Jeanette, who was seated at a table, listening to her Realtor on her cell:

"Retired doctor and his wife ready to move in. No pets, no kids, no problems. If I were you—"

"Then you'd be talking to yourself now," Jeanette said.

"Good one," the Realtor said, allowing time for a one-syllable laugh. "Their house could be finished in four months, maybe less, but they'll commit to five."

"Five? Five months?"

"That doable for you?"

BEEP! Call waiting, her rep. "I'll *make* it doable," Jeanette told the Realtor. "I've got another call. Important. Call you later."

But Jeanette wasn't up for career-talk with Helena. Not now. She clicked off her cell as The Man Who Didn't Get Laid walked toward her, minus The Walrus.

"Have we met before?" he said.

She studied his features: a sullen, almost-handsome face that reminded her of the actor, John Cusack. "Don't think so," Jeanette said. "What do you do?"

"I'm a manager who wants to *forget* I'm a manager," he said. "What are you?"

"I'm a woman in a hotel who wants to remember."

"What is it you want to remember?"

"Now, that I wouldn't share with a stranger."

"Strangers are the best people to confide in."

"Does this mean you're going to tell me your secrets?"

"I wouldn't rule that out as a possibility," he said. "How long you at the hotel for?"

"Not sure."

He pointed up at the speakers, head bobbing to the over-produced track, a big, white, auto-tuned voice, masquerading as soulful. "She's one of my artists."

"I thought you wanted to *forget* you're a manager."

"Too many reminders."

"Like the guy you were playing tennis with...he a client?"

"Wouldn't be playing tennis with him if he wasn't."

"He looks like a walrus, don't you think?"

"Molting as we speak."

"Goo goo g'joob," she said, quoting John Lennon.

"You're quick," the manager said. "You're funny."

"Want to manage me as a comic?"

"Want to take a meeting?"

She shielded her eyes from the sun and the manager.

"If you do, I'm in room 317. For a few days," he said. "But

I'm at the hotel a lot." He walked away, pointing to the speakers as his mediocre artist let loose with a melismatic shriek.

Jeanette propped her feet up on a chair. She noticed something a few inches from her toes between the brown-and-white-striped cushion and the back of the wooden slatted chair—a cigarette case?

A *beautiful* cigarette case. Silver with wide, vertical bands of tortoise-shell-colored enamel; a lighter was built right into the top. Vintage Art Deco, she thought. It felt good in her hand. She opened the case. Two cigarettes. Jeanette hadn't had a cigarette in almost fifteen years. She took one from the case, closed the lid. She put the cigarette between her lips and told herself: *One cigarette. If the lighter doesn't work, I'm not meant to have it.*

She flicked the lighter, igniting a flame.

***

Helena Lutz's three-thirty had canceled; the air-conditioner in his Lexus had conked out. The director couldn't handle the drive from Burbank to Beverly Hills with the windows open.

Yes, Jeanette could make it at three-thirty *if* she rearranged her tight schedule. She'd fessed up to being in Los Angeles, but only until tomorrow, sounding vague but purposeful. Couldn't hurt, re-establishing rapport with her rep.

They met at Sprinkles, the cupcake bakery, on Little Santa Monica, down the street from Helena's office. (Helena recommended the special of the day, orange cake with orange-vanilla frosting.) They crossed the street with their cupcakes to Le Pain Quotidien, where they drank cappuccinos and sat outside facing angry traffic.

Helena looked more like a weary, inner-city schoolteacher than the owner of a successful production company—aptly titled Driven Woman—repping ten directors and a crew she kept employed enough to have been dubbed, by *Los Angeles Magazine,* "the hardest working act in ad-biz." Harried, frumpy, no time for style, Helena was raising three boys, the oldest twelve, while coming down the homestretch of a vitriolic divorce.

"Work," she said to Jeanette. "The antidote to grief."

The last time Jeanette worked was six weeks after Michael's death; she'd regretted taking the job: directing a thirty-second spot for a women's anti-bloat tablet, at Katz's Delicatessen, in New York City. Everything that could go wrong on a shoot did—rain, flu, budget. She'd lost her usual calm with a temperamental client rep who'd insisted on casting model-skinny actresses. "These women have no stomachs!" Jeanette yelled. "How can they *bloat*?"

He yelled back, "They bloat digitally!"

"Are these cupcakes to die for?" Helena said with a mouthful of cake. "You know, sometimes I wonder what's more painful. Losing a husband through divorce...or death?"

"Death."

"At least with death there's closure," Helena said. "Not this unrelenting exchange of bitterness." She wiped icing from her chin. "Not that I'm comparing my loss to yours."

Which, of course, she was.

"I'll tell you something, though," Helena said. "As much as I detest my almost-official-ex as a husband...I would recommend him as a shrink—if you need one."

Jeanette noticed a woman-driver crying in traffic, a sign on the passenger door of her van advertising *Zen Pilates*.

Helena talked about her three boys; how much easier life would be if they were girls. A reminder to Jeanette: Business meetings were different with women than men, so often beginning on a personal note, implying potential friendship that rarely developed, a courteous offer of bottled water followed by a woman-exec sharing some private happiness or sadness, verging on tears, somehow segueing from the confessional emotion of a classic Oprah interview to business with emotional detachment. Maybe it was natural instinct—women relating emotionally first—like driving to a place, taking the longest route every time because it's the only way you know how to get there.

"Walter Stratton called me," Helena said. "He's a client rep for Gap, now. "Two thirty-second spots...he wants to hire you."

"He wants to ease his guilt."

Walter was Michael's former partner at their boutique ad agency in San Francisco. After nine years, Michael let Walter pretty much steal the agency, selling it to him during his Everything Must Go Bleeding Ulcer Sale.

"I can't work with a man who made my husband miserable," Jeanette said. "No matter how miserable my husband made him." Loyalty coursed through her like a time-released capsule, dispensing granules of instinct-to-defend-Michael...as if she were still one half of a couple.

"So how do you feel about contributing to the overpopulation of hard penises?"

Hard penises?

Jeanette stirred her latte, trying to read Helena's face.

*She **knows**? My rep knows I'm living at the **hotel**?*

"Newest Viagra competitor," Helena said.

Jeanette laughed: a laugh of relief. Like she was on the lam and her hideout had narrowly escaped discovery.

"I spoke to the Creative Director at Eagleton-Thompson. You're being considered for their initial spot."

"I'm *perfect* for it," Jeanette said, suddenly blithe.

"If you get this spot, it'll be a coup." Helena mopped cupcake crumbs from her plate with her finger. "They'd prefer a man. But tell me something I *don't* know, right?"

"Just get me a meeting, Helena."

"If I do, you'll be the first to know, kiddo," Helena said, as if it were a spontaneous utterance that amused her. (Instead of an expression she'd been using since the day she opened Driven Woman sixteen years ago.) "I look like shit," Helena said, as she ate crumbs off her fingers. "But I'll look better after I'm spray tanned." She wiped crumbs from beneath her nails with a napkin. "Ever have it done?"

"Nope."

"I stand in front of a full-length mirror, wearing nothing but a shower cap, bright light illuminating my every flaw. While a stranger sprays me with coloring that's supposed to be natural. Beets, I think. Beets and bronzing salts. I'm not sure what's in it. Long as I don't turn orange," she said, oblivious to the smudge of orange icing on her chin. "I have to avoid sweating for six hours afterwards. Color gets on my sheets the first night, but it washes out." She licked oat milk foam off her spoon. "Fifty dollars. For a tan that lasts seven days."

"Sounds awful."

"Better than sun damage." Helena's fingers reflexively grazed her cheek, feeling for wrinkles and finding them. "When my husband left me...I didn't know who I was," Helena said. "I didn't feel like *me*. What about you, Jeanette? Do you feel like *you*?"

"Only when I absolutely have to."

Helena laughed. "If it's any consolation, your skin looks great. Whatever you're doing to deal with the loss of your husband...keep doing it."

✳✳✳

The key to her house in San Francisco wasn't beneath the welcome mat where she'd left it. The key on her key ring was missing too.

Jeanette pressed the doorbell. She banged on the door.

A taxi pulled up.

"This won't take long," a man told the driver as he got out of the cab.

First, she saw the cello. Then she saw Evan, carrying the cello...walking toward her.

"What are you doing here?" Jeanette said.

"What are *you* doing here?" Evan said.

"My life is inside this house. It's where I *live.*"

"You don't live there. You never did."

Jeanette peered through the window at the living room. Empty.

She'd rented out the house furnished. Where was her furniture?

"Why didn't you tell me you were married?" Evan said.

"I'm not," Jeanette said.

"You are. You're married."

"But what about your wife?"

"What about your *life?*"

Evan walked back to the cab. Jeanette followed him.

"Play me," she said.

"You need to be tuned," he said.

"I know."

Evan got into the cab. He leaned out the window to speak.

"Housekeeping." The voice had a Filipino accent.

Al barked. Jeanette opened her eyes.

"Housekeeping," the maid said in the corridor as she rang the doorbell of the room next door.

Jeanette stared into drawn-drape darkness. Evan had found his way into her dream—took a cab there.

She'd thought about him at unlikely moments: in her car at a light, on Chautauqua Boulevard, waiting to turn onto the PCH, a crazy, deaf mute, ranting and raving in sign language at traffic, just outside her passenger window, torn cardboard cluttered with illegible desperation in his flailing hand—and she was thinking of Evan's fingers...tracing her nipples, slowly, delicately; one nipple, then the other, coating them with his saliva.

The tone is in the fingers.

His words.

My *tone was in his fingers.*

If I could be his cello for a week. A month, she thought. *While*

*he was on tour—a European tour—he'd play me every night.
He'd carry me. Carry me around Europe.*

She switched on the light. Got into her yoga pants, threw on a T-shirt and shoes. "Want to go for a walk, Al?"

Al looked up at her from his bed like he'd rather sleep. She grabbed his green leash from the door and remembered something from her dream. She scribbled on a hotel pad with a hotel pen: BUT WHAT ABOUT YOUR WIFE?

16

I'M NOT ME

Pink's eight-piece band and crew were checking in, along with ten dancers, as Jeanette and Al navigated their way across the lobby, strewn with baggage and gear, to the front desk. Laurie, who was subbing for the Graveyard Guy, handed a minibar-key to guitarist, Justin Derrico, while asking Jeanette, "How can I help you, Ms. Coles?"

A willowy, perfumed girl (Jeanette recognized the scent: Thierry Mugler's Angel) jostled between Jeanette and the musician, a solitary magenta lock of hair hanging loose from her hennaed ponytail. "Excuse me, this is important," she told Laurie. "Could you see if a guest left something for me? Something for me when he checked out?"

"Your name?" Laurie said.

"It wouldn't be under my name."

"The guest's name?"

"I don't know his real name."

"Can't help you without a name."

"Sinsation?" she said.

"Be right with you," Laurie told Jeanette as she rifled through packages behind the counter. She handed the girl an envelope.

Jeanette saw the name: *SINSATION*, scribbled across it.

"These are them," the girl said, peering inside the envelope, sounding more sad than happy to see its contents. "One more thing," she said to Laurie.

"I'm crazy-busy now," Laurie said. "I'm checking in a group and I—"

"Keith Flynn," the girl said. "Is he still here?"

"We're not at liberty to give out information about our guests," Laurie said.

"I'm not asking for information," the girl said. "Just a yes or no."

"I'm sorry," Laurie said. "But we have to respect the privacy of our guests."

"You wouldn't be respecting his privacy if he wasn't here, would you?" the girl said, as the envelope slipped from her hands. Bracelets scudded across the marble floor, halted by the base of a concertina case.

Jeanette gathered the bracelets. She handed them to the girl, seeing now: She was a pale beauty with large, blue melancholy eyes that dared you to hurt her. Jeanette had imagined Sinsation with a fleshier, less vulnerable-looking girl.

"I'm not usually like this," she told Jeanette. "I'm not *me*, tonight."

"I'm not me tonight either," Jeanette said, thinking, this girl needs kindness. And, maybe, a lorazepam.

The girl whipped around to Laurie. "When you see Keith, tell him Nessa *believed* him."

Nessa?

Woman With Lonely Legs?

Woman on the answering machine—woman that Keith had treated *too good.*

Nessa walked through the maze of baggage and instrument cases, high heels click-clacking, lonely legs in fishnet stockings.

Had she been craving more of that too-good treatment from the former basketball player? Settled for nowhere-near-good from the rapper?

Sex with Sinsation—Consolation Sex or Punishment Sex?

"I'm sorry, Ms. Coles," Laurie said. "How may I help you?"

"Someone left this on the roof." Jeanette handed Laurie the cigarette case.

"Thank you," Laurie said. "I'm sure the guest who lost this will be happy to have it back."

Jeanette walked through the lobby past tired musicians and soundless instruments; in need of touch, so they could sing.

Faded studio-parking stickers clung to the back of the rear-view mirror of a dirty brown Mercedes—*show biz barnacles*—as Charles Millburn got out of the car. Slowly. Like everything hurt.

Jeanette stepped gingerly, circumventing oil puddles between her aqua-blue Prius and the weathered Mercedes. She removed a box of dog treats from the trunk, rewarded Al with a cheese-flavored biscuit, allowing herself fleeting eye contact with the actor; long enough to decipher his look: You recognize me and I'm not in the mood to be recognized. It was a wariness acquired from a lifetime of celebrity, in need of, yet uncomfortable with, attention.

"Hi," Jeanette said. A perfunctory "Hi," feigning lack of recognition.

"That's quite a handsome dog," Charles Millburn said.

"He's a head turner, alright."

Charles Millburn walked away from her, asking, "How do you like your Prius?"

"I love it," she told the back of Charles Millburn's famous head as if he were just another guest. Not an actor she'd fantasized about when she was a sixteen-year-old virgin who stole lipstick from the beauty-supply store and doobies from her mother's stash, a sixteen-year-old virgin who masturbated in her Laurel Canyon bedroom...while sometimes gazing at a classic poster of Charles Millburn: his first film, made before she was born.

He slid his keycard into the door as if he hadn't asked the

question she'd answered. "Goodnight," Charles Millburn said, without looking at her.

"Goodnight," she said, her voice higher and sweeter than she'd expected it to sound.

One forty-five in the morning, yet she felt a sudden, almost giddy second wind—she felt like she was sixteen, again.

Two crew guys in their twenties, wearing official Ed Sheeran tour T-shirts, walked across the garage. The cuter guy eyed Jeanette. He said something to his unkempt crew buddy that she couldn't hear.

She only heard the unkempt guy's response: "She's too old."

Jeanette didn't feel like sixteen anymore. She felt dangerously close to forty-nine.

17

THE WOMAN WHO SAVES THE DAY

"We would appreciate you settling your account, Ms. Coles." A message from Curtis played on the speakerphone while Jeanette combed her just-shampooed hair, dripping water onto a Guest Services Directory. "As a courtesy to you, being a long-term guest, we can keep your account open for a month—max," he explained. "At which time we have to close it. Open a new account with a zero balance."

The dog dropped his toy platypus at Jeanette's feet. "If you got any moolah stashed beneath your bed, Al, now's the time to bark up." Her cell rang. She threw the platypus across the room. Al ran after it, up the stair to the bedroom, as she answered the phone, "Hello."

"How would you like to be The Woman Who Saves the Day?" Helena said.

"Do I get to carry a sword and a shield?"

"I'll include it in your deal," Helena said.

"Thigh-high boots?"

"Thigh-high boots," Helena said.

"What's the catch?"

"All you have to do is direct a thirty-second spot for Nuyou-tox—next week."

"Next *week*?"

"They're in a bind and they're willing to pay to get out of it," Helena said.

"Why are they in a bind?"

"The former director was rushed to the hospital during a pre-production meeting. He thought he was dying from a heart attack. Turns out it was anxiety. He couldn't handle the pressure. Now he might as *well* be dead."

Jeanette wondered if she could handle the toxic pressure of directing with so little prep time. "Maybe this is a jinx gig," she said.

"This rarely happens," Helena said.

"He's not the first director who couldn't handle pressure."

"I'm not talking about the rarity of pressure. I'm talking about salary," Helena said. "It's like a triple rainbow, such a significant increase from a previous quote."

"How significant?"

"Sixty grand for a two-day shoot."

"*Sixty*?" Al stood at her feet, platypus dangling from his mouth. "I'll do it," she said, squeaking the platypus. "I'll save my day!" She tossed the platypus onto the terrace. Al pounced on it. "I said *my* day, didn't I? Freudian slip."

"Nothing Freudian about it, kiddo. You need the money."

This was true. She had a dog to feed, a mortgage to pay, and a hotel bill.

LYRIC HOTEL

GUEST FOLIO

MS. JEANETTE COLES   ARRIVAL: September 25, 2019

DEPARTURE: OPEN

The taut guest ran like a madman on a treadmill at full throttle, the air in the small gym reeking of his sweaty rage.

"Why are you at the hotel?" he yelled.

"I'm a psychiatrist," Jeanette said, walking at a sane pace on the treadmill beside him. "In L.A. to lecture *other* psychiatrists."

"Perfect," he said, slowing the treadmill.

"Why's that?"

"I'm a psychopath."

A flabby woman—her jaw and nose bandaged—rode the elliptical bike, side-eyeing the self-proclaimed psychopath.

"I'm a *cunning* psychopath," he said, mopping sweat from his forehead where a vein throbbed.

The cunning psychopath stepped off the treadmill, not bothering to shut it off.

"In a movie!" he said. "Just got the part."

"Congratulations," Jeanette said.

"Maybe you can give me some tips," he yelled, jogging backward toward the corridor. "From the perspective of a mental health professional."

"I'm booked solid," she said. "But you're in the right city for psychopathic inspiration."

The flabby woman with the bandaged face stepped off the bike. "Bike's all yours if you want," she said. She took a deep breath like she needed a deep breath.

"I saw another woman with bandages on her face too," Jeanette said. "In the hallway."

"New TV show. Six of us...being made over."

"Well, I hope you end up with the face you want."

The woman winced from the pain of her attempted smile. "I just want to look in the mirror and like who I see."

"Don't we all," Jeanette said.

***

A cluster of funkless women sipped tea, smiling, every tooth preternatural white—whiter than the china plates and dainty white bread sandwiches, relieved of crust, at the Rose Garden Tea Room; their faces, relieved of expression, were described in the ad copy as *carefree*. Carefree because Nuyoutox had blocked nerve transmission to their facial muscles, erasing the incriminating evidence of lives being lived.

On the set at Huntington Gardens, in San Marino, the account executive's face was frozen, too, as she said, "Give Nuyoutox a try, Jeanette. I can arrange a comp for you."

"What exactly is *in* Nuyoutox?" Jeanette said.

"Stuff that lasts four times longer than Botox," the account exec said.

"Is that why their faces look four times as frozen?"

"Not frozen...relaxed. Existing lines are smoothed. Future lines *obliterated*." The account exec sounded like she was reading copy. Until she said, "It was originally used on racehorses."

"So the horses would look *younger*?" Jeanette laughed. "I guess that explains why you never see a racehorse with laugh lines."

"Laugh lines on a horse? No. Nuyoutox was for their headaches."

"Horses get headaches?"

"I'm offering you a Nuyoutox *comp*, Jeanette. You'll be happy with the results."

"But will I *look* happy?"

"What?"

"If I'm happy, I want to look happy. I'm not afraid of expression. The *absence* of it...that's what scares me."

"It all depends on who's doing the injecting," the account exec said.

An actress, hogging the only patch of shade in the garden, chimed in, "My doctor's brilliant. He Nuyoutoxed a Kardashian," she said, as a makeup man sponged foundation onto her beauty-contestant face. "It works immediately. Day of my first injection, people didn't even recognize me—that's how good it is."

"That's a good thing? That you were unrecognizable?" Jeanette said. "You're like what? Twenty-eight?"

"Twenty-six," the actress said, shaking her head in refute, suddenly depressed at being mistaken for two years older.

"What do you need Nuyoutox for?" Jeanette said.

"Lines on my forehead. They made me look worried."

"Were you?"

"Was I what?"

"Worried."

"Yeah. I was."

"And are you worried now?"

"Fuck, yes. Every day there's something new to be afraid of. I worry all the time. But at least now, people don't see it on my face."

"And that's why *you* should try Nuyoutox, Jeanette," the account exec said.

"Tell me," Jeanette said to the actress. "Just tell me honestly. What good does it do you to look like you're not worried if you *are* worried?"

"Jeanette," the account exec said, "do you really think this is the time and place to impart your negativity to the product?"

Jeanette stared at the account exec's big, Nuyoutoxed forehead. She imagined graffiti sprawled across it.

"I mean you are here to *sell* the product. Are you not?" the account exec said.

"I'm here to save the day!" A smile creased Jeanette's skin, until her face was radiantly defiant with—*expression.*

Jeanette knew she'd never work with the account executive again. It exhilarated her. And it scared her—that she didn't give a shit.

18

THE MAN WHO CAME TO DINNER & THE MAN WHO CAME TO BREAKFAST

"Everything is beautiful. Just like in the movies," Oscar said, setting a rum and Coke on the bar in front of a guest who was already drinking a rum and Coke at 10:55 A.M., and who looked like a rapper and probably was one.

Oscar was a sweet man of indeterminate age, maybe sixty, and maybe—compared to what life had been in Mexico—working at this hotel really did seem just like in the movies. Although, every now and then, Jeanette detected a tinge of irony in his words; a haunted look beneath the veneer of professional sanguinity.

"Too late for breakfast?" she said, standing at the bar.

"For you, the moon," Oscar said.

"Too early for the moon," Jeanette said, perusing a menu. "Don't know why I'm looking at this. I know it by heart."

"Next week, new menu," Oscar said. "New menu, new chef."

He lowered his voice. "He is a bastard. Don't tell anyone I tell you."

"Not even my dog," Jeanette assured him.

"He wants to fancy up the place. Bring in customers from the outside."

"Won't make the guests happy...people from the outside."

"That's what I say." Oscar placed a yellow rose in a single-flower vase. "But the new chef don't listen." He set the vase on a room-service tray beside two silver-domed plates, a carafe of coffee, two cups, and two saucers. "Ernesto's in the kitchen," he said. "He'll be out soon to take your order."

Jeanette noticed a wince of strain as Oscar lifted the tray above his right shoulder. He scurried to the elevator, his palm balancing the heavy load.

"Rum and Coke...interesting alternative to coffee," Jeanette said to the rum and Coke drinker.

"I never like to start a day the same way twice," he said, while sketching on a cocktail napkin.

"You an artist?"

"In every way shape and form."

"I used to draw...paint," Jeanette said, surprised to hear herself revealing something about who she actually was, or had been. "Went to art school."

Whatever he was about to say next, he didn't; his focus shifted to a man who was carrying *XXL* magazine and the *Wall Street Journal*. A thick, dark braid, beginning beneath his black durag, ended at the middle of his back with a red rubber band and a luxurious spill of hair, fanning a white linen shirt that was brand new or fresh from the cleaners, crisp without a wrinkle.

Jeanette thought he might be Cuban, might be in his mid-thirties, might be used to getting what he wants.

"You have breakfast yet, Luther?" he said, as he approached the bar.

Luther raised his rum and Coke. "Got my breakfast in my hand."

"Breakfast of Artistic Champions," Jeanette said.

The possible Cuban sized up Jeanette, adept at observing without revealing. He granted his lips permission to smile, diluting an intensity that had quickened Jeanette's heartbeat, the unexpected change in tempo catching her off guard.

Luther drained his first rum and Coke. "Breakfast of Artistic Champions—yeah, yeah," he said, jiggling the cubes in his glass. "That's some good interjection."

"Imagine how you'll feel about me when you've finished *all* your breakfast," she said, head-gesturing to his second drink.

"Your name's Cindy...right?" the possible Cuban said.

"Jeanette," she said, thinking he didn't sound Cuban. Maybe he was Cuban-American. Half-Cuban, half-who-cares? Whatever the combo, she was drawn to it.

"You remind me of a woman I met last time I was here," he said.

"Yeah, well...white people," she said. "We all look alike."

"But she was only beautiful," he said. "She wasn't funny. Wasn't smart."

Jeanette sat down at a table (her favorite had yet to be cleared of yolky plates and an espresso cup smudged with pink lipstick), easing onto the claret-velvet banquette. She could see that Luther had one foot in the corridor, the other in the restaurant, and was starting his second rum and Coke.

"I be doped up in my inspiration. I just need to refresh it," he told the possible half-Cuban. "Get it right. Need some motivation for like a minute and a half."

"You need more than a minute and a half, Baby Luth."

"I'm goin' back to my room. Work on the song," Baby Luth said. "Get it like it should be. Like it can be. Like it *will* be."

"Whatever it be, I want to hear it. Soon as I finish breakfast."

Ernesto entered the restaurant from the kitchen in no hurry. He was a Mexican who resembled Johnny Cash—not the Joaquin-Phoenix Johnny Cash—a mature, measured Johnny Cash with a narrow, impeccably trimmed mustache. It helped that Ernesto wore black. But all the waiters wore black, and they didn't look like Johnny Cash. Ernesto possessed a quiet machismo. And a smile that appeared only with good reason, accompanied by a subtle shrug of shoulders made solid from twenty-five years of carrying room-service trays.

He approached Jeanette's table, blocking her view of the possible half-Cuban.

"I'll have the L.A. Lite with low-fat milk, please," Jeanette said. "And blueberries."

"Blackberries are fresher."

"Blackberries then."

The possible half-Cuban sat down at the table beside Jeanette, his newspaper and magazine between them on the banquette.

"If you'd like breakfast, sir, you have to tell me now what you want," Ernesto said. "Before the kitchen switches to lunch."

"Can they make me an omelet with egg whites?"

"No egg-white omelets," Ernesto said.

"No use hurrying to order something I don't want."

Ernesto gave him the shrug without the smile. He headed toward the kitchen.

The possible half-Cuban got up from the table as Jeanette said, "You don't seem like an egg-white kinda guy."

"You think you gotta be white to eat egg whites?"

"I think you gotta be worried about your cholesterol."

"Or worried that my father died of a heart attack at forty," he said.

"I got you beat by two years. My Dad died of a heart attack at thirty-eight." She handed him his magazine and newspaper. "Don't forget these."

"I don't know how I could've thought you were anybody else," he said. "How long you at the hotel for?"

"I'm not sure."

"I'll see you again," he said, like she could count on it.

She watched the possible half-Cuban walk: a walk of assurance, a walk in black leather boots, a walk that had her wondering what he'd look like with his clothes off and if she licked him, would he taste salty?

He stepped into the elevator. Charles Millburn stepped out, anticipating the sight of his famous reflection. Maybe hoping to rearrange his hair—a mess, today, like hair on the homeless, a stringy, sooty gray. Except it was trailing the collar of a handsome, royal-blue, velour crewneck (snappy with black slacks). He carried an ancient, leather briefcase that a Fuller Brush man might have lugged door to door, as he said to a cluster of frolicking dolphins on a plasma flat screen, "I was expecting to see a mirror, here."

"Me too," Jeanette said, as she stepped into the corridor. She stood beside him, staring at the screen, disappointed to see the dolphins.

Not that she didn't appreciate dolphins. She was all for them, only not here on this wall, adjacent to the entrance of the restaurant, contributing to the extinction of one of her favorite hotel pleasures: watching guests like Charles Millburn watch themselves in the mirror as they stepped out of the elevator.

"I guess they replaced the mirror this morning," she said.

He walked toward the hallway, offering no acknowledgement of Jeanette's presence. He stopped, turned as if he'd just remembered. "We've spoken before, haven't we?" he said. "Last time you were here."

"This *is* last time," she said. "I never checked out."

"That makes two of us," Charles Millburn said. "They can't get rid of me. I'm the Man Who Came to Dinner."

"And why can't they get rid of you?" She walked closer to him (not too close), allowing him his space.

"My house has mold. And the workmen are taking advantage of me because I've been away."

"Doing a film?" she said, wishing she hadn't. Because now he knew for sure: She recognized him. And he would think of her as a fan. Instead of an equal, sharing the common experience of living in a hotel.

"As a matter of fact, I am," he said.

"Interesting part?" she said, ever so casually.

"You're nosey," he said, hostile words spoken like they were a compliment. "If you were to ask those questions to Robert De Niro, he wouldn't answer you."

"You're not Robert De Niro," she said. "And I'm not nosey."

He stared at Jeanette, trying to decide whether he was offended or amused by her. He reached no conclusion as he said, "I'm a private person."

"What if I ask, how are you?" she said. "Would you consider that nosey?"

"How are you is good," he said, pleasantly, as if his inner acting coach had advised him to lighten his character.

"Alright, then. How *are* you?"

"I'm fine," Charles Millburn said. "How are you?"

"I'm fine too."

He headed into the hallway. So did she.

"I'm playing a psychopath," he said, gifting her with the update.

Jeanette laughed.

"You're laughing," he said, miffed. "Why?"

"I met another actor in the gym who's playing a psychopath."

Perhaps he didn't want to think she'd lumped him in the same category with an actor lacking his stature. And that's why he switched the subject from him to her. "Why are you still in the hotel?" he said.

"That I can't tell you. I, too, am a private person."

Charles Millburn looked puzzled. "Nice to see you, sweetheart," he said, walking away from her.

"Nice to see you too," she told the back of his psychopathic hair.

She turned in the opposite direction, pretending that's where she was heading all along. Halfway down the hall, she looked back at him: his shoulders slumped, pace slowed as he walked toward a corner suite that faced the rear of the hotel.

Room 344.

Charles Millburn was living exactly two ceilings above her.

Jeanette picked up a lone orange from the white doily of a breakfast tray on the carpet. She tossed it high in the air... and caught it—as the door to a room at the end of the short corridor that led to it opened.

A woman, wearing nothing but a hotel robe (sash untied), stood in the doorway as a man, wearing a sports jacket, stepped into the corridor. "How's my hair look?" he said to the woman.

"Good," the woman said, her fingers smoothing wispy strands of thinning hair from his forehead.

"You sure?" he said.

"Yeah," she said. "Don't worry."

"Bye," he said.

"It was great," she said.

The man hurried down the hallway past Jeanette. And a canvas bin, filled with slept-on-fucked-on sheets, ready for the laundry room and the sexless scent of Tide.

Her L.A. Lite breakfast was on the table when she returned to the restaurant. She poured milk over muesli and blackberries as Ernesto set a warm carrot-bran muffin beside the bowl.

"The man with the braid," Ernesto said. "He called here for you."

"The man with the braid? He called here for *me*?"

"He said he just wanted you to know, he's in room 332." Ernesto gave her the shrug with the smile.

She bit into a berry.

19

PREEXISTING CONDITIONS

Sofas stacked beside armoires and end tables took up two parking spaces in the corner of the garage.

Witnesses, Jeanette thought. *To how many intimate encounters?*

"They need to be repaired. Cleaned," the Engineering Supervisor said, tossing a flowered cushion onto the sofa.

"I bet," Jeanette said as she got into her car.

She was still looking at the furniture when the garage gate opened to The Outside World.

***

The young salesgirl was in the prime of her adorable-day-or-night-with-no-prep years. "You'll regret it if you don't get it," she told Jeanette, en route to a customer in need of a compliment.

Jeanette zipped the lavender cashmere sweater (50 percent off in the upscale Melrose boutique, last one in her size) until the top of the zipper, a silver J (the *Juicy* trademark) dangled between her cleavage. She studied her cashmere-clad profile in the mirror as the door to the dressing room opened, revealing—Sophie.

"I don't be*lieve* it!" Sophie said, trying on a gray, hooded, designer sweatshirt and sweatpants ensemble, a size too big. "Do you know how worried I've been about you?"

They hugged like old friends do, long enough for Jeanette to say, "You shouldn't have worried, Soph. I called you. Left messages."

Yeah, she left messages: at Sophie's condo, knowing she was at work—like she had with every friend who'd called her, hoping to get a machine instead of a real-live human which would require real-live conversation; and the dodging of her true whereabouts. Voicemail, email, Facebook, Twitter, all of it, they'd stripped the word *friend* of meaning—friends you don't have to talk to, if-only-we-had-time friends—replaced it with illusory connection. Sophie and Jeanette's connection was far from illusory.

Sophie stared at Jeanette like she was assessing someone who had recently recovered from a serious illness, fearing the recovery was temporary.

"I'm fine," Jeanette said. "I am. I'm good."

"The universe must have wanted us to run into one another."

"That's one way of looking at it."

"What's the other way?"

"When there's a great sale, you and I sniff it in the wind."

"True that," Sophie said with a laugh. "You'd be crazy not to get that sweater." She looked at Jeanette in the mirror with an approving raise of her perfectly shaped brows, then scrutinized her own reflection without mercy. In another mirror, another city, Sophie would be considered pretty. But this was Los Angeles, and standing beside Jeanette, she felt lackluster by comparison, as she said, "You didn't even tell me you were *thinking* about renting your house out."

Jeanette had no comeback. Best she could do was pretend she was discovering a flaw in the shoulder of the 50 percent-off cashmere as she wondered, *how does she know?*

"I was in San Francisco," Sophie said as if reading Jeanette's mind. "Day before yesterday." She flipped up the hood of the sweatshirt, the price tag nesting in her blonde highlights. "I stopped by your house." She slid the hood off. "Met your tenants."

"It was such a spur-of-the-moment decision," Jeanette said, untangling Sophie's hair from the price tag.

"They said they didn't know where you were." Sophie's face turned ruminative.

Jeanette felt a familiar, almost nostalgic, affection for the two vertical frown lines above the bridge of Sophie's nose—their incipient traces were visible in college—and the dimples on either side of her chin.

Sophie had never been crazy about Michael. Maybe because Michael had never been crazy about Sophie. Especially after he'd asked Jeanette, out of the blue, "What about your friend, Sophie?" when Bobby's date couldn't make it to a Taj Mahal concert. Sophie's blonde hair was down to her waist then, and Bobby had a thing for blondes with long hair.

"If you hate each other," Michael said, his arm around Jeanette in the back seat of the car as Bobby drove to pick up Sophie for their double date, "you'll be at the concert, so you won't have to talk."

Sophie and Bobby didn't talk much; they mostly touched. Three weeks after the Taj Mahal concert, Sophie moved in with him. Not just because she was fucking him every night at his place, anyway, receiving quality orgasms (including three days during her period when she usually didn't want sex, but wanted it with Bobby)—"He's amazing. I'm in a perpetual state of juiciness"—her lease to her apartment was up, and Bobby said she might as well stay with him. Until she found the right place.

Seven months after the Taj Mahal concert, Bobby was talking marriage, talking kid, not wanting either right away. Although he already had a first choice for the kid's name: Taj—boy or girl—which he tried out on Michael, who was all for it. Bobby had yet to receive Taj feedback from Sophie.

She was smashed on margaritas with Jeanette that night, in a dim, noisy Mexican restaurant in Berkeley. "Bobby and I have so much in common—I *love* sex with Bobby. He loves sex with *me*." Sophie twirled her pink straw in margarita slush as she pondered their affinities. "We're both sensitive. *Super* sensitive," she said, emphasizing her slurred words, "to *criti*-cism. We both hate being wrong. Because we're both inse*cure*. Oh, and cooking?" Sophie said (like she and Jeanette had just been talking about cooking). "We both hate to cook. I told him I inherited my mother's lack of *cool*inary skills and how she hates to cook. And he said, 'So does my mother.' And I said, I hope I don't remind you *too* much of your mother. And he said, 'You said whenever I whistle I remind you of your dad... but there's no way you can compare my whistling the theme from *The Godfather* to your dad whistling "Old MacDonald Had a Farm"...be real, Sophie.'" Sophie emptied the last trickle of margarita from their second pitcher into her glass. "That's *another* thing we have in common. We can't stand our *fathers*!" Sophie knocked back the trickle of margarita. "I now pronounce us"—she raised her glass to a hideous painting of Frida Kahlo on the wall behind Jeanette—"*doomed*."

On the word "doomed," they burst out laughing. Sophie laughed so hard, Jeanette wiped mascara-stained tears from her cheek with a cocktail napkin that depicted a cartoon draw-ing of a man wearing a sombrero.

The following day—before Bobby could even try out the name Taj on her—Sophie left him; just like that, she left him.

Bobby would call Michael at two in the morning without a "hello" or "did I wake you?" Just, "Sophie's shoulders. I miss her *shoulders*."

Michael never admitted it, but Jeanette figured he'd blamed Sophie for Bobby's death (nowhere near as much as himself), needing to siphon his misplaced guilt. If Sophie hadn't left Bobby, then Michael wouldn't have asked him to stay in the house...so he could get away from Sophie's yet-to-be-cleared-out belongings and her scent which clung to them.

All that history. Still, Jeanette rarely divulged details of her marital problems to Sophie. On those rare occasions when she had, she felt as if she'd betrayed Michael. Like the chlamydia incident. Sophie laughed when Jeanette told her she'd gotten the STD from a funky hot tub, certain Michael had cheated on her, even with his Zoloft-deflated sex drive. The more Sophie insisted, the more Jeanette had to resist her own doubt about Michael, resenting her friend for encouraging mistrust of her husband.

She never told Sophie she was leaving Michael. She didn't want to hear her friend say, "It's about time."

"So tell me quick," Sophie was saying now. "I'm doing a bikini wax in an hour." Sophie entered the dressing room, closed the curtain. "Where are you living?"

"I'm staying...staying at a friend's house," Jeanette said, wishing she'd resisted the sale sign in the window, so she wasn't here, explaining herself to Sophie, embellishing a lie. "Friend of my rep. While she's in Europe."

"Where's the house?"

Jeanette said the first place that came to mind that was significantly east of La Cienega, east enough to be a grueling drive from the Westside. "Los Feliz area. Franklin Canyon."

Sophie pulled back the dressing-room curtain, wearing her own charcoal-colored drawstring pants and oversized tunic, the color of burnt toast (Jeanette had tried to talk her out of buying last year in CP Shades), which hid her curves and made her look heavier than she mistakenly feared she was. "Give me your number in Franklin—"

Before Sophie could say "Canyon," Jeanette said, "I promised the woman I wouldn't use her phone." She hugged Sophie.

Because she wanted to hug her—and because she wanted to hasten the goodbye. "Call me on my cell."

"We'll have lunch," Sophie said. "And you're due for a facial. My treat."

"Sounds good to me," the salesgirl said, entering the dressing room, gathering Sophie's rejects. "I could use a facial."

"I'm in Venice," Sophie said, handing the salesgirl her card.

"Sophie's worth the drive," Jeanette said.

"Did you hear what you said? You said I'm worth the drive," Sophie told Jeanette. "So get in your sneaky Prius and come see me."

"I will."

"Promise?" Sophie said, as she hurried out of the shop.

"Promise," Jeanette said, relieved that Sophie was leaving.

Not that she didn't love Sophie. It was just that, well, if any friendship could be described as a preexisting condition, Sophie and Jeanette's could. A mostly *good* preexisting condition. But here's the thing...

"I love you!" Sophie called to Jeanette from the sidewalk.

"I love you too!" Jeanette yelled back.

It's hard to feel like a new person when you're looking into the eyes of your oldest friend.

20

THE SHAPE OF A WOMAN

Baby Luth and the possible half-Cuban were finishing dinner on the hotel roof. "They got free DVDs here but they mostly all out. Leftovers be like *ancient*-stale," Baby Luth said, his mouth full of New York steak. "Girl at the front desk recommended that old movie 'bout the faggit writer what's got the lisp."

"*Capote*?"

"*Capote*, yeah."

"So did you see it?"

"I ain't gonna watch a movie 'bout a faggit writer with a lisp before I go to sleep. Girl talked me into some old *French* movie," Baby Luth said, looking at the Hollywood Hills, which until tonight he'd only seen in the movies.

The possible half-Cuban had a different view—Jeanette, walking in his direction, a glass of red wine in her hand. He offered her a sliver of a smile and full-on eye contact, wanting her to know he remembered her name. "Jeanette."

Baby Luth gestured with a string bean on his fork to the empty chair beside him. "Finish your drink with us."

Jeanette set her wine on the table.

"*Amélie*," Baby Luth said to her. "Old-ass French movie. Ever see it?"

"I did. I liked it."

"You see *Amélie*?" Baby Luth asked the possible half-Cuban.

The possible half-Cuban swallowed his last bite of whitefish, wiped his mouth with a green linen napkin. "What's it about?"

"French girl thinks she got heart trouble 'cause her father never paid her any attention," Baby Luth said. "The nigga never gave her any love, so whenever the nigga would come close and shit, her heart would beat fast."

"You like the movie, Baby Luth?" Jeanette said, sitting down beside him.

"Caught half, switched to porno."

Jeanette laughed.

"I'm sexually frustrated," Baby Luth said. "Halle Berry was here today."

"Here?" the possible half-Cuban said, doubting it. "In this hotel?"

"I saw her, saw her in the lobby, Froi," Baby Luth said. "You ever see *Monster's Ball*?"

"Great movie," Froi said.

Jeanette knew his name now, so she used it. "I liked it, too, Froi."

"Oh, man, *Monster's Ball*," Baby Luth said. Watched it on Hulu ten times."

"How many times all the way through?" Jeanette said.

"All the way through? I'd have to say...once."

Jeanette smiled into her wineglass.

"Diddy was smart," Froi told Baby Luth. "Took a small but important role, showed his acting chops. Never would've been on Broadway doing *Raisin in the Sun* without *Monster's Ball*."

"If I was behind closed doors with Halle Berry," Baby Luth said, "she'd be holdin' on to the top of my head for hours... pullin' my hair."

Froi was watching Jeanette, and she knew it; her face showed nothing but interest as Baby Luth asked:

"Know what I'd like to say to Halle Berry?"

"Thanks for paving the way for black actresses deserving of recognition from the Academy?" Jeanette said.

"I'd like to say, 'I don't care *how* old you are—just let me go down on you for ten minutes, and you won't be sorry.'"

Jeanette's eyes met Froi's as Baby Luth said, "If I could, I'd go down on Halle Berry for hours."

"I'm sure you would," Jeanette said. "Why wouldn't you?"

"Why? Why you sayin' that?" Baby Luth asked, bothered without knowing why.

"Because she's exquisite. That sex scene in *Monster's Ball*... such yearning."

"You say that like you know something about it," Froi said.

"About the movie?"

"About yearning."

"We all know something about yearning," Jeanette said.

"I was in a restaurant in Beverly Hills," Froi said. "Heard these white guys talking about their friend. Chef who was a sex addict. So I asked them, 'How is your friend a sex addict?'"

"And what'd they have to say to that?" Baby Luth asked.

"He couldn't draw the line, so he crossed over into infidelity. I told them, 'I hate to be the bearer of scary news, but sex *is* addicting.'"

"*Tell* me about it," Baby Luth said.

"When I was a teenager, day after I lost my virginity, I went to my doctor," Jeanette said. "So I could go on the pill." Jeanette sipped wine, eyeing Froi. "Doctor told me I had to be careful. She said now that I'd had sex once, I'd want it all the time."

"And did you? Did you want it all the time?" Froi said.

"Only when I was awake."

Froi laughed.

"And every now and then when I was asleep."

"Bet you'd appreciate somethin' I'm workin' on, Jeanette,"

Baby Luth said. "Tell me what you think?"

Jeanette figured Baby Luth was about to bust a lascivious rhyme on her.

"Got an idea for a man's shirt," he said. "Maybe cotton, hundred percent, maybe silk. No polyester, know what I'm sayin'? Class all the way, mad-class shirt...two mad-class shirts in one. Reversible. So when a man spends the night with a woman, in the morning, he turns the shirt inside out...looks like he's wearin' a different one altogether." Baby Luth mopped ketchup with his last french fry, leaving nothing on his plate but salt. "Nobody have to know his shit but him."

"Certainly enough men in this world who don't want the morning tattling on what they did the night before," Jeanette said.

"Gonna have my own clothing line," Baby Luth said. "Got some ideas for women's apparel too."

"You got some ideas for *songs*?" Froi said. "I keep telling you, this is premature bullshit. You want your own clothing line? Become a major artist. You want to become a major artist? Record a major album. You want to record a major album? Write songs worthy of recording."

Baby Luth got up from the table all sulky. "I'm goin' to my room to write." He walked across the patio as Froi called after him, "You gonna write, Luther? Or you gonna watch porno?"

"I'm gonna write." He opened the door to the hotel, stepped inside. "Then I'm gonna watch porno."

"Is he talented?" Jeanette said to Froi.

He can do it all...rap, sing, write—and fuck up. I need to be here to motivate him." Froi pushed aside his empty dinner plate. "I usually stay at the Four Seasons." He tossed his napkin onto the plate. "But Baby Luth hasn't earned the right yet to stay at the Four Seasons."

Jeanette wondered how Froi had earned the right to stay at the Four Seasons, cheapest room $635 a night?

"I believe in Luther, in spite of himself," Froi said. "Except for Luther, I got out of the management business couple years ago."

"Got out to do what?"

"I'm a matchmaker."

"What, you facilitate love connections?"

"I arrange marriages." Froi smiled—not a stingy smile anymore, censored by a protective mind—a smile free to express itself. "Marriages between corporate America and hip-hop stars." He gazed at the Hollywood Hills, speaking to them, "I'm going to make Cardi B as important to Tampax as Mrs. Olson was to Folgers."

Jeanette laughed, her wine swirling in her glass as if the Cabernet were laughing too.

"Twenty-one years Mrs. Olson pushin' those Folgers crystals."

Jeanette considered telling him she'd directed a commercial for Tampax but instead said, "What kind of a name is Froi?"

Froi stretched his legs, the toes of his black boots pointing toward the pool below them as he said, "Cuban."

"I knew it!" she said. "This morning, in the restaurant, I figured you had some Cuba in you."

"My mother's Cuban. Father was half white, half African American. Most people don't pick up on the Cuban part. I'm impressed."

Jeanette raised her wineglass in a toast. "To the Cuban part."

"What are you drinking?" Froi said.

"Cabernet. House."

"Woman special as you? Drinking *House*?"

Froi walked to a wall phone, pressed the restaurant button. "This Angie?" he said into the phone, his back to Jeanette.

Jeanette noticed he was wearing another white linen shirt, wrinkle-free as his probably thirty-five-year-old skin.

"I'd like a double shot of Armagnac up here on the roof. Chateau de Ravignan," he said. "And a Cabernet, your best bottle."

"No way I can drink an entire bottle," Jeanette said.

"Don't care about price," Froi said into the phone. "She deserves the best." He hung up, turned to Jeanette. "What you don't drink, you'll take back to your room. Enjoy it when you want." He sat back down beside her. "So I got some Cuba in me. Like you assumed," he said, his words punctuated by the scream of a young girl, jumping into the pool, splashing water up at them inches from their table. "But you. You, you're nothing like I assumed."

"And what did you assume?"

"This morning? When I first saw you? I assumed you were someone who wouldn't be comfortable with someone like"—Froi smoothed his hair, fingers stopping at the top of his braid—"Baby Luth."

"I have eclectic taste in music *and* people," Jeanette said, wondering how Froi's hair would look and feel unbraided.

"Tell you what I *didn't* assume," he said. "You and I would be talking tonight about oral *sex*."

"Oral sex in the context of a movie," she said. "Oral sex in the context of Baby Luth's fantasy."

"In the context of fantasy...right," Froi said.

Jeanette knew they were talking about oral sex—in the context of what might happen later—after he'd pleased his mouth with fifty-two-dollars-a-shot Armagnac, and her mouth with the hotel's best Cabernet.

A boy plunged into the pool, screaming at the girl in German.

"Unusual. Kids in this pool after dark," Jeanette said. "Reason I prefer it at night."

"You're not a sunbather?"

"I'm a *moon*bather."

"You have kids?"

"No. No kids."

"I got a daughter, just turned four."

"You got a wife?"

"No wife. What about you, Moonbather...you married?"

"No."

"You ever get lonely?"

"Sometimes, sure. I get lonely," she said. "But you can be lonely even when you're living with someone."

The boy splashed water in the girl's face.

"I like to comfort people," Froi said.

"That's good. A good quality."

"I'm affectionate."

They watched as a man, blond and pale like the kids—he had to be their father—approached the pool, a price tag on the waistband of his bathing trunks.

"I'm comforting," Froi told Jeanette. "But I got my evil side."

The girl in the pool cried as the boy relentlessly splashed water at her.

"People fuck with me, I fuck 'em right back," Froi said.

"Well, then I'm glad that was never my intention," Jeanette said.

The father admonished the boy in German.

"I think what we need about now is..." Froi said, "a change of venue."

They took the back entrance to the hotel, beside the tennis court. The flags of eighteen countries flapped as Froi opened the door for Jeanette. She felt his hand on her skin, below her nape, grazing her tank top. His hand didn't graze long. Just long enough for him to know she didn't mind being comforted.

***

The restaurant was crawling with Germans—a documentary crew. A cameraman, drinking beer at the fireplace, told Jeanette, "You have excellent structure." While Froi waited at the bar for his bill so he could sign it. And they could leave.

"German by the fireplace," Froi said, holding a glass of Armagnac—Jeanette carrying her bottle of Cabernet—as they walked down the hallway. "What were you two talking about?"

Jeanette followed Froi down the short corridor that led to his room. "I asked him how you say oral sex in German."

"You did not," Froi said, laughing, slipping his keycard into the door of room 332.

"*Mundverkehr!*" Jeanette said, her German accent absurdly strict, but sultry.

"You're really something special," Froi said. Just before another man said:

"Jeanette?"

She turned. And there he was—*in the context of **reality**—* Evan.

Evan, wearing a black hat, woven with gold; his restless hair, waves of it, streaming from beneath the hat as if they'd raced to his collarbone.

Evan with the closed-mouth smile, no bigger than it had to be; just big enough to be real, lips subtly slanting in amusement. She'd *tasted* herself on those lips.

Jeanette felt like she'd been injected with a hypodermic of emotion—so much, so fast—nervous, wanting, exhilarated, a sudden lustful mess.

Evan. Close enough to touch her.

Except she was holding a bottle of uncorked wine, on her way to another man's room, and Froi was saying, "I'll be inside," leaving his door ajar, just enough so it wouldn't shut.

She'd wanted to talk to Evan for *so* long. And what did she say?

"Hat."

That's what she said to him. Hat. She wondered if she sounded as crazy as she felt.

"Baker's hat. Italy," he said.

"Looks like you," she said.

"You look exactly like, like you did..."

"Nine and a half months ago," she said.

"This your room?" He gazed at the open door to Froi's room.

"My room? Mine? No."

"Thought maybe we'd been sleeping next door to one another without knowing."

"You're in 333?" she said, realizing he'd been on his way to his room; and she was standing in front of it. "How long have you been here?"

"Two days."

"Two *days*?" She wished she could pull her words back into her mouth.

He removed a green keycard from the pocket of his beige cords. "Played a charity event with Sting."

"When are you leaving?"

She stepped away from his door so he could get to it.

"I'm checking out in half an hour."

Half an hour?

"I want to know how you are, Evan."

"Me too," he said with a laugh.

Needy. I sounded needy. "How's your cello?" she said, aiming for easy breezy.

"My cello?" He slid his keycard into the door, opened it, and said, "Moody."

She wanted Evan to invite her into his room. *Pull* her into his room. Pull her in, kick the door shut, lean her against it—his fingers in her mouth.

"I'd invite you in..." He stood inside his room. "If we both weren't on our way to someplace else," he said, looking at the uncorked bottle of wine in her hand.

"A gift." She held up the bottle. "How long can you keep red wine once it's been opened?" she said, just because she didn't want him to think she was going to glug down the bottle with the guy next door.

"I say when in doubt, drink. Finish the bottle, but don't operate heavy machinery."

"No welding until morning," she said.

"Wait to weld until noon." Evan smiled. "It's great to see you,

Jeanette." He shut the door.

And that was that.

She stared at the PRIVACY PLEASE sign. She thought about knocking, lifted her fist to the door. But opted for self-control, walking the few feet to Froi's room instead.

Froi was stretched out on the sofa, sipping Armagnac, shoes off, cashmere socks on. The air-conditioner hummed as blue flames hissed through the empty grate of the fireplace.

"I'm sorry," Jeanette said, closing the door. "Old friend I haven't seen in too long." She sat on the easy chair.

Froi took the bottle of Cabernet from her hand, poured generously into a wineglass he'd set on the table. "To new friends…" he said, raising his Armagnac in a toast, "becoming old friends."

They clinked glasses. Jeanette sampled her wine. She sampled again. Froi talked. But she didn't listen. His words faded in and out of her consciousness like bad reception on a radio: "The Best Western" (or did he say: best women)?…"five star"… "instincts"… "ogle" (or Google)?

What she heard, clearly, was the door to Evan's room, slamming shut—slamming her back to the moment, to Froi who was saying, "Connecting. It's all about connecting."

"That's what it's about," she said.

"You like your wine, Jeanette?"

"I do," she said, suddenly aware that she'd been gulping more than sipping.

Froi cradled his glass of Armagnac in his hand, admiring the $104 swirl of amber. "You have a boyfriend?"

"Boyfriend? No…not, not right now."

"How could a woman like you not have a boyfriend?"

How was she supposed to answer that question? Her face flushed. She heard herself say, "I tend to favor quality."

Froi liked her answer. "Sit beside me," he said.

She stood, stared down at him. He patted the sofa beside his thigh, snug in black denim.

"You know what I think I should do, Froi?"

"What should you do?" He slid to the end of the sofa, making room for her.

"My friend's checking out. It wouldn't be right if I didn't talk to him just a little bit before he leaves."

"That's cool," he said. "You do what's right."

"I'm counting on you, Froi. Keep an eye on my wine until I come back."

"I'll guard it. But you got to tell me again how you say oral sex in German."

"*Mundverkehr*," she said, closing the door behind her.

She stepped into the corridor. The PRIVACY PLEASE sign on Evan's door—it was gone. She knocked on the door, hoping he was still in his room.

He wasn't.

"Everything's taken care of but the incidentals, sir," Curtis said from behind the front desk.

"Be great if you could FedEx this for me," Evan said. He set a huge bag of gourmet popcorn on the counter.

"No problem. I'll see if we have an envelope it'll fit in."

"Must be some fabulous popcorn," Jeanette said, walking toward Evan, nothing in her voice suggesting she just ran down the stairs—thirty of them—hoping to find him in the lobby.

"My wife's on a popcorn binge," Evan said.

He wasn't wearing his hat. Jeanette wanted to kiss his hair.

"She's pregnant," he said.

Surprise merged with sadness, shading the tone of her one-word response, "Really?" She tried again, aiming for upbeat. "Congratulations."

"Thought it would be a nice surprise. The popcorn. For my wife."

"An affectionate gesture."

She took in the details of him, already transforming him into a memory: his hair, free because Evan didn't try to tame it; the two parallel expression lines, horizontally creasing the center of his forehead, as if they'd stopped there for a rest before continuing their journey; his right brow, tapering toward a solitary freckle; his eyes, nose, mouth, perfectly suited for one another, in harmonious co-existence.

"I'm on my way to—" Evan didn't finish his sentence; he started a new one. "My wife and I...we didn't plan it."

"A love child," Jeanette said.

Evan nodded, but he didn't smile.

"I just wanted you to know," she said, noticing the middle button on his shirt was undone, stirring an urge to touch him; stroke his exposed skin. "I didn't—"

"Hope this is the right size for your popcorn, sir." Curtis interrupted Jeanette at the worst possible moment, handing Evan a large FedEx envelope.

She waited the five seconds it took for Curtis to walk away. "Evan..."

Evan looked up from the popcorn, as Jeanette said, "I didn't leave my husband."

He gazed at her like he was browsing his thoughts, trying to pick the right one. "I'm happy to hear that," he said. "Hear that things worked out."

"My husband left *me*," she said, seeing the surprise in Evan's eyes. "He died."

"Jeanette, I'm..." Evan ran his fingers through his hair. "I'm so sorry."

"In case the envelope's too small," Curtis said, returning to the counter with a FedEx box.

"Well, I'll let you go," Jeanette said. "Take care of yourself, Evan." She buttoned his shirt. "You're needed."

She could have sworn he was about to wrap his arms around her, hug her. But he took a step back instead of forward and said, "Take care, Jeanette."

She wanted to hold him, feel his breath in her ear—a tacit expression of import to their goodbye.

But she walked across the lobby as Evan placed the popcorn inside the envelope for his pregnant wife.

On her way back to Froi's room, Jeanette made a quick stop at her own room: to see if she looked as bad as she felt.

She did.

She felt like shit, *fragile* shit. She wished she hadn't run into Evan, tonight. At least she could have continued to wonder how it would be if they were to see each other again.

Now she knew.

He'd acted like a stranger.

As if I hadn't held him in my arms outside this very hotel while he cried about his dog, she thought. *As if he hadn't held me in this very room after bringing me to orgasm four times. As if he hadn't kissed me goodbye, then said, "I better go now before I cross a boundary I want to cross but can't."*

She'd watched him walk down the corridor. Then walk right back to her. He'd grabbed her hair with both hands as he kissed her, his mouth a saboteur of good judgment, tempting them all over again—a kiss that had her missing him before he was gone.

He's a loving man, a loving man who loves his wife. Soon he'll have a new baby to love.

"Be happy for him," she told her unhappy face in the bathroom mirror.

She tried on a smile. Her reflection failed to convince her she had reason to smile. She applied blusher (as if that would help), saw no glow, only makeup. She blended the phony flush into her cheekbones, as Al squeaked his new toy cheeseburger, dropping it at her feet.

"Thank you, Al," she said, feigning enthusiasm, so the dog wouldn't sense her sadness. "If only a squeaking cheeseburger could do for me what it does for you."

***

By the time she arrived at Froi's room, an Armani bag was outside his door with a note:

> *Moonbather,*
> *Something came up I had to take care of.*
> *Enjoy your wine.*
> *Froi*

She removed the bottle of Cabernet from the bag. Started down the corridor, but walked back—not to Froi's room—to Evan's room. A sign was on the doorknob: MAID ON DUTY, the door propped open by a red, upright vacuum cleaner.

Jeanette stepped inside. "Hello?"

She was alone in the yet-to-be-cleaned room. She scanned the traces of Evan's presence: shrink-wrap from a CD (affixed with an Amoeba Music sticker) on the kitchenette counter beside an opened package of chocolate chip cookies. An empty bottle of Heineken was on the coffee table. She picked up the bottle, put her mouth on the lip of it—where Evan's mouth had been. *This is fucked-up behavior,* she thought. *But at least I know it's fucked up...so that's a good thing.*

She took the single stair to the king bed and the snarl of sheets Evan had slept on. She was glad she had the self-control not to inhale them.

She saw his damp washcloth on the bathroom sink next to an opened, complimentary bottle of mint mouthwash. She tossed the beer bottle into the wastebasket over a disposable razor. She peered inside the walk-in closet like she was looking for clues to a missing person: wooden hangers, couple of plastic laundry bags, luggage rack; that's all.

Then she saw it. On the carpet, behind the easy chair, against the railing that bordered the living room from the bed—Evan's hat.

She brushed it off as a maid entered the room, carrying an armful of fresh towels.

"I was just looking to see if this room was bigger than mine," Jeanette told the maid.

"Your room nicer. Bigger."

"I'll stay where I am then."

"You need towels?" the maid said.

"Towels? Sure."

Jeanette left the room, carrying two hand towels, two bath towels, the bottle of Cabernet, and, on her head—Evan's hat.

***

The night was not without orgasm. Courtesy of her fingers on her clitoris; and Evan on her mind—a fantasy revival of their night together—although, en route to her second climax, her fantasy featured a surprise cameo appearance:

"Just let me go down on you for ten minutes," Baby Luth told Jeanette. "And you won't be sorry." She let Baby Luth lick her inside and out, his tongue flicking for about thirty seconds—then booted him from her imagination.

She brought back Evan.

Evan's fingers traced the curve of her bare hips, her own fingers understudying his caress as she remembered his words:

A man designed the cello—so he made it in the shape of a woman.

"I want you inside me," Jeanette said, on her bed in the darkness of 144.

*I **am** inside you*, Evan said in her mind.

Evan stayed while she came, stayed as she moaned his name at the ceiling, and the sudden strings of an electric guitar wept through the wall of the room next door.

She opened her eyes. Evan was gone. His hat was still on her head.

21

MONKS AND DOGS

It was windy in Albuquerque at 5:00 A.M., the sports section of the *Albuquerque Tribune* scudding across the sidewalk, when Evan arrived at the hotel with the rest of Sting's band, wishing he had his hat.

At 11:00 A.M., a wake-up call infiltrated his fourth hour of sleep. Evan tried to remember what city he was in. He brushed his teeth, phoned the hotel in Los Angeles.

"No hat was found in your room, sir," Housekeeping informed him, same as yesterday.

He dialed Housekeeping at the hotel he'd just brushed his teeth in, requesting an ironing board, so he could iron his performance outfit for tonight's concert.

That's what he was doing now, ironing. And thinking, how he hated losing things, forgetting stuff, mentally retracing his activities, trying to remember where he'd put his hat, his cigarette case; his mind.

He'd tried sleeping on the plane but couldn't. Couldn't concentrate on the Murakami novel he'd started reading three weeks ago—still on the fifth chapter—reading the same page twice, his real-life narrative pushing fiction from his mind like a territorial bully. He'd close his eyes, let his thoughts wander.

They'd find their way, on their own, to Jeanette.

There had been weeks, entire months when he hadn't thought of her; easier at home, where days and nights were crammed with commitment, balancing music and family. It was on the road that he'd think about Jeanette. The woman he'd assumed was single, who'd turned out to be married, was, now, a widow. And he had to admit he was relieved, not that her husband had died, of course. Relieved that she hadn't left her husband because Evan the Detonator had *stirred everything up.*

There were times, when his cell rang, he'd been afraid: it might be Jeanette calling to say she'd left her husband, wanting...needing to see him. But after running into her—outside his hotel room, for Chrissake—he realized:

A. Jeanette had put their one night in its proper perspective.

B. He'd said goodbye abruptly, closing the door in her face... because he was about to grab her—pull her into his room.

There was a moment when he'd almost knocked on the guy's door—guy who'd bought her the wine, guy who'd wanted to fuck her, *did* he?—to invite Jeanette into his room. So they could "catch up" before he checked out.

And there was another moment in the lobby—while he was trying to mail the popcorn to his wife and saying his second goodbye of the night to Jeanette—he'd almost hugged her, held her, inhaled her...after she'd buttoned his shirt.

Early on in his career, at one of his first session gigs (with Terence Blanchard), he'd overheard some veteran jazz musicians talking about a horn player who was embroiled in his third bitter divorce. That's when he learned about monks and dogs. Monks were faithful to their wives on the road; dogs weren't. Dogs were always baffled by the wreckage of their relationships.

Evan was a monk. Never a dog. Except with Jeanette, when he hadn't been either. More like some rare hybrid monk-dog. But was monk-dog a prelude to full-fledged dog?

On the road in Austin, with Diana Krall, he'd met a woman

backstage during a meet-and-greet, friend of a friend (bass player). The three of them had gone out for drinks with a couple of musicians from the tour. The woman was cute, young enough for her extra pounds to suggest fleshy, not fat. She liked Bailey's Irish Cream, and she liked Evan, punctuating their conversation with a twirl of her long, coily hair around her finger; a squeeze of his thigh beneath the table. She didn't excite him like Jeanette, but he did have to fight the urge to invite her back to his room. His urge for Jeanette had a power—

He looked down at the yellow silk shirt he was ironing. He'd burnt it.

His cell rang. He shut off the iron. Picked up the phone from the crumpled bedspread.

"Hello."

"Thank you, honey." It was his wife. "Thank you for the popcorn."

"Did it make you laugh?"

"Yes then Sarah made me cry."

How does she do it? Evan thought. Not even a breath between good news and bad.

"Our daughter's a thief," Nancy said. "She stole a hat from a shop in—"

"Sarah stole a *hat*?"

"Walked out with it on her head."

"She get caught?"

"*I* caught her. Bragging on the phone."

"That is so weird, Nance. When did this happen?"

Nancy sighed. "Day before yesterday, but I found out this morning."

"Day before yesterday, I *lost* my hat," Evan said, examining the burnt iron imprint on the back of his shirt.

"Sarah said the store was going out of business anyway. It was their last day, as if that makes a difference."

"Don't you find it interesting, Nance...that I lost a hat on the same day?"

"Do you care that our daughter stole something?"

"Of course, I care. It's just that it's, it's almost like..." He couldn't resist a laugh. "Some kind of hat karma."

"Hat karma would be if Sarah *found* a hat, not *stole* it. We need to talk about punishment."

"Can we talk about punishment later, Nance? I've got to leave for a sound check."

"I'm not going to deal with this alone, Evan."

"I'll call you tonight after the concert."

"I love the popcorn...love you."

"Love you," Evan said.

Halfway through the concert, as he was accompanying Sting on a particularly poignant rendition of "Fragile," Evan ran his bow along the strings of his cello—and felt the back of his shirt rip where he'd burnt it ironing, thinking of Jeanette.

22

ISN'T THAT
WHAT MEN WANT?

Marvin Gaye's soulful rendition of "The Star Spangled Banner" (at the 1983 NBA All-Star Game) wafted from the second floor; some guy upstairs, with impressive chops and the cultivated taste of a DJ savant, was singing along, mimicking Marvin's phrasing, when Laurie called from the front desk.

"Just a reminder, Ms. Coles. It's time again. For you to settle your account so we can close it. Open a new account with a zero balance."

"Hold on a sec," Jeanette said.

She didn't want to miss the elegant flamboyance of Marvin Gaye, and the guy on the second floor, wrapping up the anthem: "For the laaa-aaand of the freeeeeee...and the home... of the...home of the bray-ayve."

Jeanette hurried to the terrace. She issued a two-finger whistle of approval up at the second floor.

***

LYRIC HOTEL

GUEST FOLIO

MS. JEANETTE COLES   ARRIVAL: October 25, 2019

DEPARTURE: OPEN

"So how's life in Franklin Canyon?" Sophie said, the second Jeanette answered her cell. The question surprised her. She stopped right there in the middle of the stairway that led to the parking garage, forgetting for a moment: she'd told Sophie she was living in the canyon.

"See what happens when another month goes by and we don't talk," Sophie said. "You don't even recognize my voice."

"Of course, I recognize your voice," Jeanette said, as a man walked up the stairs toward her. He looked like Questlove. "The fundamental things apply as time goes by, Soph." The man smiled at Jeanette.

Questlove (for sure) continued up the stairs.

"I'm almost booked up, so I'm saving a slot for you," Sophie said. "Three weeks from tomorrow—your birthday facial."

"My birthday...already. Can you believe it, Soph? Forty-nine—lying in wait for me."

"I'll exfoliate the dead cells of forty-eight."

"Can't ask for more than that from a friend. If I did it wouldn't be right."

"I'm penciling you in for one-thirty," Sophie said. "Gotta go. My lash tint is here. Bye."

Jeanette opened the door to the garage, nearly hitting a guest in the head—the manager who wanted to forget he was a manager. She looked to see if his fingernails were still painted green. Yup.

"I just checked in," he said. "And you're the first person I see."

"You still trying to forget your occupation?" she said.

His cell rang; he gave it a dirty look. "I wake up in the morning and I say, What now? Can I brush my teeth before a client calls with a crisis?" He took the call. "Talk to me." He closed his eyes, listened, shaking his head back and forth in disgust, then spoke with the strained calm of a divorced father on custody day, "I was never in favor of you opening for her, you know that. Hold on." He rested the phone against his thigh, and asked Jeanette, "What room are you in?"

She told him as she walked across the garage.

"The audience didn't come to see *you*," he said into his cell, as if there had been no pause in the conversation. "They came to beat the parking rush."

A new assortment of damaged furniture was outside the Engineering workroom: couple of bedside tables; an armoire; the chipped white-iron frames of two coffee tables, one on top of the other (legs in the air); a faded green cabinet sprouting pointy, iron posts (empty of the customary TV, DVD player and sound system). Three wooden end tables caught Jeanette's attention—like the ones in her room on either side of the sofa—ringed with glass and bottle imprints: relics of partying and just plain loneliness.

Jeanette approached the open door to the workroom. The Engineering Supervisor, barricaded by TVs and assorted appliances, tinkered with a DVD player.

"Hi," Jeanette said.

He looked up: a weary prick who didn't care who knew it, deficient in front-office appeal, perfectly suited for a small workroom in a corner of the parking garage where he could mutter his opinions, unchallenged, to the bolts and nuts and nails. "Hi," he said, dipping his head back into his work.

"What's the story with the end tables here?"

"Probably gonna get rid of those."

"Yeah?"

"Probably."

"If you do, can I have them?" Her fingers traced the rim of a stain on one of the tables: faded red wine. "I don't need the whole table, just the tops."

"You want the tabletops?" he said, searching a box, crammed with tools.

"If you could saw the tops off for me, I'll be happy to pay you for your time."

He processed her request.

"If you could saw the tops into four parts, that'd be great."

"You want each top sawed into four parts?" he said, deadpan.

"I'd really appreciate it."

He removed a screwdriver from the box. Tossed it back. Found one that was a keeper. "Can't do it today."

"At your convenience."

"Can't do it tomorrow."

"When you can."

"They're pretty banged up."

"I know. That's why I like them," she said.

The Engineering Supervisor resumed his tinkering. Nothing surprised him anymore, not at this hotel.

✳✳✳

The Creative Director had arrived from New York this morning. The fifty-two-year-old exec was expensively groomed, paint job on his closely cropped hair was good—light brown with just enough gray to deceive—but his shiny, white veneers were too big for his thin-lipped mouth. He wore a seersucker suit as he lunched with Director Number Three (he would interview three more directors before sunset) at Angelini Osteria, in West Hollywood, corner table, staring across the linen tablecloth at Jeanette, trying to make up his mind about her: Could she effectively, in sixty seconds, sell a product that promised a better boner than the competition?

Rigidyne.

That was the name of the newest Viagra competitor. Neil was the name of the exec with Eagleton-Thompson. "I had breakfast with another director we're considering," Neil said to Jeanette as a waiter poured sparkling Italian mineral water. "I have to tell you, he impressed me."

"I'd like some olive oil please," Jeanette said to the waiter.

"The account executive, Forrest Kinney. He's worked with him before."

"I don't know Forrest," Jeanette said.

145

"I know him well. Know how he thinks. We've worked to-gether on a number of major accounts. And I'll be honest with you...Forrest thinks a man is more apt to get the appropriate tone. Thinks an actor would be more comfortable with a man directing, considering the product."

"I'll be honest with *you*," Jeanette said. "I've never met a man who had a problem talking to me about his hard-on."

Neil laughed.

Jeanette realized if this weren't business, and they were seated at the hotel bar, by now he would have asked, "What room are you in?" But this was business. And the product just happened to be a pill that hardened penises. She was appreciating the perfectness of the timing of this meeting, what with her living in a hotel which was frequented by numerous hard penises—some even made hard by her—knowing if anyone could do the product justice she could, as Neil said: "I wouldn't be meeting with you if I wasn't a fan of your work."

"Thank you."

"I was impressed with your treatment. I like your take on the spot."

"I don't."

He looked at Jeanette like he wasn't sure he'd heard her cor-rectly.

"I've been rethinking it," she said.

"So, then, we're already having our first disagreement about your work. I like it, and you don't?" he said, laughing.

"Yeah. And I refuse to back down."

"Now you've got me curious," he said, smiling, his veneers reminding Jeanette of piano keys, his left front tooth a pol-ished middle C.

"More sex," Jeanette said, as a waiter poured olive oil onto her bread plate. "Less talk."

"Would you like to order now?" the waiter asked Neil.

Neil dismissed the waiter with a wave of his hand, his fo-cus on Jeanette.

"Isn't that what men want?" Jeanette said, dipping warm bread into the oil. "More sex, less talk? Isn't that what the product should allude to?"

Neil leaned back in his chair, intrigued. "So, you want to what? Put the man in bed with the woman?"

"I want to put them in an *alley*."

"An alley?"

"Shoot it in black and white—noirish. Click-clack of high heels on wet pavement. Her shoes. His shoes. Camera pans to their hands as—he pulls her into the alley. Leans her against the wall—kisses her. Her red polished fingernails scraping his black cashmere coat."

"Sexy," Neil said. He sipped his iced mineral water. Then said it again, "Sexy."

Jeanette knew she was on her game, momentum propelling her. "Suddenly—voices. From the sidewalk," she said, leaning across the table like she was confiding in Neil. "A young couple walking. They see the man and woman kissing...then breaking their kiss, turning to them, and to us—revealing their faces. Young Couple is surprised. So are we. Man is in his sixties, Woman almost fifty. Man grabs Woman's hand as they run from the alley, across the street to—a hotel."

Neil bit into a sliver of ice.

"Cut to hotel lobby," Jeanette said. "Man and Woman kissing in the elevator as door closes. Over the door—*RIGIDYNE*. Elevator rising, floor numbers lighting up, 1-2-3-4!" Jeanette slammed her palm on the table, underscoring her words. "Elevator door opens. Man and Woman, still kissing. Only now...a husband and wife, in their sixties, wait to board the elevator. Husband coughs nervously. Man and Woman stop kissing... walk down the corridor, holding hands. Husband and Wife stand in the elevator, four feet apart, watching Man and Woman...envying their passion, as the elevator door closes. And again, we see the word—*RIGIDYNE*."

Neil stared at Jeanette, expressionless; he ripped a piece of sourdough. He buttered the bread, set it on his plate. "Can you make this work with an actor who's in his seventies?"

"I'll make it work with a man in his eighties, if you get me Robert Redford."

"How about Charles Millburn?"

"Charles Millburn?"

She wondered if she'd sounded as silly-girly as she suddenly felt.

"Is he available?" Jeanette said, professionalism camouflaging all traces of silly-girly.

"Possibly next month. We're in negotiations."

"Charles Millburn could have…" She mopped olive oil with her bread. "Provocative potential."

Neil opened the menu. "I'll talk to Forrest. He trusts my judgment." He squinted at the menu, a blur without his glasses. "What do you recommend?"

Jeanette opened the menu. She smiled at the entrees. Man, oh, man. She wanted this job. But she was calm; she was cool as she said, "Ossobuco." And imagined the delicious possibility of directing Charles Millburn in a commercial for top-notch hard-ons.

23

POCKETS OF WARMTH

A tango slow-floated from the speakers of 144, Astor Piazzolla's "Milonga del Angel," coloring Jeanette's mood like she knew it would.

She'd purchased a sketchpad and charcoal pencils, two weeks ago, but hadn't removed them from the bag. Until today. She picked up a pencil, put it down; picked it up again as if holding the pencil might bring her closer to using it.

Ten tangos later, the circular, glass dining table was cluttered with crumpled paper: mounds of dissatisfaction. She stood. Stretched. Pet the dog. Showered. Moisturized.

She sat on the sofa, wearing her terry cloth hotel robe, listening to the music of Lianne La Havas (her smoky voice a vulnerable conduit of hurt yet hopefulness), while gazing, again, at a blank sketchpad. Four songs later, she clicked on Laura Nyro.

"Oooh la la la...oooh la la la la," Laura sang as Jeanette heard a man and a woman, in the living room next door, their muffled laughter seeping through the thin wall that separated Jeanette from the exuberance of their verbal foreplay. She picked up a charcoal pencil from the fat, flowered arm of the sofa.

As Laura Nyro sang, *"Time to design a woman..."* Jeanette began to draw the vague outline of a face.

***

"We went to Rodeo Drive today," the wife said. "Can't say I enjoyed it."

"Me neither," the husband said. "Although I didn't dislike it as much as my wife."

The couple from Indiana stood at the bar, holding hands (first held hands forty-two years ago, they'd said). They were waiting for food to go, so they could avoid the room-service charge.

"Those people who work at Armani," the wife said. "How do they know who has money and who doesn't? The way they treated us..."

"People don't generally go to Rodeo Drive for kindness," Jeanette said.

"Where exactly does a person go for kindness in Los Angeles?" the man at the bar, two seats down from Jeanette, said.

"There are little pockets of warmth in this city," Jeanette said. "But you won't find them in any tourist guide."

"Everything is beautiful, just like in the *movies*," Oscar said, emerging from the kitchen, carrying two silver-domed plates. "Medium rare *exactly*!" he told the couple.

"Are you sure I can't buy you two delightful Indians a drink?" the man who was seated beside Jeanette asked the couple, the preciseness of his British accent loosened by Bombay Sapphire. (He was deep into his third double martini.)

"I've been called an Indi*anian*. Never an Indian," the husband said. "If we didn't have an early flight tomorrow, we'd take you up on your offer, believe you me." He carried the room-service tray into the corridor, wife at his side.

Jeanette watched the couple as they waited for the elevator. The wife broke a french fry in two (half for herself/half for her husband), brushed a speck of something from his cheek with her wedding-ringed finger—and, suddenly, Jeanette missed the husband she no longer had, reminding herself (before despair could stake a claim to her balanced state): she'd missed the husband she no longer had when he was alive.

"They're quite the lovey-doveys aren't they," the Brit said to Jeanette.

"Nice to see," she said.

"Nice to see you, too," the Brit said.

"Why are you in Los Angeles?"

"I'm a composer," the Brit said. "I've been commissioned to write a ballet."

"I take it you're from jolly old England," the man two seats down from Jeanette, said, casually inserting himself into the conversation. "Whereabouts?"

"London," the Brit said. "Before that, I lived in Manchester with my wife." The Brit turned to Jeanette, unwilling to share her with the man beside him. "She still lives there."

"You're divorced?" Jeanette said.

"Separated," the Brit said. "Separated at the hip—like Siamese twins." He sipped his martini, then confided softly, "Our hips haven't touched in quite some time."

"I'm sorry," Jeanette said.

"Kind condolences are appreciated," the Brit said, helping himself to a few wasabi-coated peas from a bowl on the bar. "It's a self-sacrificing thing"—he examined the pea like he was appraising a pearl—"being a parent."

"So they tell me."

"Everything changes."

His black hair, streaked gray, was combed straight back, looping around his earlobes. Jeanette imagined the Brit wearing a tux and white silk scarf. He was almost debonair—if he wasn't so drunk, confessing into her ear like someone dared him, "I haven't had a blow job in eight years."

Whoa.

She hadn't anticipated such confessional intimacy. Not this soon. If she were at a bar in the outside world, she would be moving to another seat about now. But she was here at the hotel, where she was *living*, eager for insight into the male species, inquiring with the measured interest of an anthropologist:

"Eight years, long time. Were you and your wife having intercourse?"

The Brit constructed a cross on his cocktail napkin with the toothpicks from his previous martini as he answered with a dry laugh, "In a fashion."

"And you, did you go down on your wife?"

"I loved to go down on her. *Loved* it. But she didn't want it anymore," he said, the sloshed elegance of his voice transforming sexual explicitness into astute self-awareness.

The other man at the bar stared into his Jack Daniels like he was afraid to look up from it.

"Sad," the Brit said. "You'd think the closer you got with someone...the more time that went by...the freer you'd be when you had sex." He downed his martini. "But it doesn't work that way."

"No," Jeanette said. "It doesn't."

"You can have freer sex with a stranger you've known for just one night," the Brit said.

He's smashed, but he's right.

The Brit stood; he braced himself against the granite bar top. "Do you know why I'm telling you this?" He didn't wait for Jeanette's answer. "Three reasons," he said. "One, I am hammered. Two, I know I'll never see you again." He walked toward the corridor like he was determined to pass a sobriety test.

"What's the third reason?" Jeanette said.

"Three," the Brit said, his balance deficiency prohibiting a graceful pivot, "You are a little pocket of warmth."

The elevator door opened. The Brit stepped in; the man with the green fingernails stepped out. "Let's think about what's good for the band, not *fun* for the band," he said into his cell, as he entered the restaurant. "You make a difference or don't bother." He took the Brit's vacated seat. "Everything is urgent with my clients," he told Jeanette.

"Your usual, Mr. Devlin?" Oscar asked, clearing the bar of the Brit's martini-detritus.

"Yes, please, yes," Mr. Devlin said, setting his cellphone beside a bowl of mixed nuts.

Jeanette unfurled a cocktail napkin, placed it ceremoniously over his phone. "Out of sight, out of mind," she said.

"Wish it were that easy," Mr. Devlin said. "I tell my clients you say it's urgent, but I want you to think about whether it's interesting. Tomorrow, you tell me if it's interesting enough to be important."

Before Oscar could set the drink on the bar, Mr. Devlin took the tumbler from him. He clinked glasses with Jeanette.

"Urgency. Interesting. Important," Jeanette said.

"I'll drink to that," Mr. Devlin said. And did. "You look healthy. Glowing."

"I just worked out," she said. Her yoga pants and white T-shirt were still damp with perspiration. "I'm sweaty."

"I like it when a woman sweats."

"I'm a little pocket of warmth," she said.

If Jeanette had been looking at the other man at the bar, she would have seen that he was laughing quietly to himself.

"Are you married?" Mr. Devlin said to Jeanette.

"No."

"I'm married. Fourteen years."

"You just missed a couple who've been married *forty* years."

"Were they talking to one another?"

"Seemed very much in love."

"You have to watch out for married men. They're not trustworthy."

"Are you saying you can't be trusted, Mr. Devlin?"

"I was bad. I was naughty." He sipped his Scotch. "But my wife took me back."

"And now you can be trusted?"

"I have to monitor my behavior." His eyes drifted past Jeanette to the corridor. "So where's that set list you promised me?"

Jeanette followed his glance to a young, light-skinned black man; he had the likeable, clean-cut face of a popular camp counselor. The slender arms of a young, white woman were wrapped around him, her hands clutching his shoulders, her cheek against his back. "We're still finalizing it," he said.

The woman let go of the musician. He took her hand as they walked down the corridor. And Jeanette caught a glimpse of her—

Nessa.

"Keyboard player," Mr. Devlin said to Jeanette. "Guy's brilliant."

"He with a group?"

"He is if they don't break up on this tour."

"And the woman?"

"Don't know much about her. Neither does he." Mr. Devlin stared into the tumbler like it was a crystal ball; his green fingernails encircled it. "That didn't stop him from thinking he can't live without her. He met her a week ago...married her yesterday."

"Remarkable," Jeanette said.

"Not that it should surprise me," Mr. Devlin said. "He's needy."

"Maybe she needs to be *needed*."

Jeanette considered revealing what little she knew about Nessa. But she'd be betraying a confidence (wouldn't she?), a confidence Nessa had no idea she'd shared, yearning into a hotel answering machine, never thinking she was speaking to anyone, except the man she'd been craving.

Jeanette changed the subject, so she wouldn't talk about the new bride. "You ever stop working?"

"Hard for me to unwind. I'm thirty-eight and I have high blood pressure. My wife says I should learn to delegate."

"Couldn't hurt."

"I know what's good for me and I don't do it."

"Maybe someone should manage *you*."

"I'm unmanageable." He got up from the bar with his Scotch. "I'm going to drink this in my room. Where I won't run into anybody but me."

"Congratulations. You're doing something that's good for you."

"I'll tell you what would benefit my well-being. You coming to my room...and rubbing my stomach."

Jeanette laughed.

"I'm going to get in my boxers and sit on my sofa," he said, lowering his voice, speaking words just for her, presenting his plan as if it made perfect sense. "Then, you come to my room, get on your knees, and rub my stomach."

"What's in it for me?"

"The fun of innocent flirtation. Just a little tummy rub. That's all."

"You have to be good, Mr. Devlin. Your wife took you back."

"I can be good. But I don't think *you* can."

"That a challenge?"

"I could say something naughty to you, but I think you'd like it."

His cell rang.

"Toss your cell in the trash," she said. "Throw it away—right now. In the wastebasket behind the bar, with the sucked-on lime wedges and Pina Colada droppings...and I'll go to your room."

He looked at Jeanette, looked at his ringing cell.

"You're worth it," he said. "But my priorities are fucked." He answered the cell, "Talk to me." He closed his eyes, listened, nodding his head. "We all need our comfort," he said into the phone. "We all need our blankie...but how bout you pass the fuckin' drink tray and deal with solutions that aren't liquid for a change—hold on." He signed his bill, then said to Jeanette, "I guess a tummy rub is out of the question?"

She shrugged. "I *can't*. Your priorities are fucked."

"To be continued," he told Jeanette.

He left the restaurant, sipping Scotch. He was still talking on his cell as he stepped inside the elevator. "You need to re-examine your priorities."

The remaining man at the bar nabbed the seat beside Jeanette—pronto. "Mind if I sit here, before someone beats me to it."

"Might as well," she said.

"Real flurry of activity at your end of the bar," he said. "One more, please," he told Oscar, holding up a tumbler of ice, depleted of Jack Daniels. "Can I buy you another glass of wine?" he asked Jeanette.

"Just started this one."

"Put the lady's wine on my bill," he said to Oscar.

"You got it!" Oscar's mood downshifted. "The new chef," he said to Jeanette. "He's giving us a *test*."

"What kind of test?"

"On the new menu. We got to know how each dish is prepared—memorize it."

"Why?"

"Because he is a bastard, that's why. *Worse* than a bastard," he said, reaching for a fifth of Jack Daniels on the mirrored shelves.

"Must be a full moon, tonight," the man beside Jeanette said.

"I checked," she said. "A mere sliver."

"You don't remember me, do you?"

She scrutinized the bland evenness of his features. "Something's familiar. Are you a musician?"

"Do I look like I could be?" he said, hopefully.

"You're too well-rested."

"We met a couple months ago. Here. At the bar."

"I've got a good memory for faces." She picked up her wine. Set it back down on the bar without drinking. "What do you do? Maybe that'll jar my memory."

"I'm a market research manager. In Greenville, South Carolina." He waited for Oscar to set a fresh drink in front of him, then announced proudly: "I'm the Michelin Man!"

"I remember meeting someone who worked for Michelin,"

Jeanette said. "But he *looked* like the Michelin Man."

He laughed; he drank.

"Man I met dealt in antique money," she said.

"Yeah. That's *me*."

"No. This man had a different face."

"Yeah. That was *my* face!" I've been *made over*—for a new TV show."

Jeanette smiled like the secret of a really good magic trick had been revealed. "So you were one of those bandaged faces, milling about the hallways."

"Like a bad dream after a late-night piece of pie," he said. "Remember that TV show *Extreme Makeover*, where sad sacks had cosmetic surgery in the hope that a new face would perk up their lives?"

"No. Never saw it."

"Well, this is a kinda copycat of that," he said. "You get made over surgically, then they throw a party in your hometown where everybody cries from happiness 'cause you're not ugly anymore."

Jeanette laughed. "So what parts of you are new?"

He pointed to each new part: "Chin. Cheeks. Upper eyelids. Neck. Nose. Teeth."

"That's all?" she said, laughing.

"My hair's a different color. Blonder. I don't wear glasses any-more. Plus, I lost close to twenty-five pounds."

"So how do you feel?"

"I'm still getting used to me."

He took a handful of nuts from the bowl, set them on a cock-tail napkin. He looked at them as if he'd just remembered: The new him didn't eat salty nuts. "I have a meeting tomorrow with a movie producer," he said.

"Movie interest in your makeover?"

"He's interested in antique money. But you never know."

"No, you never do, do you?"

"My name's Ned." He shook her hand. "Ned Finger."

"Finger. Interesting family name."

"I was the middle child, too. My mother gave my father the middle Finger."

Jeanette laughed; Ned Finger laughed with her, grateful for the opportunity to do so.

"Would you like to refresh your memory?" he said. "See what I looked like before my makeover?"

"Got a photo?"

"Better than that. Got a copy of the show in my room. Brought it with me. You know, just in case I hit it off with the movie producer. Thought I might leave it with him, put the bee in his bonnet, so to speak." Ned Finger drank his whiskey like it was laced with courage potion. "Care to finish your wine with the *new* me...while we watch the *old* me?"

Every emotional memory in his brain prepared him for rejection. So, when she said "Sure," he was surprised. And he was nervous.

24

THE AWAKENING OF THE MICHELIN MAN

The makeover show revealed more than she wanted to see: brutal close-ups, arrows designating the unacceptable features in need of repair, glimpses of the reparation, complete with the awakening of the Michelin Man from anesthesia bandaged, swollen and incoherent.

The party was interesting—friends, family, co-workers, gathered at a Greenville steak house for the debut of The New Ned Finger—camera panning from awe to shock to tears.

"That's my mother by the salad bar," Ned said, as he sat beside Jeanette on the sofa in front of the TV.

Ned's mother looked like she'd witnessed a miracle: seen Jesus in the garbanzo beans. Her son no longer resembled her or her long-gone ex-husband.

The steakhouse was owned by Ned's brother who bore an uncanny resemblance to Ned, pre-makeover. Depression must have descended upon the brother in the midst of a party celebrating the riddance of the unattractive features he was still saddled with.

"The woman crying in the polka-dot blouse. She's the mother of my daughter," Ned said.

She was a petite woman with short, no-nonsense hair, wearing lipstick the same pink as her polka dots; her hands cupped her cheeks, mouth agape, like a secret Edvard Munch painting (completed just before his mental breakdown). The camera panned to a girl, maybe eight or nine. "That's my daughter," Ned said. Her undefined chin was reminiscent of her father's before his makeover. "She's the only one who misses my old face."

The show ended with a close-up on Ned beaming into the camera, saying, "This is surely a life changing experience. A real humdinger."

Ned clicked off the TV.

"So has it?" Jeanette said. "Has it changed your life?"

He rose from the sofa, ejected the DVD. "If I hadn't had my makeover, I wouldn't be here now, talking to such a pretty woman."

"That's sweet."

"I sincerely mean it."

Jeanette knew that he did. "The woman you said was the mother of your child—"

"First time we slept together she got pregnant. I take care of her and my daughter."

"And you live with them?"

"No. But I love my daughter. She's the best thing that ever happened to me. Besides my makeover," he said, smiling, unlatching a showroom of new white teeth—the teeth reminding Jeanette of the ad exec for Rigidyne. Her mind wandered to the possibility of directing Charles Millburn, remembering he was on location, playing a psychopath. *Will I get the job? When will I know? When?*

"I had a girlfriend I loved, once," Ned said, sitting on the sofa, a flowered cushion away from Jeanette.

"And did she love you?"

"I found her in bed with a guy. Tall guy, nice-looking guy.

At a friend's party."

"What did you do when you found them?"

"My buddies said I should've gotten angry—*hit* him. But I just walked out of there fast as I could. Drove home in the rain."

"You sound like you're sorry you didn't hit him."

"Maybe if I had, things would be different. Maybe she'd love me...maybe I'd be with her. Maybe we'd be husband and wife. I don't know. That's not who I am. Maybe it's who I should be. But I'm not."

Jeanette stroked the back of the hand that couldn't hit the guy who'd fucked his girlfriend—a brief caress he kept his eyes on—until her hand returned to her wineglass.

"I was in a restaurant today," Ned said. "And this girl came in with George Lucas—the director. I was embarrassed for her." Ned drank his whiskey, although there was none left, just watery cubes. "Why would a girl want to be with George Lucas? He's weaselly-looking."

Jeanette laughed. "So you think George Lucas needs a makeover?"

"The only reason the girl was with George Lucas was because of what he can *do* for her."

Jeanette figured he was yakking about George Lucas because he was nervous and didn't know what else to yak about—trying to muster the courage to touch her.

"If you, Jeanette, and I were to go to a really nice restaurant together, I'd know and you'd know, it was because we were having a really cool time together. Having fun—like we are this evening. Not because of what I could do for you."

"Maybe I'm just angling for a new set of Michelin's for my Prius," she said, smiling at his forehead, comforted by a frown line that had escaped eradication.

"You're not that kind of woman."

His surgically lifted eyes gazed earnestly at her. She stroked his implanted cheek; his altered, streamlined nose.

"My nose still has some thinning out to do," he said.

"Is your face still sensitive?"

"A tad sensitive, yes. Yes it is."

"How 'bout your mouth?"

"My mouth? It, it's hunky-dory."

She stroked his newly defined chin. Then kissed his hunky-dory mouth. She stretched out on the sofa, making room for him.

"Good thing I lost all this weight," he said, lying on the sofa beside her. "You, you're...you're gorgeous."

"You're gorgeous too," she said.

"Me? Gorgeous? Thank you. Would it be all right if I pulled your yoga pants down? Just a little?"

She slid her yoga pants down to her thighs, exposing a thong, patterned with red and yellow roses.

He stared at the yellow roses on her crotch—he'd never seen anything so alluring...not in real life. He inserted his hand beneath the bouquet. His fingers roamed the entrance to her vagina.

"How does this feel?" he said.

He searched for her clitoris like he was trying to find a doorbell in the dark. Jeanette placed his fingers on the clitoral bull's-eye. But his digits strayed from the target as he said, barely above a whisper:

"Touch him."

Him?

"Touch him," he said, like a neglected little pal was living inside his khakis.

She palmed the bulge.

"Oh, wow," he said, closing his eyes. "Oh. Oh...wow."

And before his little pal could be freed from his pants—he came.

They lay in silence. Until Ned said, "Thank you."

"I didn't do much."

"You were here...that was plenty."

She pulled up her yoga pants.

"I apologize for not reciprocating," he said.

She got up from the sofa.

"You are so much more sophisticated than I am. *So* much more sophisticated," he said. "Is there any advice you can give me...sexually speaking? You know, advice about giving a woman an orgasm?"

"What about the women you've been with? Have you satisfied them?"

"You're the first woman since my makeover," he said. "To be perfectly frank, when I had my old face...well, there weren't many women. And the few that there were, they, they may have been faking."

"Are you telling me—the man who was born The Middle Finger doesn't know if he's ever given a woman an orgasm?"

"I can't be 100 percent sure. I *think* I have. I *must* have. I'm forty-years-old. I'm a *father*."

"Watch this," Jeanette said, like she was about to somersault across the room. But she didn't somersault. She took off her yoga pants, lay down on the carpet. She slid her hand inside her thong. And closed her eyes.

If her eyes were open, she would have seen that his expression was not unlike the marveling witnesses to his makeover on the TV show. He watched from the sofa—transfixed.

She was masturbating. Right in front of him. Right on the carpet of his junior suite. Her fingers beneath the roses patterning her thong, moving round and round (her clitoris, he supposed). He wished he could see exactly what her fingers were doing (if only there was a gizmo that could measure the pressure of a finger against a clitoris as easily as, say, measuring air pressure in a tire, take the guess work out of it). He was amazed at how quickly she'd transported herself—to a place he knew he'd never taken a woman.

He made notes on his mental clipboard.

Her expression: kind of a mixture of pleasure and pain.

Her eyes: shut, blocking distraction from her focus.

Her mouth: open, like she was waiting to be fed.

Her legs: straightening.

Her toes: pointing.

Then—

A subtle spasm, a quick jerk of her pelvis, her legs too—the roses on her crotch jutting toward him in 3-D—one, two, three, four, five times.

Her body went limp.

Her breathing subsided.

A lazy grin eased onto her face.

She opened her eyes like awakening from a dream. A *wonderful* dream. She looked up at him from the carpet. Her hand emerged from her thong, then rested on her décolleté.

"Mr. Finger," she said, softly.

"Yes," he said.

That was a woman who did not fake orgasm.

25

PERKS

Twin Good Witches of the North waved sequined wands at the bellman—no Jeanette wasn't dreaming—it was Halloween (impossible to ignore in West Hollywood); the transvestites's frilly gowns skimmed the lobby's marble floor as they waved their wands at Jeanette.

"There's no place like home," Jeanette said, clicking her heels together three times as she opened an envelope that Ned Finger had left for her at the front desk. She removed its contents: a one-hundred-dollar bill. Not just any one-hundred-dollar bill. A one-hundred-dollar bill dated 1861—*Confederate* money.

The carpeted stairs were wet from a shampooing, blocked by a yellow plastic cone featuring the red outline of a man falling. Jeanette entered the elevator, studying the one-hundred-dollar bill. The words *Confederate States of America* framed an illustration—slaves, loading cotton bales onto a wagon.

"What floor?" the other passenger said.

"One, please." Jeanette looked up from the money long enough to recognize the veteran rapper, Busta Rhymes. He pressed the first-floor button. Jeanette and Busta rode in silence, until the door opened, and he said: "After you."

Jeanette stepped into the corridor. Busta followed.

"You ever see Confederate money?" Jeanette said, handing Busta the bill.

He scrutinized the illustration. Squinted at the details. "This for *real*?"

She read him a printed note that had accompanied the money: "'Fine condition, crispness remaining, light aging staining at top borderline but does not detract much. Small nick at left bottom border barely edges borderline, decent note with full borderline which is not commonly found. Basically, a clean note with evidence of moderate circulation.'"

"Where'd you get this?"

"Someone gave it to me as a gift. Man who sells antique money."

Busta handed her back the bill. "Gift for what?"

"I'm a life coach," she said. "The man was in need of coaching."

"You worth more than a hundred dollars."

"That I am," she said. "But a hundred dollars from 1861 is worth more than a hundred dollars."

"Whatever it's worth, you worth more."

"That's because I'm in fine condition. Got some light aging at top borderline...but I'm basically clean—with evidence of moderate circulation."

"You're a funny woman," Busta said. "I'll see you again, most definitely." He strolled down the corridor as Jeanette's cell rang.

"Hello."

"Rigidyne."

It was Helena.

"Did I *get* it?" Jeanette said.

"You *deserve* it."

"I do. I truly deserve it."

"They didn't want to go with a woman."

"I didn't get it?"

"They agree with you—a Rigidyne hard-on needs a woman's touch."

"I got it? I got the *job*?"

"Congratulations! I'm late for a meeting. Just wanted to give you the good news."

"Helena—"

"We'll talk in the morning, kiddo."

"Did they get Charles Millburn?"

Helena hung up.

✷✷✷

There was a snag in the Charles Millburn negotiations. "The association with erectile dysfunction could impair Mr. Millburn's attainment of future roles requiring an illusion of virility," his lawyer had explained. "My client deserves compensation parity to his risk."

"He's older than my *grand*father," Agency Producer Mutt Stone said, updating Jeanette on the speakerphone (putting nasal emphasis on "grand"). "Charles Millburn should be grateful we're giving him the opportunity to be associated with the *obtainment* of pussy."

Jeanette laughed as she clicked a photo onto her laptop; the client's second choice was a former soap star—white haired, Evangelical-eyed—who had done well for them pushing a pill that combated diarrhea.

"Easy to imagine him with the runs," Jeanette said. "But an *erection*?"

"Let's not imagine that until we absolutely have to," Mutt said.

The shoot would take place in Los Angeles, accommodating Charles Millburn's schedule, in the event they had Charles Millburn to accommodate. He had a window between commitments. Not a bay window. A half-opened slat of a louvered window: one night. Doable, since there was no dialogue. The date of the shoot was set for—well, what do you know? Her birthday!

The Rigidyne gig without Charles Millburn would be like birthday cake without ice cream. Birthday cake was nice, but it was the vanilla ice cream slathered on top that made it worth the calories.

***

It wasn't until Sunday night, after a weekend of sketching and painting (acrylic), splurging on color and room service (a rarity), so as not to interrupt her focus, that she felt inspired enough to remove the rectangular piece of wood from her closet—one fourth of the top of an end table—identical in size to the other eleven pieces the Engineering Supervisor had sawed, delivered, then stacked on the shelf beside the plastic laundry bags, iron, and extra blanket.

She contemplated the faint, circular burgundy stain in the lower right corner of the scarred wood. She turned it upside down, vertically, then horizontally, shifting the burgundy sphere.

Room service waylaid concentration. Angie, back from a visit to the Philippines, six pounds heavier, had returned to a worry: The new chef had hired a new girl. And she was French. Ernesto had seen them kissing in the kitchen by the freezer. Already, the new girl was working a party on the roof tonight instead of Angie, circumventing experience, usurping big tips.

Jeanette signed the bill, adding a generous tip, including a sample tube of Clarins *Extra-Firming Neck Cream*. "A salesgirl at Saks gave me two samples," she said. "One for me, one for you."

Angie laughed. "I will use it tonight!" On her way to the door, she turned to Jeanette. "Of course, what I said about the new girl...this is between you and me."

"Of course," Jeanette said.

Paint beneath her fingernails, Jeanette ate a puny piece of overpriced, smothered-in-pesto veal, all the while gazing at the rectangular relic of an end table as if she were engrossed in a good book.

***

TALENT. It was written on the label of the DVD—a generous application of the word, considering the roles didn't require speaking. After weeding hundreds down to several callbacks, the agency had FedExed their picks, matching the required specs: Sensual Woman, 49, with a body that still turns heads; Envious Sexless Wife, late 50s Weight Watcher who overate at dinner; Envious Sexless Husband, 60-ish small business owner with a paunch but doesn't care; Young Guy On Date, early 20s, shy, good looks; Young Woman On Date, early 20s, style and mind of her own.

Jeanette popped a DVD into the machine, clicked "play." She immediately clicked "stop." She phoned Sophie, rescheduled the birthday facial to a *pre*-birthday facial, promising to elaborate on her new job when they saw each other. Sophie had one available slot, thanks to a cancellation—a woman whose lips had swelled from a collagen injection gone awry, her sudden resemblance to a Thick-Lipped Gourami fish taking precedence over a waxed-tidy bikini line.

Jeanette did not like what she saw on the DVDs. The candidates for Sensual Woman, 49—they were all early 30s.

She called Mutt Stone but he was in a meeting; she emailed her disappointment, requesting actresses who were forty-nine.

Mutt's secretary called back with a question from her boss. "Mutt wants to know—Does she *have* to be forty-nine?"

"Yes," Jeanette said. "She *has* to be **forty-nine**."

"Have you *seen* women who are forty-nine?" the secretary said. "Because I've *seen* women who are forty-nine."

"I need to talk to Mutt," Jeanette said.

Half an hour later, Mutt emailed Jeanette:

Sorry. Client feels a younger woman would be an implied perk of the product.

26

SERENELY SOPHIE

Abbot Kinney Boulevard used to be described in the tourist guides as a "Venice hot spot for artists, poets and hipsters." The very people who gave the city its bohemian flavor had been pushed out by the wealthy techies. Amid the expensive boutiques, cafes, restaurants, and the few remaining artsy, oddball little shops, along Abbot Kinney's broken sidewalks, a humble haven survived: Serenely Sophie.

Fears and frustrations ran amok beneath Sophie's serene surface, but diligent maintenance of fragile calm allowed for her gentle pampering of a loyal clientele; it commenced the moment she opened the original paned door of her 1920s bungalow, framed in pink roses and wisteria, lending Sophie an aura of blissfulness that, in a different setting, might be interpreted as exhaustion.

Here was the salon, all of it: love seat on the left beside a table draped with white satin, displaying scented candles (some lit, some for sale); treatment table on the right, adjacent to Sophie's top-of-the-line machines and array of skin-care products. Another paned door, curtained in lace, opened onto the small adjacent room, one step up the hardwood floor to Sophie's office/kitchen.

The salon was originally in the front bungalow, until the rent got so high, Sophie moved to the rear bungalow, relinquishing her prime front location to a tearoom/chocolate shop: Aphro-teasiac.

This afternoon, Serenely Sophie smelled like oranges, ylang-ylang and lavender. That great spa scent, endorsing the wisdom of every dollar spent on a respite from reality's harsh glare, no matter how brief.

Jeanette lay on the treatment table as Sophie mulled the options, "Let's see, I can do a papaya enzyme peel. But not if I do ultrasound...works the products deep into the skin."

"Whatever you think, Soph."

Jeanette closed her eyes as Sophie shined a mag-light on her complexion.

"Maybe microcurrent," Sophie said. "You need a series of treatments to get the full benefit. But even after one, your skin will look firmer."

"Firmer, I'm for it."

"Power peel, first. Then microcurrent."

Sophie busied herself with preparation as Jeanette, eyes shut, updated her on the Rigidyne gig. She felt the soothing touch of Sophie's fingers massaging herbal cleansing milk into her forehead.

"Call me old-school," Sophie said. "But when Howie gets a hard-on, I want to know the source of that hard-on is *me*."

"Right."

"I mean arousing a man...that's half the fun."

"Sometimes more than half."

Sophie washed cleansing milk from Jeanette's face with soft puffs of organic cotton. Already, Jeanette felt herself unwinding.

"Tell me if it gets uncomfortable," Sophie said, over the whir of the dermabrasion machine. "I'll lower the setting."

It felt like sand was being gently ground into her face, as Sophie ran the probe of the machine along her skin.

"So have you gone out with anyone?" Sophie said, her voice tinged with concern. "Anyone at all yet?"

Jeanette grunted, "Uh-uh."

"Might be good for you, you know. To start seeing men."

Jeanette deflected the subject, "How are things with you and Howie?"

"Couple weeks ago, we were walking into Cedars-Sinai, and guess who we saw leaving the hospital?"

"Who?"

"Don't move your mouth while I get the skin above your lips."

Jeanette clamped her mouth shut.

"My ex-husband, in a wheelchair," Sophie said. "A nurse was wheeling him to a cab."

Jeanette mumbled, careful not to move her lips, "Andy in a wheelchair?"

"They always wheel you out when you've had an operation," Sophie said. "Andy's second on his ravaged septum."

Four years ago, Sophie divorced a husband whose coke-enhanced hostility had garnered so many enemies, he'd been booted from his law firm—tail between jittery legs—sacrificing a partnership in the firm, semi-bouncing back with a partnership in an outpatient-rehab facility.

After the divorce, Sophie was exclusively attracted to non-threatening underachievers. Like the dog groomer she'd met at Whole Foods, squatting beside him, while they scooped goji berries and chia seeds from adjacent bottom bins. "Talk about bottom feeding," Sophie had joked to Jeanette. "My standards have plummeted. All I'm looking for is a reasonably attractive man who isn't insane."

What Sophie found was The World's Dullest Man. Howie, a reasonably attractive textbook publisher, wasn't insane, but he did collect mustard memorabilia.

"Howie was surprised Andy didn't look more like an asshole," Sophie said as she exfoliated Jeanette's skin. "I told him, you have to picture Andy out of the wheelchair. Without a hospital band on his wrist—punching a refrigerator."

"Why were you at the hospital?"

"Howie's snoring problem. He spent the night so they could see if he has sleep apnea."

"Does he?"

"No."

"That's good."

"I guess. They don't know why he snores."

"Michael snored when he drank too much. I'd sleep on the sofa bed."

Sophie zapped microcurrents of electricity into Jeanette's face, pinching folds of her skin with thin, metal prongs. "I do think it would be good for you to start seeing men."

"Mmmhmm," Jeanette mumbled.

She scrutinized her face in a handheld mirror; Sophie waited for her reaction.

"Maybe," Jeanette said. "Maybe it looks a *little* firmer."

"Definitely," Sophie said. "It definitely looks firmer."

Jeanette set the mirror down and picked up a Trader Joe's bag. "I just finished this," she said. She removed from the bag—one-fourth of the top of an end table. Propped it up against the love seat.

Sophie studied it.

"Well?" Jeanette said, eager for Sophie's opinion. "What do you think?"

She stood beside Sophie, the two of them looking at an acrylic portrait of a man, painted on the scarred end table: a man with pleasant features and a shock of brown hair. Above him, a circular burgundy stain ringed a full moon in a dusky sky. Beneath him—a caption, painted in the same deep blue as his eyes.

"Really grabs your attention," Sophie said.

"So you like it?"

"His expression. His eyes. All wide and innocent, like he's hiding his guilt," Sophie said. "And the caption." She read the words out loud:

"*'I'M MARRIED…I HAVE CERTAIN BOUNDARIES.'* What gave you the idea?"

"Came to me one night, when I least expected it. Been so long since I've painted, I wanted to see if—"

"What is this wood from?"

"Old end table I found."

"Found where?"

"Parking lot of some hotel."

"You could *sell* this, Jeanette."

"You think?"

"Aphroteasiac. Small shop but busy." Sophie opened the blinds on the door. (Her signal to arriving clients: She was ready for her next appointment.) "I bet the owner would be happy to hang it in her shop."

"Yeah? I'll stop by."

"She's closed today. I can show it to her tomorrow, if you want."

"Sure, why not?"

Someone, outside, tapped impatiently on the pane of the front door.

"My brows and power peel," Sophie said.

"Thank you, dear Sophie, from the bottom of my pores."

Sophie laughed and hugged Jeanette. "Maybe your Rigidyne commercial will start you thinking about sex again."

"Never a problem *thinking* about sex, Sophie."

Jeanette stepped outside as a frazzled woman entered the salon, in dire need of pampering.

"I need a firmer face for tonight," the frazzled woman said.

Sophie shut the blinds; in dire need of pampering too. But hiding it.

27

THE STUFF THAT DREAMS ARE MADE OF

A cello resonated with consoling melancholy from somewhere on the first floor—Jean Sibelius's "Was it a Dream?"—drifting into her very bathtub, as she soaked in the plump foam of lavender-scented bath balm. Cello? Or violin? Jeanette loofa-sponged one shoulder, then the other, concluding: *cello*.

Jeanette walked barefoot down the hall, like a wide-eyed somnambulist, soap-bubble residue clinging to her damp skin beneath her terry cloth robe, the sublime voice of the cello luring her to its source—room 138, sign on the door: PRIVACY PLEASE.

She stopped at the room-service tray on the carpet of the corridor that led to the door and the cellist behind it. On the tray: a red rose, two coffee-stained espresso cups (one rimmed with red lipstick), and a dessert plate scattered with strawberry stems and a dollop of whipped cream.

She nabbed the rose, scurried back to her room.

Red rose still in her hand, she dialed room 138. Three rings and the strains of the cello ceased. On the fifth ring, a man answered, "Hello."

"Who is this?" Jeanette said.

"Who is it you want?" the man said.

"Are you the one who's playing the cello?"

"I *was* the one. Until the ringing of the phone interrupted my playing." He sounded Israeli. Sounded angry.

She racked the phone, pricked her finger on the rose.

✳✳✳

Sleeping Jeanette was dreaming on the very edge of the king bed in room 144; but in her dream, she was in her first home with Michael in Berkeley. Only they were looking at the back-yard of their last home in San Francisco—their house—the house she'd rented out. And she was thinking:

What will Michael say when my tenants come home?

"What is it you want to tell me?" Michael said.

Doesn't he know he died?

"Tell me now," Michael said. "It's the perfect time."

Maybe he didn't die—maybe I just thought he died.

He was talking to her like nothing had changed. She would have to tell him: **Everything** had changed.

Because he was alive; she would have to tell him.

She was glad he was alive. Only, she didn't feel happy. She knew that she looked awful, afraid to peer into the mirror, afraid her face was different.

I should look in the mirror—after I tell Michael we're getting divorced.

She hit him. Hit her husband. A loud, angry slap across his cheek.

She punched him. Pounded his shoulders...to see if he felt it.

*Did he feel it? Did he feel **anything**?*

Jeanette woke up/sat up simultaneously. She walked to the bathroom in the dark.

Al was in the kitchen, slurping water from his hotel dog bowl as she returned to bed. "Al," she said, patting the comforter.

176

"Sleep in my bed tonight."

Al jumped onto the bed. He lay down beside her. Jeanette wrapped her arm around him; his coat smelled a little like rosemary. "Pretend you're a guard dog," she said. "Protect me from my dreams."

28

WHO KNEW?

A big, pale-yellow stick of butter—the faded remnant of an ancient advertisement—was painted on an equally ancient brick building at the end of an alley.

"Rigidyne meets *Last Tango in Paris*!" Jeanette shouted.

The butter was, fortuitously, across the street from a 1940s hotel in the broken heart of downtown Los Angeles. Formerly a luxury hotel, now a resident hotel, a resident explained: The tiny fridge in his room, chilling insulin, had once chilled champagne for well-heeled guests. Jeanette knew how to maximize the surviving grandeur. The original elevators were intact, complete with brass arrows above the doors, indicating each floor as the elevator rose from one to ten.

After three long days of scouting locations with Production Company Producer, Roberta Frasnay, and Tucker Smith, Director of Photography, Jeanette had what she needed.

Until the conference call.

"Ocean. Palm trees. *Ocean*," the Rigidyne rep said from New York: a call that included Roberta and Producer Mutt Stone.

Jeanette had assumed they were in conceptual agreement on the term "noir" when the Rigidyne execs okayed her shooting in black and white, like she'd pitched.

"She can have her black and white," the Rigidyne rep said (as if Jeanette wasn't on the phone, knowing, of course, she was). "She can have her noir. Long as it's upscale-romantic...associates the product with upgrade of lifestyle."

"Are you saying flaccid to erect is not an upgrade?" Mutt said.

Jeanette laughed. Roberta Frasnay said, "Ha."

The Rigidyne rep merely stated with absolute seriousness, "The renewed capability of erectile achievement should connote other heretofore unattainable rewards."

The following morning, Jeanette, Roberta and Tucker were back scouting locations, Roberta combating the pressure with copious drops, beneath her tongue, of the homeopathic sedation, Rescue Remedy. Jeanette had worked with Roberta before. A dependable, loyal workaholic with impressive biceps, she wore no makeup, liked a tan too much to care about sun damage, and favored short hair because it dried faster when she washed it.

Tucker popped Advil for a tooth that was literally aching for root canal. But he was a trouper, the DP's commercial credits dating, appropriately, back to "Where's the Beef?"

Two days later, Jeanette had a Four-Diamond hotel in Santa Monica—palm trees, ocean view—couldn't get more upscale-romantic. But what really won her over was the long, stone driveway leading to the entrance. And the wrought iron gate with the brass letters that spelled: *H O T E L.*

Unfortunately, the elevators were dismal. Forget arrow above the door. Not even floor numbers except for the service elevator. (She could piece that together in editing.) The alley across the street ran adjacent to a cold, white, modern office building. No faded advertisement for butter. But she did have an eighty-foot Moreton Bay Fig tree, historical landmark, in fact, outside the entrance to the hotel.

She stood beneath the tree's sprawling branches, imagined the visual possibilities—and pressures. The shoot was in five days. Her cell rang; she heard anxiety in her "hello," wondered if the person on the other end heard it too.

"I have news," Helena said.

"Good or bad?"

Jeanette couldn't tell. Helena sounded preoccupied, like another client was on hold.

"Charles Millburn," Helena said. "He's all yours."

Good news? No. It was *how-great-is-this?* news. A *who-knew?* occurrence. As in, who knew she would grow up to direct the actor she'd fantasized about when she was a girl? And who knew he'd be playing a man who was reaping the benefits of a pill-induced hard-on?

If Jeanette could backflip, she would. Backflip down the stone driveway...all the way from the Moreton Bay Fig tree to the wrought-iron gate that proclaimed: *H O T E L.*

She wanted to drive to Aphroteasiac, buy chocolate, see how her painting looked in the tearoom—Sophie was right; the owner was all for displaying it, but the place would be closed by the time she got there. So she drove to K Chocolatier in Beverly Hills, where she bought dark chocolate truffles, a hand-poured dark chocolate bar, and—how could she resist?—blueberries coated in dark chocolate (hey, they were more than celebratory, they were loaded with antioxidants). Then, she drove to Amoeba Music in Hollywood, where she purchased nine CDs and one DVD: Truffaut's *The Woman Next Door.*

Peggy Gou's upbeat electronic dance track, "Starry Night," played in room 144, as Jeanette binged on music and chocolate (two truffles plus half the bag of chocolate blueberries). And as "Minor Swing" by Django Reinhardt, Stéphane Grappelli & The Quintet of the Hot Club of France filled the junior suite—Jeanette danced with the dog.

29

CLOSING TIME

"Still time for a beer?" The man sounded like he wasn't about to rush for a beer or anything else.

"Last drink of the night," Oscar said, from behind the bar. "You *got* it."

"I'll have a Sam Adams," the man said, his baby-blue shirttails hanging loose over faded jeans.

The bar was empty except for Jeanette, who was halfway through a glass of champagne. He sat two seats over from her.

"Not that I don't wanna sit next to you," he said, a boyish grin on a weary face, like a lively guest at a dwindling party. "I'm figurin' some lucky guy's about to return to his seat beside you, tell me to scram."

"No lucky guy," she said. "Just enjoying a glass of champagne before the bar closes."

"I like your style," he said.

It was the startling blue green of his eyes that grabbed her attention—had her thinking of the ocean along Route 1 on the way to Big Sur—as he scooted to the seat beside her and said, "I'm Clancy."

She was trying to place his accent, place his age too: younger than her, not by much. "Where you from, Clancy?"

"New Orleans, born and lazed."

"You a musician?"

"My talent's in my *ears*. Not my fingers," he said. "I'm a recording engineer."

Oscar set a bottle of Sam Adams and a tall glass on the bar. "No need to dirty another glass at closing time," Clancy said. He took a long drink from the bottle. He was a leftie—and Jeanette saw no ring on his untalented fingers.

"So how's life in New Orleans?" Jeanette said.

"I split after Katrina. I know how to survive disaster," he said. "My life was stormy *before* the hurricane."

He swigged. She sipped.

"I'm in Kansas City now," he said. "Ain't New Orleans. But it has its advantages."

"Like what?"

The boyish grin was back. "Garage-sale capital of the world."

"That a fact?"

"Indisputable."

Oscar set their checks on the bar.

"You know, I hate to keep a man workin' longer than is necessary," Clancy said, signing Jeanette's check before she could object.

Oscar *did* look tired.

"I'm going to let the bartender close up, drink my beer on the rooftop."

"Rooftop still open, Oscar?" Jeanette said.

"Closed," Oscar said. "Closed twenty minutes ago."

"Looks like I'll be drinking my beer in my room." Clancy stood as he picked up the beer. "Closing time has deprived us of getting to know one another."

"Right place, wrong time."

"Story of my life," he said. "But, what do you think about prolonging our brief acquaintance?"

She waited for him to ask. He did.

"Would you like to finish your champagne with me in my room?"

There were those ocean eyes—maybe if she got close enough, she'd see specks of seaweed—and she wondered what his story was, so she didn't say no. Didn't say yes, either.

"If it would make you feel more comfortable..." he said, "we can leave the door to my room *open*."

"Or we can sit outside your room in the hallway. Have a picnic."

"Whatever puts you at ease, darlin'."

She got up from the bar.

"I just invited this woman to finish her champagne with me in my room," Clancy said to Oscar. "Can I trust her?"

"Abso*lutely*," Oscar said with a wink and a smile.

***

Clancy slipped his green keycard into room 227; Jeanette followed him into his junior suite.

"I meant it," he said. "About leavin' the door open...if you'll be more comfortable."

"I wouldn't be in your room if I thought I would be uncomfortable."

"Well, I don't mind leavin' it open a sliver," he said. "Don't wanna give you the wrong impression is all."

"What wrong impression would that be?"

"That I might have expectations other than conversation."

"You just need a friend away from home to finish a drink with...right?"

"That's what I need," he said, easing onto the sofa.

She set her champagne glass on a *Welcome to Los Angeles Hotel Guest Informant* book, as she sat on the overstuffed chair.

"Mind if I take my shoes off?" he said.

"Whatever puts you at ease darlin'."

"I know *one* thing about you," he said, pleased. "When I talk you actually hear what I say."

"So why are you in Los Angeles, Clancy?"

"Business." He slipped off his loafer. "Potential partnership in a recording studio."

"And if it happens, you'll move to L.A.?"

"Not thinking about that till I have to."

"Now that's a talent," she said. "Not thinking about things until you have to."

"I live in the moment, the right here and now. I *appreciate* life." He removed his left shoe, placed it on the carpet precisely against the right one. "People tell me I live every day like it'll be my last."

"Your home in New Orleans..." She noticed a bit of cork floating in her champagne. "Did you lose it in Katrina?"

"My place in the Quarter, it survived. But I'd already lost it. Lost what mattered most *before* Katrina." He set the bottle of beer on the table. "My own fault," he said. "I had an affair— then I had a divorce."

He sauntered in white sports socks to the kitchenette.

"How long was your affair?"

"Little over a year." He held up a wicker basket of junk food. "Cookies? Chips? How 'bout some M&M's one month past the expiration date?"

"Expired M&M's," she said. "Wonder if they melt in your mouth *and* your hands."

"Might as well give 'em the consumer test." He tossed the pack of M&M's onto the table as he said, "Woman adored me."

"Which woman? Your lover or your wife?"

"Good question," he said. "I was referring to my lover." He sat back down on the sofa. "She'd check my clothes for strands of her hair so my wife wouldn't find them."

"What color hair?"

"Red. Soft," he said, like he missed that soft, red hair. "I never worried about lipstick on my clothes. She was like you, didn't wear lipstick."

He must be used to women telling him his eyes are gorgeous.

Probably since he was a boy.

"Know what she said?"

Jeanette shook her head "no."

"She said she couldn't be like me—*unfaithful.*" Clancy swallowed beer, stifled a burp. "Not if she loved a man who knew how to love her."

Jeanette turned on the radio: DJ giving a rundown on the club scene. "So how'd your affair end?"

"A present," he said. "Present she gave me."

"Boy, you must have really hated that present."

Clancy smiled. "I loved her present," he said. "She didn't want me to bring it home...have to lie to my wife."

"What was it?"

"Little CD cabinet. Doors from some funky old fence in the lower Ninth." He gazed at the TV like he could see his ex-lover's gift on the blank screen. "She said whenever I came to her place, I'd see it. Know it was mine."

"Sounds like she didn't want anything jeopardizing your affair."

"Did I listen to her?"

"I'm going to guess...no."

"I insisted on putting it in my recording studio." He drank beer; he drank some more. "One night my wife came by. She liked the cabinet so much, she wanted another one for home." He set the beer bottle on the table. "She asked where I got it."

"And you're wondering why you didn't listen to the woman with the soft, red hair."

Clancy nodded. "I told my wife I bought it at a flea market."

"Good answer."

"Good answer, yeah. Till she moved the cabinet from the wall, picked up the CDs she knocked behind it with her purse." He propped his feet on the table; his little toe peeked from a hole in his white sock. "That's when my wife saw the words carved on the back: 'For Clancy—Love, Lisa.'"

"Maybe you *wanted* your wife to find out."

He stared at the wet imprint of the beer bottle on the table. "Don't think so."

"What happened with Lisa?"

"She fell in love with a man who knew how to love her." Clancy tore open the pack of M&M's. "Week before my wife left me." He poured M&M's into his palm, ate them one right after another.

"We humans are a complicated species," Jeanette said, as she recognized the tune on the radio: Joe Henry's sensual ballad, "Animal Skin."

"*I see in you an animal trace*," Joe Henry sang. "*That's quick in your blood...and it's deep in your face...*"

"Ever been married?" Clancy said.

"I was."

"How'd it end?"

"I don't feel like talking about my marriage."

"Feel like dancin'?"

She opened the door to the terrace, stepped outside. She started to dance slowly without him.

"Hey, wait for me," Clancy said, joining her on the terrace.

He watched her dance in front of the red geraniums (the flowers seemed to be watching too from the planter boxes along the railing), her feet still, body swaying, hands reaching toward the moon.

"When we were walking to my room," he said, "I thought you might be a dancer."

"Really?" She liked that. But she didn't think she looked anything like a dancer.

"You *move* like a dancer," he said.

"Well, I hope so," she said. "I'm a choreographer."

"Knew you had to be something like that," he said, as he put his arms around her waist; she placed her hands behind his neck. They moved to the music.

"Who were you sadder to lose?" Jeanette said into Clancy's baby-blue shirt. "Your lover or your wife?"

"My wife."

"Because you sounded like you miss your lover."

"I miss them both," he said. "You're a lovely woman."

"Yeah?"

"I don't even know your name."

"Jeanette."

And Joe Henry sang:

"*Oh let your arms make a deep night for me. Enclosing my world so I cannot see...*"

"You're a lovely, lovely woman, Jeanette. Lovely and sensual."

A heavy, thumping bass from the street below—sudden as an earthquake—a rapper spewing anger to a menacing track, boomed from the speakers of an Escalade.

"Drive-by vibe-crusher," Jeanette said.

"I don't know who you are," Clancy said. "But here I am in a hotel with a strange woman. And I'm feeling...*safe.*"

She looked into his ocean eyes, saw no seaweed as he said:

"I know you'd never stab me."

Some part of her brain ordered another part of her brain: run that by me again. He said what? *I know you'd never stab me.*

"It's a compliment," he said.

"You think?" she said. She stepped back into the room.

He followed her. "When I was in my twenties," he said, "a stranger walked up to me in New Orleans. On Canal Street—and stabbed me." Clancy shut the glass door to the terrace. "He stabbed me in the stomach...then disappeared into the crowd."

"That's *awful.*"

And it suddenly dawned on her: Clancy's offer to leave the door to his room open—had been for *his* comfort. Not hers.

"I almost died," he said. "But it left me with a sexy scar."

He sat on the easy chair, unzipped his jeans. He lifted his shirt—revealing a diagonal scar across his stomach.

It was huge. She didn't know what to say. Never could she

have imagined that she would be in a hotel room with a man who'd unzipped his pants, and she would be overwhelmed by the size of his *scar*.

"I got a tattoo on the fifteenth anniversary," he said. See?" He pointed to a vertical tattoo beside the scar. "See what it says?"

"I can't make it out," she said. "Looks like a seahorse from here."

"A seahorse?" He laughed. "No, Jeanette. It's a word—*life*."

L

I

F

E

Tattooed on his wounded stomach.

"A celebration I'm still here," he said.

She took a very long drink of champagne.

"Now you know why I live every day like it's my last."

She nodded.

"Why I gave myself permission to have an *affair*."

Well, there was a rationalization for an affair that deserved a category all its own.

He zipped his jeans. Got up from the chair.

"It's made me wary," he said.

"Wary," she said. "I can see where it would."

"But when I *trust* a woman…" He placed his hand gently on her shoulder. "It's made me an appreciative lover." He stroked her arm. "A generous lover," said the man whose talent was in his ears, not his fingers.

Okay, what was happening here? Was she witnessing some world record for speed of emotional growth? Had he gone from being afraid to close the door with her in his room to feeling safe enough to fuck her?

"Appreciative, generous," she said. She downed her champagne. "But I have a conference call in half an hour."

"So late?"

"Paris," she said, walking to the door. "Director of a ballet company. I'm up for an important gig."

"Take it as a compliment…that I showed you my scar," he said. "I only do that with people who put me at ease."

"I *will*. I'll take it as a compliment," she said, uneasily. She opened the already ajar door, wide enough for a graceful exit as Clancy said, "Expired M&M's."

He held up his hand, stained with chocolate, yellow, and red food coloring. "They *do* melt in your mouth *and* your hands," he said. He gave her that boyish grin. "Good luck with your choreography gig."

"Toes crossed," she said. "Good luck to you, too, Clancy. Good luck with everything."

"That's why I'm *alive*, darlin'—I'm a lucky guy."

Jeanette headed down the corridor. Clancy shut the door. He locked it. Then unlocked it. He opened the door, checked to see if the PRIVACY PLEASE sign had fallen off. It hadn't. He closed the door, locked it again.

Al greeted Jeanette like there was no one else in this world he'd rather see. She sat on the carpet beside him. Looked into his soulful canine eyes. "Being single at almost forty-nine is different than being single at almost twenty-two."

I'm smarter now. Aren't I? My instincts are more informed. Aren't they?

"Al, I just made a brand new rule for myself—no sex with any man who says he knows I'll never stab him."

Al wagged his tail along the carpet like a drummer's brush softly grazing the drumhead. "What a good rule," Jeanette said. "What a *good* rule."

30

THE WAY TO FEEL

Dr. Aaron Lutz—psychologist.

She told herself, curiosity was why she was sitting in the Brentwood office of the almost-official-ex-husband of her rep. Jeanette had wondered what kind of man Helena once loved but now detested. And, well, she just might benefit from talking to a shrink. Although shrinks were plenty fucked up themselves.

A framed photograph on the desk faced Dr. Lutz, for his cold eyes only. Photo of the three sons he'd had with Helena?

"So..." Dr. Lutz said. "Tell me what brought you here, today."

"I met a man who survived being stabbed in the stomach by a stranger," she said. "A stranger stabbed him...then disappeared into the crowd."

Dr. Lutz stared at her blankly, as if all his sessions began with that very concern.

"He's so grateful he's alive," Jeanette said. "He had the word *life* tattooed alongside his scar."

"The tattoo, that's a bold statement," Dr. Lutz said.

"Me? I have dreams that I have a tattoo of the word *widow* beside my pussy."

Well, that piqued his interest. She saw it in his subtly raised eyebrows.

"That, too, is a bold statement," Dr. Lutz said. "*Are* you a widow?"

"I can't define myself by that word."

"But your husband...he died?"

"Almost nine months ago."

"That's very recent. I'm sorry," he said. "How did he die?"

"His SUV," she said. "He was trying to avoid a truck. Day after I...I told him I wanted a divorce."

Dr. Lutz gave her an empathetic grimace. "What was your husband's name?"

"Michael." She said his name so softly, she wondered if Dr. Lutz heard her.

"You're dealing with some complicated emotions," he said. "Michael died before the two of you could have closure."

Closure. She remembered Helena talking about her divorce from Dr. Lutz, musing, what was more painful? Losing a husband through death or divorce?

"Closure," Jeanette said to Helena's almost-official-ex. "Like you can put twenty-five years of life with someone into a Tupperware container, snap the lid, and nothing's going to spill over the sides?"

"Tell me about the part that's"—his fingers formed air parentheses—"spilling over the sides of the CorningWare."

"Tupperware," she said.

He nodded.

She wasn't sure what would make her feel better: to say it or not.

*Sometimes I feel like **I** caused the accident,* she said silently to herself.

She looked at the clock on the wall—five minutes fast—first thing she'd noticed when she entered his office. She waited for Dr. Lutz to extract more angst from her. But he waited for her to extract it from herself.

"Sometimes I feel like *I* caused the accident," she said.

"So the pursuit of your own happiness," Dr. Lutz said. "You think that's what caused your husband to die?"

"Are you married?"

"No," he said.

"Divorced?"

"Yes." His left cheek twitched. "I am."

"When you were married, did you ever have the feeling that you didn't feel like...like *you* anymore?"

"We're not here to talk about me," Dr. Lutz said.

"I *loved* Michael." She stuck her finger into the soil of a potted plant on the desk—dry. "That's why it took me years to tell him I wanted a divorce." She glanced, again, at the clock on the wall. "Your clock is five minutes fast," she said.

"I know."

"You should fix it. All your patients will assume they've arrived late. And that will increase their anxiety."

"Are you angry at your husband for dying?"

"I wanted a divorce so I could *stop* feeling angry. Angry and unhappy."

"It's a common emotion, anger," he said. "When someone we love dies."

She heard a knock on the office door as Dr. Lutz told her, "It's okay to be angry." He shouted to the person on the other side of the door, "I'm in *session*."

"I don't *want* to be angry," Jeanette said.

The knocking on the door escalated to banging.

"I'm sorry," Dr. Lutz said. "My receptionist is out having a procedure."

He opened the door just wide enough to see who was on the other side. "This won't take long," he told Jeanette. He stepped into the reception room, closed the door behind him.

The framed photograph on his desk—she couldn't resist—she turned it around, saw the photo: Dr. Lutz, tan and smiley, on a sailboat, his arm around a woman at *least* fifteen years younger than Helena. Jeanette placed the photograph back where it was, as a man in the reception room yelled:

"You're an *asshole*, Lutz!"

Jeanette hurried to the clock. She removed it from the wall, reset the time back five minutes—exactly where it should be.

"An asshole with a hemorrhoid for a heart!" the man in the reception room shouted.

Jeanette hung the clock on the wall. A door slammed. She sat down as Dr. Lutz entered the office. He closed the door, locked it.

He took his seat behind the desk—like someone *didn't* just call him an asshole with a hemorrhoid for a heart. "So...where were we?" he said.

"Anger. You said it's okay to be angry. I said I don't want to be angry."

"There's no right or wrong way to feel," Dr. Lutz said. His left cheek twitched.

Words rushed from her mouth demanding to be expressed without waiting for her consent. "I'm a mess. Mess of guilt. Mess of longing. I'm a, a tangle—tangle of *want*. I want to be wanted. But I want to be wanted by someone I want to be wanted by. I, I want big chunks...stretches. Long stretches of time when I feel *alive*. I want the *right* to feel **alive**!"

"There's no right or wrong way to feel," he said.

Again.

"I'm sorry," Jeanette said. She removed a water bottle from her purse, took a swig. "But we have to stop now."

His shrink eyes could not mask his surprise. In all his years of practice, Dr. Lutz had never heard a patient say those words to him.

"And you know what would be good for my mental health?" she said. She watered the parched plant on his desk. "Paying you a reduced fee for your reduced concentration."

He didn't disagree.

31

FUCK 49

Does she have to be 49?

Definitely.

It had arrived—her birthday. 48 when she went to sleep. 49 when she woke up. 49 felt no different than 48. Except it was one year closer to 50, not two anymore. She'd read somewhere online: The beauty of being 49 is a woman knows that she can survive heartbreak.

Hooray! Hurrah!

She scrutinized her face in the bathroom mirror for new lines. Nothing that wasn't there the night before—except a sleep crease across her right cheek. Like some pimp had taught her a lesson: Don't be holdin' out on me. You're 49, bitch, admit it.

"Fuck 49," Jeanette told her sleep crease.

✳✳✳

Her Fuck 49 Birthday began with a pre-production breakfast meeting: just Jeanette, Roberta, and Tucker. The DP, recovering from root canal, in too much pain to talk, wrote his comments in a style best described as stream-of-Vicodin consciousness.

The agency and client execs would arrive later due to cancelled flights, both yesterday and the day before. The airline's vague and ominous explanation: "safety issues"—a happy plus for Jeanette. Jet lag would weaken their nitpicking stamina during the 10:00 P.M. to 7:00 A.M. shoot (she hoped).

Jeanette paced herself for the long night ahead. She viewed a bit of *The Woman Next Door*, rewinding the scene she always rewound—the kiss between Gérard Depardieu and Fanny Ardant. She studied it: Fanny fainting, slumping to the pavement from its power, the intoxication of his lips on her lips.

The marimba ringtone of Jeanette's cell intruded on all that French passion. She put the kiss on "pause." Checked the number on her cell. She returned to her Truffaut state of mind...as Fanny Ardant emerged from her kiss-induced haze.

Jeanette watched the entire scene. Then she listened to the message on her voicemail:

"Woo-hoo!" Sophie said. "A customer at Aphroteasiac wants to buy your painting! So call the owner with the price. Oh, the owner...she wants to hang more of your art. Says it's super compatible with chocolate!" Sophie sang, "Happy birthday to—"

BEEP!

Jeanette bit into a dark chocolate truffle, savoring its whipped center and, again—watched Gérard Depardieu and Fanny Ardant...

Kiss.

***

The new waitress was probably pretty when she wasn't tense; Jeanette had never seen her relaxed. Her high-strung temperament, underscored by the impatient rhythm of her French accent, was in sharp contrast with the here-to-please-you demeanor of the other servers.

"The chef, he is sorry you think the tarte Tatin is burnt,"

she told Jeanette on the hotel roof. "Most guests *prefer* it well-done."

Jeanette had tried to speak French with her, two attempts: 1) While ordering a Salad Niçoise. 2) While politely mentioning the sorry condition of the burnt tarte Tatin. The waitress's corrections of her French grammar had short-circuited both conversations—a rare occurrence in Paris. (Most Parisians appreciated the effort, even complimented Jeanette on her accent.)

"Just the tea then," Jeanette said.

The waitress carried the rejected tarte Tatin across the patio like it was a dead mouse on a china plate.

Lazy steam rose from the swirling surface of the Jacuzzi. Jeanette rolled up her jeans, removed her black sequined ballet slippers; she stepped into the hot froth, as far as the second step, wanting the heat to soothe, not drain her. Water sloshed her calves as her cell rang. She recognized the number, answered the call, pronto.

"*Bonsoir,* Madame Mom!"

"What a lovely surprise, Jeanette. You answered your phone... and on your birthday," her mother said. "Happy, *happy* birthday, darling."

"Couldn't have done it without you."

"You know who you remind me of when you say that?"

"Who?"

"Me, of course."

"Where are you? Italy or Paris?"

"I'm in Italy again."

"What is it? One in the morning there?"

"Can't sleep. Neighbor almost killed herself over a man."

"Husband or lover?"

"Lover. Married. She caught him in bed with a woman who wasn't his wife. It's all very Italian, sweetie."

"How are things with *your* Italian?"

"My Italian and I will be spending the Christmas holidays in Argentina with Massimo's brother and sister-in-law."

"Lucky you, having a boyfriend who facilitates travel."

"Luck is the residue of design," she said (just like Jeanette knew she would), quoting Jeanette's late father, who'd taken the quote from Branch Rickey of the Dodgers and put it on his business card; perfect for an Art Director. "I'd invite you to Paris to stay in my apartment if it wasn't rented out." (Small, but great location in the 14th arrondissement.) "And there's barely enough room in the house in Argentina for me and Massimo."

"Too tumultuous for me anyway," Jeanette said.

"Speaking of tumultuous, how are you celebrating your birthday?"

"Directing a commercial tonight...Viagra competitor."

"Hard way to spend a birthday," her mother said with her customarily subtle delivery, leaving the recipient of her humor unsure if the joke was intentional. "And what about Thanksgiving?"

Thanksgiving? She'd forgotten until now, a voicemail from Pete, last week, inviting her to Thanksgiving dinner in San Francisco.

"Don't know what I'm doing yet."

"It's in three days, Jeanette. And you don't have plans?"

"Ah, but I have work. They wanted to go with a man—but I convinced them to go with *me.*"

"I'm proud of you, you know that. But what about when you're not working? What are you doing for pure pleasure?"

The French waitress yelled to Jeanette from the deck below the Jacuzzi as she set a puny slice of cheesecake on the table. "Courtesy of the chef."

"*Merci,*" Jeanette said.

"Where *are* you, Jeanette?"

"A hotel in Los Angeles...for the shoot."

"Should I worry about you, dear?"

"You'll look younger if you don't."

"I won't worry, then," she said, a smile in her Mom-voice. "I love you, Jeanette. You only turn forty-nine once. Someday you'll *wish* you were forty-nine—so *celebrate.*"

"I love you, Mom. Now get some sleep."

"Tell me you'll celebrate."

"I'll celebrate—I will. Sweet dreams."

"*Sogni d'oro...golden* dreams, my darling daughter. Better than sweet."

Jeanette clicked off the phone. "*Sogni d'oro,*" she said to the Hollywood Hills.

***

In the dream, Jeanette was walking down a dark alley...toward a woman who was standing in the middle of it.

"You should cut your hair," the woman said.

"I *did* cut it."

"It's the same," the woman said. "Same as always."

Jeanette felt the ends of her hair trailing the back of her bra. Her hair was long again. Like it used to be. How was that possible?

The woman walked down the alley.

Jeanette followed her.

The woman stopped; she looked in the mirror of her compact, scrunching waves of her hair—cut exactly like Jeanette's hair before it had grown back (overnight). The woman turned to her. That's when Jeanette realized, the woman was—

Evan's *wife.*

"What is it you want?" the wife said.

"I want your husband."

"You already have a husband," the wife said, without anger or jealousy. No emotion, none.

"I used to have one," Jeanette said.

"Did he die?"

"Yes."

"And you want *my* husband?"

"Can I have him?"

198

"He's right there," the wife said, gazing across the street.

Jeanette saw Evan's silhouette in the dark. She ran toward him, afraid the wife would try to stop her. But the wife just stood in the alley, watching. So, Jeanette kept running. Running until she saw his face—

Only it wasn't Evan.

It was Charles Millburn. "You're late," he said. "We started without you."

Was that rap music playing? Jeanette wondered who'd made that decision. Because rap was all wrong for the spot. She was about to tell him but...

She woke up to the sound of Drake—"*bad things, it's a lotta bad things that they wishin' and wishin' and wishin' and wishin' and wishin' on me*"—angsting through the floor of room 244. Jeanette turned to the clock; she'd slept for thirty-five minutes.

Roberta Frasnay would be picking her up in an hour.

✳✳✳

On her way to the lobby, the elevator door opened, revealing an almost subliminal glimpse of—nooooooo—Charles Millburn. Almost subliminal because that's how fast Jeanette pivoted, reversing her course. She didn't want to talk to him; didn't want Charles Millburn to know she would be directing him—until tonight.

32

HAPPY BIRTHDAY TO ME

Agency Producer Mutt Stone was cuter and younger (twenty-seven?) than Jeanette had imagined from their conversations, his cuteness a distraction from his shrewdness, which could devastate or placate an opponent. Mutt drank Starbucks drip in the Santa Monica hotel with the rest of them, having finally arrived from New York: Creative Director, Art Director, Copywriter, Senior Account Exec, Junior Account Exec, and Rigidyne Rep, gathered in "Video Village," a corner of the lobby (couple of sofas, chairs, water cooler, Cokes) set up just for them where they would view the shoot on monitors, wrapping up the eighty-ninth minute of a pre-pro meeting with Jeanette and Roberta.

Rigidyne Rep: "Let me stress this. *Romantic*-sexy—not dirty."

Senior Account Exec: "I don't see dirty as a concern."

Junior Account Exec: "I see sexiness with style. Sexiness that invigorates."

Art Director: "But without sacrificing the noirish tone."

Agency Producer: "Great, then we're all in agreement. Okay!"

Mutt said to Jeanette. "Why don't I introduce you to Charles Millburn."

One historical landmark leaned against another. Charles Millburn stood among the gnarled roots of the 120-year-old fig tree, resting his silver pate against a venerable branch, eyes closed as a makeup woman dabbed foundation onto his nose. And Mutt said, "Charles Millburn…Jeanette Coles."

Charles Millburn opened his eyes. He saw Jeanette. He looked confused.

"You?" he said.

"Me," she said, like she'd been dealt a straight flush and was about to smooth call him.

"You're my director?" he said, processing the revelation, unsure: Is this a good thing or bad?

"You two know each other?" Mutt said.

"We don't know each other at all," the actor told Mutt, then said to Jeanette, "I had no *idea* you were a director."

"Why are you dressed in white?" she said.

Charles Millburn was wearing a white V-neck sweater, white shirt, white slacks, and white loafers.

"Client feels it offsets the darkness," Mutt said.

"But we agreed on the black cashmere coat," Jeanette said.

"Client prefers something 'jauntier.'"

"Jaunty-*noir*?" she said.

"You'll be the director who invented a genre," Mutt said.

"He looks like he just stepped off a shuffleboard court."

"You'd be surprised what a man and a woman can do on a shuffleboard court under the spell of a Madrid mist," Charles Millburn said. "Many mists ago, Gina Lollobrigida and I—now there was a woman who looked like a woman."

"We don't start until his wardrobe reflects the tone of the piece," Jeanette said.

"You're feisty," Charles Millburn said.

"And *you*—are a very attractive man." She leaned toward the makeup woman, whispered in her ear, "That wiry follicle peeking from his nostril—clip it."

***

"Cut!" Jeanette said.

Charles Millburn ceased kissing the Juvederm-plumped lips of Sensual Woman Early 30s. He was sporting a wardrobe compromise: royal-blue shirt, black herringbone slacks, black loafers. The actress filled her white knit dress like helium fills a balloon. A wide black leather belt hung low on her hips, nasty-nice with black spike heels that flattered her calves and tortured her toes; her auburn mane, highlighted with gold, cascaded down her back—she looked like Charles Millburn's hottie-granddaughter.

Or as the Rigidyne rep relayed from Video Village: "Couple credibility concerns."

The Make-Out scene in the alley was a challenge—Jeanette was two hours into the challenge—the actors failing to convince: sex between them was probable *or* possible.

"When he strokes her hair," Roberta said to Jeanette at the monitor, "his hand is lookin' mighty veiny."

"Charles," Jeanette said as she approached the actor. "I want you to run your fingers *through* her hair."

Tucker nodded in agreement, popped a Vicodin.

"*Bury* your fingers in her hair," Jeanette said. "You're still too hesitant."

"I'm close though. Much closer, I think."

"Not close enough. I need your *passion*."

What she didn't need was Agency Producer, Mutt, hurrying into the alley.

"Greetings from Video Village," Mutt said to Jeanette. "May I impart a brief suggestion to Mr. Millburn?"

"You may impart," Jeanette said. "Briefly."

"Thank you," Mutt said. He turned to the actor. "We're behind schedule so pardon my bluntness—you're *horny*, Charles.

You're horny so you want to rip this woman's clothes off. You want to throw her on a bed, have sex with her, then tell her to get dressed so you can rip her clothes off again and start all over."

"That's not my style," the actor said, his tone suggesting his inner monologue: *you silly boy.*

"I'm sure few men know more about getting a woman into bed than Charles Millburn," Jeanette said.

"My director speaks the truth," the actor said.

"I need to talk to Charles," Jeanette told Mutt. "Alone."

Jeanette placed her hand on the back of Charles Millburn's royal-blue shirt; they strolled down the alley. "I have a confession to make, Charles. Two confessions, actually," she said. "One, it's my birthday."

"Happy birthday, honey."

"Thank you," she said. "I've chosen to work on my birthday because I wanted the experience of working with *you.*"

He nodded as if her decision made sense. "Now what's the second confession?"

"When I was a teenager, I had a poster of you. Hanging on my bedroom wall right next to my bed. From *When Day Becomes Night.*"

"Wonderful film," he said. "Gutsy writing. You couldn't get that film made today."

"I would come home from school, lock myself in my pretty pink bedroom. Then I'd turn on the radio—plop down on my bed beside this great, big, stuffed elephant my boyfriend won me at Disneyland."

"Dumbo," he said.

"I would lie there listening to the music, gazing at your face on my wall."

"That's very sweet," he said.

"While I masturbated with Dumbo's *trunk.*"

He could have sworn she said, "masturbated with Dumbo's trunk." But maybe she didn't.

"Dumbo's trunk on my white cotton underpants," Jeanette said cheerily. "Circling my clitoris."

Charles Milburn just stared at her, like he was waiting for someone to give him his lines.

"Now—we're *ready*!" Jeanette shouted to the crew. "Buckle up 'cause here we go!"

The instant Charles Millburn ran his hands through the golden-highlighted mane of Sensual Woman Early 30s, Jeanette saw a difference. He had a commanding, well—*sexiness that invigorates.*

"Prolong the anticipation," Jeanette said, watching the actor on the monitor. "You want that kiss. Savor your desire, Charles."

Savor, he did. Then he brought the actress's face toward his and kissed her. Not only was he in the moment, he was *lost* in it.

"Sensual Woman," Jeanette said, softly, to the actress. "Keep your arms at your side. Good, good—now you can't resist. Run your fingernails down the arms of his shirt. I want to hear those red nails *scraping.*"

Charles Millburn embraced the actress, sliding his hand beneath the back of her belt, low on her hips.

"Sensual Woman," Jeanette said, "wrap your leg around Charles's leg...that's right. Now dig your heel into his—"

"Eeeeew," Sensual Woman said, pulling away from the actor.

"Cut!" Jeanette said. "What? What's the matter?"

The actress shuddered. "Erection."

Jeanette, Roberta, Tucker, Mutt, the entire crew stared down at Charles Millburn's herringbone slacks—the actor had a boner you could shift from park to drive.

"You asked for horny," Charles said to Mutt with a flourish.

"What exactly did you say to him?" Mutt asked Jeanette.

"I just gave him a suggestion, that's all."

"Must have been some suggestion," Roberta said.

Jeanette couldn't contain her delight; her teenage masturbation confession had *aroused* Charles Millburn. It was as if a time-travel machine had transported her from her Laurel Canyon bedroom, transformed her from a teenager into an adult—just for this shoot. "I think we should take advantage of his excited condition," Jeanette said.

"Excuse me," the actress said. "But nobody told me I would have to deal with an actual *real-life* hard-on."

"Consider yourself fortunate," Charles told the actress, "to be working with an actor who gives of himself."

"Enough talk," Jeanette said. "We don't want to lose the heat."

"Oh, I think the heat will sustain itself for quite some time," Charles said. "This stuff really works."

"What stuff?" Jeanette said.

"Rigidyne," Charles said. He smiled. "They won't be sued for false advertising."

"He took the product," Mutt said. "He fucking took the product."

"I thought you were a method actor," Jeanette said.

"Whatever the part calls for," Charles said, marveling at the sturdiness of his erection.

"How long will that thing last?" Roberta said, like his *real-life* hard-on was battery powered.

"Your guess is as good as mine," Charles said.

"We need some kind of time frame," Mutt said.

"Well, what does it say on the bottle?" Jeanette said.

"Seek medical attention," Charles said, "if erection lasts more than seven hours."

"Seven?" the actress shrieked. "Seven *hours*?"

"Results may vary," Charles said with a shrug.

"He took the product," Mutt said, as if repeating the problem would somehow suggest its solution.

Tucker tapped Jeanette on the shoulder, handed her a note. She read the DP's Vicodin-sloppy scribbling:

Side effects may include a dick that's a pain in the ass.

Jeanette was about to laugh when she saw the gang from

Video Village—halfway down the hotel driveway—hurrying toward her.

"I think now is a good time to regroup," she said.

***

"If he were wearing a coat like the script specified…" Roberta told the Rigidyne rep.

Rigidyne Rep was a bald man with skin the color of canned albacore tuna (packed in oil). "So we put him in the coat, now," he said.

"And you don't think people will notice he's suddenly wearing a coat?" Mutt said.

"He was chilly. He went to his car off-screen, got his coat," Junior Account Exec said, buzzed from too many espresso brownies and the knowledge that he was the youngest person at the table.

"If he's rushing to a hotel to have sex—why did he stop to get his coat?" Senior Account Exec said.

"We can establish the coat in the alley," Copywriter said, eyes closed like he was talking in his sleep.

"There's no time to re-shoot," Roberta said.

"Quick shot of his coat in the alley on the pavement," Junior Account Exec said.

"Why is the coat on the pavement?" Senior Account Exec said.

"He was hot from Sensual Woman. So he took off his coat," Junior Account Exec said, with rookie-on-a-roll confidence.

"No," Copywriter said, eyes still closed. "She took it off *him*."

"Then we need to show that," Creative Director Neil said, wiping coffee stain from his piano-key teeth with a napkin.

They were at a table on the patio (Craft Services had commandeered it for the shoot), agency people and Rigidyne Rep, multi-tasking: eating, arguing, scanning their smartphones, anxiety ousting logic, fluttering from worry to worry like lost hummingbirds.

Jeanette listened to their concerns, thinking: In the big scheme of things, when placed on life's humongous scale of problems, this one weighed in at delightful. She felt no pressure; she counted the Koi fish, swimming aimlessly in the pond beside her. When she'd counted twelve fish, she said, "It would have to be the opening shot, so we'd lose him pulling her into the alley, lose the momentum."

"I think we're in sync," Junior Account Exec said, ignoring Jeanette as he addressed Rigidyne Rep. "Our top priority is camouflaging the tumescence."

"What the hell is a tumescence?" Rigidyne Rep said.

"From the word tumescent," Junior Account Exec said, like he was about to trounce the competition in a spelling bee. "It means swollen."

Rigidyne Rep swatted the air between him and Junior Account Exec. Then he turned to Jeanette. "Millburn will be wearing the coat from here on in."

It's my birthday, Jeanette thought, remembering her mother's words. *Someday I'll* **wish** *I was 49. Might as well turn this into a party—celebrate!*

"What if we show it?" she said.

"You want to shoot the tumescence in color...everything else in black and white?" Mutt said, welcoming a little comedy relief.

"I'm serious," Jeanette said. "Why not show the power of the product? Break new ground. It's not like we'd be showing an actual penis."

They stared at her, all of them, wondering if she, indeed, was serious.

"Just a bulge housed in handsome herringbone," she said. "And this isn't a porn star we're talking about. This is a legendary actor. A former Academy Award nominee. An *artist*. A man who's admired—*respected*."

They looked over at the buffet table where Charles Millburn was spooning broccoli onto his plate, oblivious to his erection; Sensuous Woman, the other actors (Jeanette had yet to shoot), and crew people, keeping their distance like he was a registered pedophile.

"Let me lend a sane perspective, here," Rigidyne Rep said. "No television station in this country is going to air a spot that's erection inclusive."

"Be a hit on YouTube," Jeanette said. "I'll shoot enough coverage so you'll have that option."

"I don't want that option—I don't want to see *hide nor hair* of it," Rigidyne Rep said. "What's your plan?"

"My plan?" Jeanette said. She stared into the pond, counted five more fish. Then she leaned across the table and told him:

"I'll shoot around it. Above it. Below it. From behind. I'll treat it like it's the sun eclipsing the moon—and even the slightest glimpse could cause blindness."

Everyone looked at Rigidyne Rep. They waited for him to speak.

He removed three walnuts from a brownie, dropped them, one by one, into his cup of cold coffee. "Can't ask for more than that," he said.

In the morning, after the shoot had wrapped, Jeanette assured Charles Millburn his hard work—and his hard-on—had paid off. He was too tired to smile as he got into a Town Car, about to be driven to St. John's Hospital, adhering to the Rigidyne warning: SEEK MEDICAL ATTENTION IF ERECTION LASTS MORE THAN SEVEN HOURS. Clocking in at seven hours and twenty minutes, Charles Millburn's erection was still going strong— the only part of him that wasn't exhausted.

⋆

Her first thought when she awoke to the drawn-drape darkness of 144: Charles. She hoped he was okay. It was 8:15 P.M. He would have requested a DND on the phone if he were still asleep. Best to check with the front desk; she didn't want to be the one to wake him. She leaned across Al, curled beside her on the bed, dialed the desk.

"Charles Millburn's room, please."

"Mr. Millburn checked out this evening," Curtis said.

"This evening?" she said.

"Just a few minutes ago, Ms. Coles."

"Thanks, Curtis, and you can remove the DND from my phone now."

"Will do."

She hung up. Padded to the bathroom. She brushed her teeth, washed her face. Toned. Before she could finish moisturizing, Al barked at the door.

"Someone there?" Jeanette said.

"Sorry to disturb you," a bellman said from the hallway. "Package for you. I'll just leave it outside your room."

Jeanette slipped into her robe, opened the door.

A large white gift box, tied with pink ribbon, was on the carpet. She picked up the box, returned to her room, kicking the door shut. She set the box on the table. She finished moisturizing to prolong the suspense of opening an unexpected gift.

Jeanette shook the box gently. She removed the pink curlicue ribbon, placed it around Al's neck.

Finally, she lifted the lid. It was a gift, alright. Nestled in pink tissue paper, a big fleecy gray—stuffed elephant.

Dangling from the tip of the elephant's trunk was a card, its brief message written in fountain pen:

Thank you.
Charles

33

THE GODDESS OF THANKSGVING

She sat at the bar, the bar on Thanksgiving, wondering where she would be today if Michael were alive. No matter how civilized the process of their divorce might have been, their run of five consecutive Thanksgivings at Pete and Olivia's would have come to an end, that's for sure.

Pete's loyalty would have been to Michael. And Pete's wife, well, Jeanette had never connected with Olivia, who mostly connected with her four-year-old daughter, believing she possessed a wise, old soul. Last Thanksgiving, it had been a strain for Jeanette to reign in her sarcasm while Olivia raved about her daughter's sophisticated palate (at three she'd developed an appreciation for Camembert), the daughter with the old soul she was still breast feeding. It was enough to make Jeanette lactose intolerant.

Michael would have been at Pete and Olivia's today. Not Jeanette. Not at a dinner of mostly couples, wondering why she and Michael, a seemingly happy, longtime twosome, had split into *one*somes; singles on Thanksgiving.

The only reason they invited her this year was because Michael died.

"Dead, huh?"

The question startled her. She turned to the man who'd posed it, the only other person at the bar, seated three stools away, pegging him for a guest; otherwise he'd be having his holiday dinner at a table.

"Awfully quiet for Thanksgiving," he said.

Jeanette nodded.

"Thirty percent occupancy," he said. "Fella working the graveyard shift told me last night."

"People usually stay with relatives on Thanksgiving," Jeanette said. "And musicians on the road, most of them are home today." She slid a large bowl, covered with foil, from her placemat, making way for the goat cheese salad that Oscar set in front of her.

"Chef was expecting a big turnout—his loyal following," Oscar said with a wink. "From when he worked in the *valley.*"

The diners didn't appear to be guests. Six-thirty, and the chef's loyal following amounted to two occupied tables—seven people. An empty table set for nine, in the middle of the room, resembled an art installation: *No One Came to Thanksgiving.*

"I take it you're staying at the hotel," the man at the bar said to Jeanette.

"I am," she said. "And you?"

"Nope. I just like eating alone at hotel bars on Thanksgiving." He drank his chardonnay. "I'm joking of course," he said. "I'm here on business."

He was a stocky man who looked like he should have mechanic's grease under his fingernails, but they were impeccably manicured. His rust-colored shirt, patterned with green fern fronds, belonged on the chest of a more charismatic man. He resembled those vintage amusement park photos—smiling face atop a cardboard torso suggesting a colorful alter ego—Jeanette thought as she said, "What do you do?"

"I custom-make shirts."

"Perfect," Jeanette said. "I was just *admiring* your shirt. The fabric, beautiful pattern."

"I know," he said, moving down a seat, separated from her by two barstools, instead of three now. "Found it in a fabric market in Amsterdam...Lapjesmarkt. What a scene that is."

"The Stark Forest Dance Group," Angie said to Jeanette, as she dashed behind the bar. "Serving them in the banquet room." She topped off Jeanette's Cab. "Most people I've served all day."

"Haven't seen the French waitress," Jeanette said.

"Chef sent her home. Not enough customers," Angie said, in hushed confidence. "And she was bitchy to a party of four."

"Miss," one of the chef's so-called followers called to Angie. "My turkey is tender like satin. But it's cold," the woman said.

The shirtmaker leaned across the bar toward Jeanette. "I've always found satin to be cold to the touch."

Jeanette smiled as she buttered a biscuit.

"I stay in hotels a lot," the shirtmaker said. "Perk of the job... travel all over the world to my clients."

"Eclectic clientele?"

"Celebrities," he said, moving down another seat, leaving just one barstool between them. "And people who can afford to live like celebrities."

"My mother," Jeanette said, "she used to make shirts."

"Well how 'bout that."

"Shirts, every now and then a dress." Jeanette unzipped her *Juicy* cashmere sweater, exposing an ecru jersey tank top. "Mostly shirts for musicians."

"When was this?"

"Late sixties through the eighties...Laurel Canyon. Her studio was a guest house in our backyard."

"The musicians...any I might have heard of?"

"Lowell George, Stephen Stills?"

"Stephen Stills, sure."

"John Mayall. Pharoah Sanders. Steve Reich. My mother

sewed for them while she listened to their music." Jeanette returned a forkful of salad to her plate, the pull of a memory stronger than the desire to eat. "Steve Reich bought six boxes of Girl Scout cookies from me—Thin Mints."

"You remember the flavor of the cookies?"

"I remember the flavor of everything. I've got a head crammed with flavor." She smiled into her wineglass en route to her lips. "Tess the Tailor—'Quality tailoring for quality musicians.' My mother's slogan."

"Clever. Memorable," the shirtmaker said, mopping his soup bowl with a biscuit.

"That's my mother...clever and memorable."

"So no more quality tailoring from Tess?"

"Occasionally, when it pleases her to make something fantastic for me. Or her boyfriend."

"Turkey and all the trimmings coming right up," Oscar said, reaching over the frond-patterned shoulder of the shirtmaker, removing his empty soup bowl from the bar.

"I'll have mine when the lady has hers," the shirtmaker said, scooting over another seat, finally beside Jeanette. "That way I'll feel like I'm eating with someone on Thanksgiving."

"You *got* it!" Oscar said.

"Question," the shirtmaker said to Jeanette. "Why are you dining alone in a hotel on Thanksgiving?"

"I just like eating alone at hotel bars on Thanksgiving," she said, quoting him.

He smiled like he thought he might have lettuce between his teeth. (He didn't.)

"I'm here like you, on business," she said.

"Business being what?"

"I direct commercials."

"Really? I make shirts for a fellow who does voice-overs. Boy, does he rake in the bucks. Large man, lot of fabric. Likes his shirts loose." The shirtmaker looked at his glass of chardonnay as if he was surprised at how little was left. "So what's it like?" he said. "Directing a commercial."

"I'd rather talk about shirtmaking." She removed the foil from the bowl beside her placemat.

"What's in the bowl?"

"My homemade applesauce," she said, her voice alluding to its deliciousness. "Midnight, I was thinking how I would miss it. How it wouldn't feel like Thanksgiving without it." (Michael had loved the smell of her applesauce cooking; in each place they'd called home, he'd loved it.) "So I went to the twenty-four-hour Ralph's on Sunset."

"You made applesauce in your room last night?" he said, impressed.

"Today...finished an hour ago. "Still warm," she said, setting the bowl on the bar between them.

"Sure smells homemade."

"There's something Zen-like, clarifying, the act of peeling an apple."

"Here's a bold suggestion," the shirtmaker announced, pausing as he bolstered himself to make it, "How about we sit at a table? Turn this into a *real* Thanksgiving dinner."

"I accept your bold suggestion," Jeanette said, getting up from the bar. "We're moving to a table," she told Oscar, as he exited the kitchen, carrying two slices of pecan pie and a slice of pumpkin.

"Just like in the *movies*," Oscar said to Jeanette, hurrying toward the three lone diners as if the restaurant were filled.

So, here's what the shirtmaker told her about himself over turkey and all the trimmings: He resided in Boston, grew up in Buffalo; he was allergic to cranberries. He liked inventing things, always coming up with ideas he thought could take off big—if he had the time and capital to follow through—like the gadget he thought would appeal to "women on the go," having high hopes for it, unable to describe it to Jeanette because at this "stage in the game," it was best kept a secret. His uncle had gotten him into shirtmaking against his father's wishes; he preferred not to talk about his clients by name, but made an exception when it came to George Clooney ("just as good a guy as you'd think"). The shirtmaker was crazy about opera, crazy about Amsterdam, crazy about Jeanette's applesauce, spooning a second helping onto his plate, as he said, apropos of nothing, "So how old do you think I am?"

Jeanette dipped turkey into applesauce. "I'm not good with numbers."

"Fifty, the big five-o. Do I *look* fifty?" he said, his face pleading for a "no."

He looked older than fifty, she thought, finishing off her sweet-potato tart. "If you hadn't told me," she said, "I never would have guessed."

Her answer pleased him. He ate his green beans and sliced almonds. "You think I should color my hair?"

He was doing okay in the hair department, mostly gray and plenty of it.

"Gray hair hasn't hurt George Clooney," she said.

"That's because he's George Clooney. And I'm..." He finished his explanation with a shrug.

"You're who?"

"I'm just Kenneth Tench."

"Don't paint your hair. I like it."

"Thanks, thank you."

They ate without talking, until he issued a small laugh like a happy cough.

"What?" Jeanette said.

"I was thinking...my daughter was right."

Married or divorced, Jeanette wondered. "How old is your daughter?"

"Twenty-one. She told me, my—this woman I've been see-ing...contemplating living with...my daughter didn't think it was a good idea." He ate some applesauce, ate some more. "If I were living with this woman, I would be feeling guilty now."

"Guilty? About what?"

"I'm attracted to you." His eyes darted from her gaze to the cornbread stuffing on his plate. "Now I don't have to feel guilty."

Jeanette wiped sweet potato from the corner of her smile. "This woman you're contemplating living with...your daughter doesn't like her?"

"She thinks I got involved with her too soon. Too soon after my wife died."

Widowed. It hadn't occurred to her: He might be widowed. "When? When did your wife die?"

"Thirteen months ago. Thirteen," he said, as if he couldn't believe the passage of time.

"How soon after—"

"I met the woman three months after my wife passed away. My daughter said I didn't allow myself to grieve."

"And what do you say?"

"I don't expect my daughter to understand."

"She doesn't want to think you can replace her mother. Certainly not so quickly."

"I can't replace her." He sipped water. "This woman"—he drank more water, half the glass—"she says my wife would *want* me to find someone, someone to love."

"Would she?" Jeanette said, peering into a vase containing a single yellow lily, seeing no water. "Is that what your wife would want for you...to love another woman?"

He thought about that as long as it took the party of three to file out of the restaurant.

"My wife would want me to love another woman who was good for me."

Jeanette poured water from her glass into the vase and said, "My husband died."

"I'm sorry," he said, although he looked almost relieved to hear it. "Then you know what I'm talking about."

"Grieving..." She inhaled the scent of the lily. "Such a, a personal sadness. You're on your own with it...all those feelings."

"All those feelings," the shirtmaker said. "When did your husband die?"

"Nine months ago."

"What did he die of?"

Jeanette slid the vase back to the center of the table. She thought about what she wanted to say and what she didn't want to say, the process of consideration making her wish she hadn't told him. She didn't want to be swept into an undertow of sorrow on Thanksgiving. She wanted to feel—*thankful.* "Whatever I say, you'll say something like: that must have been awful. Then I'll say, yes it was, was awful...and I'll want to switch the subject back to you, so maybe I'll ask, how did your wife die? And you'll tell me. And I'll say, I'm sorry, it's not fair. And we'll volley our details of anguish...your images in your head, mine in my head...both of us back there in the past. Instead of the present—here, where we need to be—thankful we're alive."

He was blown away by her. He wanted to say something empathetic, wise, candid. But what came out of his mouth was, "Whew." Before he could improve upon it, Oscar was at the table asking Jeanette:

"Ready for dessert...or are you sweet enough?"

"Not until I have some pumpkin pie," Jeanette said.

"And you, sir?" Oscar said.

He was still trying to come up with something empathetic, wise, and candid. "I'll have what the lady is having."

"You got it," Oscar said.

"It might sit on the table until I have room for it," Jeanette told the shirtmaker. "But I refuse to be pie deprived on Thanksgiving."

They watched Oscar clear the table; his right hand balanced the tray of dirty dishes above his shoulder, the fingers of his left hand snapping en route to the kitchen, as if hurrying him along.

"So you like my shirt, huh?" the shirtmaker said.

Jeanette reached across the table, rolled down his sleeve

(he'd rolled them up to his elbows during dinner), smoothed the frond pattern on his wrist. "It's all that a shirt should be, Kenneth Tench."

He laughed, enjoying that his name had been in her mouth. "You would love the fabric I found in Thailand."

"Describe it to me."

"I'd rather you see it...it's in my room. I'm showing it to a client tomorrow." He waited for her response.

She waited for him to elaborate.

"Beautiful to look at, beautiful to touch," he said. "Would you like to see it?"

"Ask me again after the pie."

***

Jeanette stood in the living room of his junior suite, eyes closed because the shirtmaker had asked her to close them. He also asked her to remove her sweater, turning up the flames in the gas fireplace, so she wouldn't be chilly in her tank top. Her bare shoulders were being teased with a fabric as delicate as she'd ever felt against her skin.

"You can open your eyes now," he said.

He held a bolt of pale lavender silk, having loosened just enough to drape around her shoulders like a shawl, her skin showing, faintly, through the fabric.

"The color," she said, "so subtle."

"They call it a blend of lavender and pale nutmeg."

"Like some luscious, creamy dessert," she said, sliding it down her shoulders and up again.

"Handwoven, hand-dyed," he said, loosening silk from the bolt, facilitating her passage as she walked across the room.

She turned on the radio, found the jazz station and the soundtrack to her mood: "In the Wee Small Hours of the Morning" by Rob Schwimmer. It wasn't just the song that moved her; it was the playing. The pianist seemed to be caressing the keys, eliciting tenderness from them. Tenderness and empathy. Like he felt deep longing, deep as Jeanette's—an intimate longing he could only confess to his piano when the whole wide world was fast asleep.

She closed her eyes, felt the lyrical flow of his playing, the perfect combination of musician and song, moving her internally and externally, the music coursing through her; a beautiful sensual aching. She felt it in her thighs, her hips, even her waist, her shoulders... her hands traveling along each inspired part until she was running her fingers through her hair, slow dancing in place.

The shirtmaker sat on the sofa, watching her, the bolt of fabric in his hands like a remote control.

"Now you close *your* eyes," Jeanette said.

"I have no problem with that suggestion." The shirtmaker closed his eyes.

She took the bolt of fabric from him, walked to the dressing area. "Don't open them until I tell you," she said.

In the wee small hours of the morning...that's the time you miss her most of all...

The pianist was nearing the end of the song, his touch on the keys delicate as, well, lavender/pale-nutmeg silk. And Jeanette was standing in front of the shirtmaker, saying, "Okay, you can open your eyes now."

He opened his eyes.

She had on nothing; nothing at all but her earrings, and the lavender/pale-nutmeg silk, wrapped around her curves, looking like a sculptor's muse or obsession or both—the slimmed-down bolt of fabric at her bare feet.

"The Goddess of Thanksgiving," he said.

Jeanette laughed. "I could sleep in this silk."

"I could *watch* you sleep in this silk."

She handed him the bolt of fabric. "Follow me."

He trailed her, unfurling silk up the two steps leading to the king bed. She tossed the comforter aside as she lay on the sheets, looking up at him, like there should be rose petals beneath her hospitable body.

He stood there, savoring the sight of her in that silk from Thailand on his hotel bed in West Hollywood. "You've given me reason to be thankful," he said.

"Happy Thanksgiving, Kenneth Tench."

He picked up the phone from the night table. "I'm going to order us a couple more drinks."

"The trouble with room service," she said, "is someone knocks on your door...and you got to open it."

He put down the phone.

"Let's see what your beautiful shirt looks like unbuttoned," Jeanette said.

He lay on the bed, facing her, watching her, separating a frond beneath the center button as she undid his shirt. He kissed her.

She was in the mood to be kissed. She wanted a wee-small-hours-of-the-morning kiss. A kiss that started out tender... lingered enough to build; a kiss that took its cue from the soul as well as the loins, from imagination, not intellect—a kiss that in a breath could turn ferocious and invade her.

His kiss was dry, tentative. His lips hadn't heard from his soul or his loins.

"Do I taste like pumpkin pie?" he said.

"You taste like hotel mouthwash. What do I taste like?"

"You taste like...a pretty woman."

She inserted her tongue into his mouth, flicked it around in there, his tongue too shy to meet hers. She withdrew her tongue, and he gave her another closed mouth, dry kiss. He reached across the night table, turned off the light.

"Better," he said. He stroked her shoulder with his index finger, observing it like he was writing a message in invisible ink. "Do you like when I do this?" he said, as if she might not, self-judgment disallowing the tactile pleasure of caressing her.

She unzipped his pants. Reached into his boxers, palming an indecisive cock, almost hard but not fully committed, as she said, "Do you like when I do *this*?"

"Yes," he said. "Yes," he whispered.

She put his uncommitted cock into her mouth, wanting to arouse him so he would lose his inhibitions, satisfy her in return.

He mumbled something.

She removed his cock from her mouth so she could say, "What?" Then plunged it back between her lips.

"Tryptophan," he said. He patted the roundness of his stomach. "Too much turkey."

She looked up at him from between his legs as she removed a pubic hair from her tongue.

"Can we just cuddle?" the shirtmaker said.

Jeanette lifted her face from his thigh, slid up the sheets to him.

"I like to be cuddled," he said, his arms enveloping her.

She slipped her hand around his waist; her palm rested against his lower back. "Don't Explain" was playing now, Dexter Gordon—his sax almost speaking the words:

Hush now don't explain...you're my joy and pain, as the shirtmaker brushed her hair from her face with his fingers and said:

"I miss my wife."

He patted Jeanette's head; he spoke softly:

"Do you miss your husband?"

Jeanette tried to speak.

Maybe it was his heartfelt tone, the unexpected directness of his question, the beauty of the song, "Don't Explain"...a man's arms around her in bed—man who missed a wife who was no longer alive—he'd broken the levee to her grief. And her grief had a sound...a guttural, almost primal cry of loss.

"I know," the shirtmaker said, pulling Jeanette closer to him, as she sobbed into his chest. "I know," he said.

Jeanette wasn't sure how long she cried, but she cried as long as she needed; the shirtmaker's chest was wet with her tears.

"It's been a while since I comforted a woman," he said, grateful she was in need of comforting, so he couldn't fall apart himself this Thanksgiving.

Jeanette lay with him until she heard the rhythm of his gentle snoring. She pried herself from his arms, unraveled the lavender/pale-nutmeg silk from her body.

She stood beside the bed, tucked him in, adjusting the top sheet, covering his chest which had so graciously accepted her tears. She put on her clothes, then quietly shut the door to his room behind her.

***

She could still smell the applesauce she made today in her junior suite. She sat in bed, petting the dog, and writing a letter. A letter to Michael—as if he would somehow receive its message—page after page, writing her thoughts as they took shape. On the fifth page now. Writing him that sometimes she felt responsible for his death, and she wanted to stop feeling responsible. Writing him that sometimes she felt angry, angry at him for dying...which made her feel more guilt, and her guilt was hurting her and certainly not helping him. Writing him that she wanted to feel the fullness of the present, appreciate her precious time on this earth...because he had shown her just how tenuous life is. Writing him that she has been alive for forty-nine years and three days. And nothing made her feel more alive than celebrating her aliveness. Writing him that she doubted anyone felt fulfilled every day, but he had deserved more; he had deserved more life. Writing him that she'd sold a painting. Writing him that, sometimes, she felt as if her very being was undergoing a slow remodeling—adding on little by little, expanding, yet maintaining her original design.

She fell asleep with the light on, the pages of her letter on the bed, the dog's mouth imprinting the final paragraph:

My dear, smart, big-hearted, selfish, encouraging, controlling, prescient, regretful, up, down, bold, insecure, impossible husband—I never stopped loving you. On our worst day, our most abysmal night...I never stopped.

She slept nine hours. Her only dream was a good one.

34

SOUTH OF THE MOON

The agency suggested stunt hands. Charles Millburn's large, thin-skinned hands conjured an arthritic lecher, inching the back of Sensual Woman's dress, destination ass.

"And as long as we're bringing in younger hands for him, how about a younger ass for her?" they said.

The client disagreed with the agency, believing: Charles Millburn's "experienced" hands sold the product, although agreeing on a younger ass.

"You already lost seventeen years of ass," Jeanette reminded them, "when you cast Sensual Woman early *30s*—instead of 49."

The debating of stunt hands/stunt ass amounted to a waste of Eastern and Pacific Time. The shots of Charles Millburn's hands pursuing "mature ass" were edited out (too "overt," the client concluded) in favor of the actor's "experienced" right hand creeping beneath Sensual Woman's hemline.

The debut airing of the spot had been set: December twenty-third. It would be at least two weeks before they had an approved cut, and post-production (re-color correction, sound, graphics) would take another week. Tough deadline in the best of circumstances; cruel and unusual punishment in the days leading up to Christmas.

Christmas. It loomed.

"Winter Wonderland" was on the speakers in the hotel lobby, the tempo too upbeat for Karen Carpenter's melancholy voice.

"Dad needs your number," the Graveyard Guy said into the phone, as he gazed at the Christmas tree in the corner, all lit up and gaudy, so many gold baubles it looked fake. "He wants to call you."

That's how slow it was in the hotel. Slow enough for the Graveyard Guy to be on a personal call at midnight.

Jeanette sat on a club chair beside a basket of apples, dog at her feet, pretending she was reading *Los Angeles Magazine* instead of listening to the Graveyard Guy saying:

"Whoa, whoa, whoa, whoa. How is he supposed to get in touch with you? Cynthia...what do you mean Dad can't call you? He wants to visit you."

Probably his sister, Jeanette figured as Karen Carpenter sang:

"*A beautiful sight...we're happy tonight...*"

"Okay. Right...right...right," the Graveyard Guy said. "Does this mean you can't have visitors? Or you don't want to see Dad? Hold it. No, I'm not going to tell him...listen...listen. His health is declining...I'm, no. I am not telling Dad if you see him you'll use again."

Rehab, Jeanette concluded, absently turning a page of the magazine she wasn't reading.

"His heart can't take it, that's why. He's going to visit you... listen to me. Just listen to me. If you'd listen to me first"—he turned away from the tree, his back to Jeanette—"I'm at work. You think I'm going to call him now? He's asleep. No, no, no. Listen, listen. You crazy? Listen, listen, hold on, hold on. Relax. Let's say he doesn't come tomorrow. Will you see him on Christmas?" His shoulders sagged beneath his jacket as he let out a weary sigh, and Karen Carpenter sang:

"*In the meadow we can build a snowman and pretend that he is Parson Brown...*"

"Right...right," the Graveyard Guy said.

"He'll say, are you married? We'll say, no man..."

"But see the thing...all right. No. Listen. Okay, now. Listen. Hold...hold"—he answered an incoming call—"Lyric Hotel, how may I help you?" He massaged his tense neck. "No sir, we're north of Melrose...south of the moon." He resumed his personal conversation as if it hadn't been interrupted. "Listen, Cynthia. Listen...listen to me."

It wasn't the Graveyard Guy's familial holiday-angst that had Jeanette tugging Al across the lobby; she had a sudden urge to paint. And to not hear Karen Carpenter singing: *"To face unafraid the plans that we made...walking in a winter wonderland..."* sounding like she was losing the will to imitate good cheer.

Jeanette hurried Al up the stairs as the Graveyard Guy said, "At least call Dad, tell him you'll *try* to see him on Christmas."

✳✳✳

She finished breakfast while reading an article in the *Los Angeles Times*: a celebration of Minimalism at the Getty (discussions, concerts), her focus diminished by a conversation in the otherwise empty restaurant.

"I told my wife we can hang our Christmas stockings above the fireplace in our room," a man said. "Be our first Christmas in Los Angeles...far cry from Michigan."

Jeanette glanced up from the paper. The man standing at the entrance to the restaurant was alone. And he was talking to her, "Our daughter's in a movie," he said, walking toward Jeanette. "We're here for the premiere, figured we might as well stay for Christmas."

He stood at her table: a rundown-looking daddy, in his forties, with a short dyed-brown ponytail that curled at the base of his skull like a giant snail. "Minor role," he said. "But my wife and I couldn't be prouder."

"Congratulations," Jeanette said, her focus on the newspaper, eyes zeroing in on two consonants, two vowels: *E v a n.*

"I hope you don't think I'm out of line when I say this."

Jeanette wasn't listening to Rundown Daddy because she was reading about cellist, Evan Jameson. Jameson...was that his last name? She didn't know. But it was probably *him*, playing with a string quartet, part of the Minimalism celebration tonight, subbing for their regular cellist who was recuperating from a snakebite.

"You have beautiful skin," Rundown Daddy said.

Jeanette looked up at him. "What?"

"Your skin is beautiful. I'm sure my wife would agree."

"Thanks," Jeanette said, wanting the waiter to reappear so she could sign her check, go back to 144, call the front desk—ask for Evan's room.

Just to see if he's here. Here at the hotel. That's all.

"Tonight we're going to a club, Girlicue," Rundown Daddy said. "A friend said it would be fun."

"Girlicue," Jeanette said. "Think that might be a lesbian club."

"My wife likes to dance with women," he said. "Not as intimidating as men. Maybe you'd like to meet us there."

"Got plans, but thanks."

"If they fall through, drop on by."

He was leaving; she wished he would walk faster. But he stopped walking and said, "You wouldn't happen to know where Girlicue is exactly, would you?"

"I'm pretty sure it's south of the moon."

"I'll ask Siri," Rundown Daddy said, as he got into the elevator.

"Ask Siri if she wants to dance with your wife."

He looked like he was about to laugh as the elevator door shut.

Jeanette beelined for the phone on the maître d' stand beside the stacked menus. She dialed the front desk, felt a sudden surge of energy as she said, "Evan Jameson's room please."

Ernesto emerged from the kitchen.

"Just talking to the front desk," Jeanette said.

"Take your time," Ernesto said with a bored shrug. "Nobody's calling for room service." He strolled back into the kitchen.

"Are you sure?" Jeanette said into the phone. "Sure he doesn't have a reservation for today?"

Her mood swung downward. She knew she was *way* too disappointed.

A wreath, which wasn't on the wall yesterday, framed a mirror above the fireplace. Jeanette inhaled the pine (already losing its scent, three and a half weeks till Christmas), needles dry against her nose. She saw her face in the mirror, framed by the holiday wreath, a face deep in thought as she wondered: Could she still get a ticket for tonight's concert?

35

SEE HOW YOU FEEL AFTER THE HOLIDAYS

Hideous traffic on the way to the Getty. Hideous. She arrived one minute before showtime; the concert was sold out. Just as she was about to leave, serendipity tapped her on the shoulder and it was wearing perfume. A woman outside the auditorium had an extra ticket. Not only that, the woman *gave* Jeanette the ticket; wouldn't let her pay for it. Like some kind of sign: She should be here. There she was, again, looking for signs, reminding herself—she didn't believe in signs.

Jeanette hurried down the aisle...as Evan took his seat on stage with the quartet: two violinists and a violist—Evan, second from the right in the semi-circle, cello against his chest (cello contrasting beautifully with his butter-yellow, short-sleeved shirt and ivory corduroys), the "hips" of the cello between his knees.

Jeanette's aisle seat, second row center, gifted her with an unobstructed view of Evan's face; his features more chiseled—was it the intensity of his focus?—on stage. She watched him breathe...the subtle rise of his shoulders as he inhaled, the easy settling of them as he exhaled. She watched his right hand bring the bow downward gently across the strings, his left hand fingering the notes. She watched him close his eyes, tilt his head back slightly, sustaining a haunting tone. Then—with a quick release of his fingers—silence.

Silence for so long, Jeanette became aware of the rhythm of her own breathing...until the quartet played a melodic line, and her breath merged with the pulse of the music, a prolonged, unadorned harmonic that bled into another silence.

The piece consisted of just a few, repetitive chords: quietly, delicately, capturing the audience's attention; securing it through each silence.

Silence. Music.

Tension. Release.

Jeanette wasn't sure how long the hypnotic exchange of silence and music held her captive. She anticipated the stroke of Evan's bow, his touch on the strings, restrained.

His left forearm pulsated as he fingered a chord, sustaining a soft moan of a tone. A gentle power—music...flowing through him from mind and soul to fingertips. She'd assumed he was a good musician, but nothing had prepared her for being in his presence while he coaxed beauty from the cello.

That's what he did to me. Didn't he do that? Coax beauty from me?

And Jeanette—she couldn't help it—imagined his fingers inside her.

He lifted his bow from the cello, his fingers from her fantasy.

She studied him in the silence, supporting the neck of the cello with only his thumb. Transfixed on Evan's opened hand, she asked herself:

Can he bring me to orgasm from the stage? Can I climax right here—in the aisle seat of the Getty auditorium?

Evan's index finger touched a string. Just that one finger; a tender, subtle pressure...Jeanette imagining that one finger— tenderly, subtly—encircling her nipple, his thumb joining in, pinching; presenting her nipple to his lips.

Silence. Music.

Tension. Release.

Again. And again.

She waited in the renewed silence, wanting Evan to finger the notes, bow the string, smooth. Controlled.

Silence.

Music.

Tension.

Release.

Evan focusing. His fingers tapping the strings of the cello...

Tap. Tap. Tap.

Jeanette focusing; imagining...his fingers tapping her clitoris...

Tap. Tap. Tap.

Evan pressing the strings. Holding an exquisite tone. Holding...holding...*holding,* stroking, his bow *stroking*—now lifting his bow, his fingers from the strings, muting the music with a gentle opening of his hand, leaving Jeanette yearning in the silence—"*Don't stop!*" she wanted to yell, yell to him right there on the stage: "*Do it.* **Do** *it, baby. Stroke those strings. Finger them. Finger* **me.** *Let...me...***come.**"

She was getting there. On her way. Close. Close to achieving orgasm in seat 101, Row B-Center of the Getty auditorium—when the audience applauded.

The piece had ended.

The woman seated beside her spoke over the applause.

Jeanette turned to the silver-haired woman with the turquoise, drop earrings.

"All those silences. Difficult for me to sit through," the woman said. "I don't know about this minimalism."

"Minimalism made me wet," Jeanette said.

The woman wasn't sure she'd heard right.

But Jeanette just laughed, applauding as Evan and the rest of the quartet joined hands. And took a bow.

***

The lobby was crowded with people browsing at CDs for sale; a smaller group waited to meet the musicians who would walk through on their way out of the auditorium.

Jeanette stood among the browsers. She wanted to see Evan before he saw her. Pick the right moment—when everyone else had flattered him and said goodbye—before she said hello. Just hello...that's all, a friendly hello. Nothing wrong with that. It would be weird if she *didn't* say something to him; weird if she *didn't* let him know she was here. Right? It's a natural thing...to acknowledge her presence at the concert, acknowledge her appreciation of his musicianship—a *natural* thing. These thoughts jockeyed for position inside her first-come-first-served-standing-room-only head. She surveyed the crowd: eclectic, smart, somewhat stylish, the youngest around twenty. She scanned the room for the oldest, lost interest in the demography, distracted by a woman who was standing alone in a corner near the door—pregnant.

Alright, stop. Stop it. Just because the woman is pregnant and, maybe, waiting for someone...why jump to the irrational conclusion, or possibility—Evan's wife?

It had never occurred to Jeanette: his wife might be here. Or that she'd be so pretty. Or so pregnant—twins...triplets? *Three* babies?

A man, wearing a black beret and pink, retro-circular shades, approached the pregnant woman. He put his arm around her as they headed for the door. Jeanette smiled at the foolishness of her anxiety.

Musicians from the quartet, the violist and one of the violinists, entered the lobby. Jeanette watched them as they amicably accepted praise from their fans. A woman chatted easily with the violist; she turned to the violinist, included him in the conversation. It was then that Jeanette realized she was looking at yet another pregnant woman; her small mound of a belly protruded against a cable-knit sweater. She had a pleasant face, attractive in a non-threatening way, no one Jeanette would give a second glance to—unless Evan was walking up to the pregnant woman, placing the hood of her sweater on her head...kissing her lips.

Evan's **wife**.

There she was—bringing her hand to her belly, a wince of discomfort erased by a tiny smile of acceptance. Evan—there *he* was—placing his hand beside his wife's hand, feeling the life beneath his wife's skin...the life they'd created, the two of them, their baby. Evan's and his wife's *baby*.

A young Asian woman offered Evan a CD and a pen, flustered in his presence. Evan signed the CD, saying something that had the fan giggling with appreciation. Then he took his wife's hand, started across the lobby.

Jeanette turned so fast, she almost gave herself whiplash. She pushed through the crowd, "Sorry, excuse me, excuse...so sorry"—rushed out the door, gulping night air.

She ran across the terrace; down the stairs, over the beige, cleft-cut travertine, imported from Italy; the soles of her Sauconys slapping fossils ingrained in the stone. She didn't stop running until she was standing at the tram, waiting for the door to slide open so she could board it.

As the tram descended the hill, Jeanette gazed down at the traffic clogging the 405. She glimpsed her face, reflected in the window, stared at her abject humiliation.

✶✶✶

Forget about wine.

Jeanette required more than 15 percent alcohol; circumstances demanded 80 proof. Tequila, Canicas Blanco, lubricated the bluntness of her thoughts, so her mind could accommodate them: the *reality* of the wife—*seeing* the wife, wife pregnant, Evan's hand on his wife's belly, his lips on his wife's lips—all of this, she pictured, wishing she'd gone with her instinct: gotten drunk in her room instead of the bar.

Because Rundown Daddy was about to sit beside her, assigning the seat on the other side of him, gesturing like there was a name card designating the spot, to a woman as fit-looking as he was tired.

"Girlicue was closed," he said to Jeanette, like they'd spoken five minutes ago. Then he said to the woman beside him, "I told you she was lovely."

The woman leaned across the bar past Rundown Daddy. "My husband was right," she said to Jeanette. "You *do* have beautiful skin. You wouldn't happen to know where I could get a good facial, would you?"

Jeanette reached for a pen on the bar, jotted Sophie's name and number on a cocktail napkin. She read her sloppy writing: evidence she was as drunk as she felt. She scooted Sophie's number down the bar and said, "I trust this woman with my only *face*."

"I told you she'd know someone," Rundown Daddy said to his wife. He turned to Jeanette. "Not that my wife needs anything to make her more radiant than she already is."

"I'm Carolyn." Carolyn reached across her husband and shook Jeanette's hand.

"We've been married a long time," Rundown Daddy said. "All of a sudden, just recently....guys have started coming *onto* Carolyn."

"Larry. We just met the woman. I'm sure she doesn't want to hear that."

"Twenty-eight-year-old hotshot brought his Porsche into the body shop—"

"Larry owns a body shop," Carolyn said, as if translating her husband's words from a foreign language. "In Michigan."

"Not important," Larry said. "What's important is this twenty-eight-year-old hotshot was knocked out by you."

"I was helping Larry that day. Woman in the office had

personal problems," Carolyn told Jeanette.

"He was so knocked out by Carolyn, he started emailing her."

"That bother you?" Jeanette said, grabbing a handful of wasabi-coated peas from the bowl. She tossed them onto the bar in front of her like she was playing jacks.

"It makes me proud," Larry said. "When men find my wife attractive...women too."

"Larry," Carolyn said.

"I just want to tell her about that masseuse we met in Florida."

"I'm sure she doesn't want to hear it."

"This young woman was gorgeous enough to be a model in South Beach, but she had healing skills. Chose to work with the elderly. Anyway, she was almost half my wife's age and she thought Carolyn was the most beautiful woman she'd ever met."

"Not that she'd *ever* met, Larry."

"Well, she started emailing Carolyn, too. She was *smitten* with her."

"Larry, you're embarrassing me."

But Carolyn didn't seem embarrassed. Jeanette had the feeling they'd recited this routine before. She remembered his words at breakfast: My wife likes to dance with women, not as intimidating as men—was he pimping Carolyn? Hoping for a threesome (only way he could cheat on his wife, *include* her)? Or did he just want to watch? Maybe that's why Rundown Daddy was so rundown—too much watching.

A man trying to hook his wife up with her; that would be a first. That's what was happening. Wasn't it?

"He just can't believe I get more compliments now," Carolyn said, "than when I was—"

Before she could say "younger," a little-girl voice said, "Where's the bartender?"

The little-girl voice belonged to a full-grown woman. She leaned against the end of the bar like the weight of her fake breasts was pulling her otherwise petite physique down into the granite counter. Her blond, silky-haired boyfriend, his skin half a shade darker than albino, had somehow fit his hand into the hip pocket of her skinny jeans.

What is this? Couples Night? Jeanette asked her drunk self.

"Join the club," Larry told the couple. "Have a seat. We're all waiting for the bartender."

"We just want to take a bottle of champagne back to our room is all," the little-girl voice said.

"Celebrating?" Larry said.

"My all-time best week at work," she said.

"What do you?" Larry said.

"I'm a stripper...days. On La Cienega. 'Live Nude Girls Girls Girls.'"

"And are you nude nude nude?" Larry said.

The boyfriend answered, his Swedish accent lending him a goofy earnestness, "Nude except for pasties and a G-string."

"Business is like so amazing at Christmas time," the stripper said.

"You would think the customers would all be sad," the Swede said.

"Sad because they're inside a nude club instead of outside caroling?" Jeanette said.

"Sad because they're watching all these great women," the Swede said. "Then they have to go back home to their families."

"People are in the mood to feel joy during the holidays... spend money," the stripper said to the Swede. "You *know* what it's like to have a girl like me—they don't."

"Every day I am with her," the Swede said to Jeanette, "it is like a surprise I had no idea I would ever receive."

"You are so sweet," the stripper said to the Swede. "And I know sweet from bitter," she told Jeanette, her little voice getting littler. "I learn from him. He's 32. Before we met...I was just having like 26-to-28-year-old fun."

Jeanette downed her tequila, got up from the bar.

"Leaving?" Carolyn said, disappointed.

"Been a long night," Jeanette said, signing her check.

The stripper took Jeanette's seat at the bar, sat sidesaddle, facing the Swede.

"Why don't you and I change seats, hon," Larry said to his wife. "I'm sure there's some questions you'd like to ask this fascinating young lady."

Jeanette steadied herself. She felt the 40 percent alcohol flowing through 100 percent of her body as she whispered into the stripper's ear, "Try not to talk like a little girl. It limits your options."

Jeanette managed a fine performance of a sober woman walking who *didn't* want to scream. She stepped into the open elevator, wondered if the stripper and the Swede would be celebrating by themselves tonight. As she pushed the button for the first floor, the stripper garnered enough vocal power to yell all the way from the bar to Jeanette:

"Have a Merry Christmas or whatever!"

∗∗∗

Her cell woke her. Who would call at this time of night? She opened her eyes to drawn-drape darkness, saw the time: almost—noon? She reached for the phone, knocked it from the night table, rousing Al who got out of his bed with a reluctant stretch, preferring a more leisurely rise and shine.

She grabbed the phone from beneath the bed skirt, recognized the New York number (already three o'clock at the ad agency), ignoring her policy of never taking a business call before brushing her teeth. "Hello," she said, morning mouth at noon, her husky voice a tattler, divulging her half-awake condition.

"Good news," Mutt said.

Good was all she could handle.

The latest Rigidyne cut had been approved by one and all—agency *and* client had exhausted the aggressive obstinacy required for vigorous nitpicking—a happy side effect of the holidays. There

237

was still re-color correction, sound correction, graphics, East Coast headaches, not hers.

"The client is extremely high on you," Mutt said as Jeanette's bare foot flattened Al's squeaking toy platypus. "They're launching a campaign they think you'd be ideal for."

Jeanette opened the drapes to conclusive evidence of daylight, although the sun had yet to receive a wake-up call behind the clouds. "What's the product?"

"A pill for women," he said. "Curbs the appetite *and* the period."

"Why not curb a woman's need to talk, too?" Jeanette said, sarcasm the most alert part of her.

"If there was a pill that could do that...men would be schlepping their wives to the doctor for a prescription—*worldwide*."

"But seriously," Jeanette said, sliding open the terrace door. "Why am I ideal for a pill that prevents women from eating and menstruating?"

"They want to give it a sexy flair."

"Got to go, Mutt. I need to change my tampon. Then get me some pancakes, buckwheat with blueberries."

He laughed.

"Side of scrambled eggs," she said. "Potatoes too."

He laughed again. Like she was kidding.

She wasn't.

"No need for a definitive answer now," Mutt said. "See how you feel after the holidays."

36

CHRISTMAS AND THE BEADS OF SWEAT

It was too hot for a Santa hat on a head sprouting clumps of dirty dreadlocks; an incongruity with shorts and a bare chest in most places on the planet. Sensible daywear for Venice, as favored by the stupid-eyed, white dude Rollerblading along Abbot Kinney Boulevard, dragging his weary pit bull on a leash, the dog huffing and puffing, sporting a Santa hat too—like it wasn't insult enough, having to keep pace with the skater in this heat—the two of them, beast and beast, whizzing toward Jeanette who dashed for the curb.

Aphroteasiac was a cozy little place (seating capacity: eighteen) devoted to chocolate and exotic tea. A peach-colored wall featured vintage, sepia-toned photographs of soft, buxom women eating chocolate in dreamy states of absorption: on a divan, a picnic blanket, brass bed.

At a table, beneath the photos, a woman, the antithesis of buxom, sat hunched over a book, *When Food Is Love*, furtively eating chocolate sea-salt caramels.

Jeanette sipped iced tea at an empty, burnished wood counter.

Half a counter, actually; enough room for three stools, facing the street. The intense sun shooed her to a cooler seat at a table with an enticing view: a display case of chocolates, including mango-basil, passion fruit, lychee, and lavender. Silk jewelry boxes, brimming with chocolates, were on top of the case beside a sterling silver frame containing a single sentence, penned in calligraphy, on antique stationery:

Have you had your Aphroteasiac today?

"The owner should be back any minute," a young, fleshy, Hungarian beauty told Jeanette from behind the counter, her Hungarian accent as rich and filling as the chocolate truffles she poured from a bag onto a plate of samples.

A cowbell clanged as the door opened. Sophie entered, sweating through her wrinkled summer dress. "Jen!" she said. "What a happy surprise!"

"My favorite kind," Jeanette said.

They hugged.

"I'm just waiting for the owner," Jeanette said. "Brought her a new painting."

"You're on a roll, girl. This is such an upper."

"I stopped by the salon to show it to you, knocked on your window."

"Just got back from the gyno. My vagina walls...only part of me that's getting thinner." She sat at the table with Jeanette. "It's not right."

"Not right at all," Jeanette said.

"Can you believe this heat?" Sophie said. "Look at me. I'm wearing a summer dress and it's almost Christmas."

"Pretty dress."

"'Ross for Less.'"

"You should wear dresses more often, Soph."

"My waist looks big and my underarms look flabby."

"No one thinks that but you."

"No one spends as much time looking at me as I do," Sophie said. "What are you drinking?"

"Flowery Oolong."

"Simona," Sophie said to the Hungarian beauty, "I'll have what my friend is having." Sophie sipped from Jeanette's iced tea. She slid the glass back across the table. "I am so not ready for hormones."

"Rev up on lube."

"Wonder if they sell lube in bulk at Costco."

Jeanette laughed. "They might."

"Wouldn't it be great if I could fatten my walls by just sticking eclairs up there."

Sophie and Jeanette laughed, their mutual laughter a familiar and comfortable sound to them both.

Not to the bingeing reader, who shot them a look of disapproval. She dipped her head back into her book, her hands shielding her peripheral vision like blinders on a horse.

"Is this place not heavenly?" Sophie said. "So much enticement." She gazed at a shelf lined with canisters of teas and cocoa. "Dangerous having it so close." She turned back to Jeanette who was removing one-fourth of the top of an end table from a Trader Joe's bag.

"Now, tell me the truth," Jeanette said. She set her latest painting on the table in front of Sophie.

Sophie studied the painting: a portrait of a woman against a two-tone background, the top half earthy-brown, speckled with sand; the lower half pale blue—as if sky and land had reversed itself—the woman's expression pensive, almost quizzical, underscoring the caption beneath her.

"Well?" Jeanette said, anxious for Sophie's reaction.

Simona spoke before Sophie could. "I loved your last one. But this"—Simona set Sophie's tea on the table—"it's fantastic. The owner, she will go so crazy for it."

"Well, we'll see," Jeanette said.

"The woman's expression it is—perfect," Simona said. "Like she's surprised by what she's thinking." Simona's sultry Hungarian inflection shaded each word as she read the caption: *"I WANT YOUR HUSBAND."*

Sophie was still studying the painting as she said, "I wondered about your last piece—'I'm Married...I Have Certain Boundaries.'"

"Yeah?" Jeanette said, glancing at Simona who was heading to the back of the shop, thinking she looked like a young Ingrid Bergman. "What were you wondering?"

"Could you pass the sugar?" Sophie said.

Jeanette passed a silver bowl of brown sugar cubes across the table.

"I thought I was being paranoid," Sophie said, spooning a sugar cube into her tea, still looking at the painting. "But now, with this one..." She stirred her tea. "You're toying with me—aren't you?"

Jeanette laughed, a laugh of confusion. "What?"

Sophie looked up from the blunt stare of the woman in the painting. "Just tell me."

"What is it you want me to tell you?"

"Tell me—I *know*, Sophie." Sophie's words were flat, zero emotion; all fact: "Tell me—I know you had sex with Michael."

Jeanette was stunned. Too stunned to jump from comprehension to reaction.

Would she throw her iced tea at Sophie? Throw her tea at Sophie's face? Sophie's dress? That was movie behavior. And that would require spontaneous reflex.

Jeanette absently set her tea on the edge of the table. The glass fell, clattered to the floor, spilling a stream of Flowery Oolong and ice.

"No worries," Simona yelled from the back of the shop. "I'll get a mop."

"You really didn't..." Sophie said, softly voicing her conclusion as she reached it: "You didn't know. I thought that was why you weren't calling me. I thought maybe he told you before he—"

The cowbell clanged. Jeanette looked over at the door. The bingeing reader was leaving as Sophie said:

"I thought you were sending me a message through your *art*."

Jeanette turned back to Sophie; she was staring, again, at the caption beneath the portrait: *I WANT YOUR HUSBAND.*

"Maybe I just needed to confess," Sophie said. "Rid myself of this awful—we only did it once." Sophie looked into her oldest friend's eyes. "It was so unexpected. Completely unexpected—I swear."

"When, Sophie? *When?*"

"That weekend I was in San Francisco for the trade show. I dropped by your house. I didn't know you were on location. Directing a Midol, I think...or Monistat—who cares *what* you were directing?" Sophie drank tea in a thirsty hurry. "Any other day," she said, "any other time in my life...it never would have happened. My self-esteem was at an all-time low. I'd been rejected the night before. Horrendous rejection—this Ryan Gosling-looking lawyer I'd thrown myself at. And Michael, he..."

Jeanette picked up a cube of sugar, staring at it like she'd never seen a cube of sugar before as Sophie said, "Michael had gone off his Zoloft without telling you and—"

"Oh, *Sophie*."

"He wanted to see if he could...I, I was like his *guinea pig* or something."

"God, Soph. My *friend*." Jeanette stood; she sat back down. "That, that whole chlamydia episode. Me convincing myself I'd actually gotten it from a hot tub. And Michael *letting* me convince myself...when my chlamydia came from you. Didn't it? *You*, Sophie. You who insisted—Michael had sex with another woman."

"I couldn't tell you the woman was me. How could I? I was afraid it would destroy our *friendship*."

A rear screen door slammed shut. Jeanette got up from the table, as Simona approached with a mop and pail.

"Tell the owner I'll be back with another piece soon, Simona," Jeanette said. "I'm giving this one as a gift to my friend here."

"That is so nice of you," Simona said.

"She *deserves* it," Jeanette said, heading for the front door. Sophie rushed after her.

Jeanette stepped outside into the heat and glare. Sophie trailed her, blurting, "He didn't come *inside* me."

"Is that supposed to make me happy?"

"I didn't have an orgasm."

A siren wailed as a black and white police car rolled past them down Abbot Kinney. Sophie shouted over it:

"He *hated* himself afterwards."

Jeanette waited for the siren to fade.

"And you, Sophie?"

"I hated myself. But I hated Michael even more for *cheating* on you."

Jeanette didn't know whether to laugh or cry. She put on her sunglasses, took the stairs to the sidewalk.

Sophie called after her, contrite—the voice that had sought sporadic forgiveness from Jeanette for twenty-eight years. And had always received it. "I love you, Jeanette."

Jeanette kept walking.

37

SIGNS

One in the morning; she was still tense.

Even after a workout and two glasses of wine, Jeanette wanted to pound her fist into a wall. She would if she were a man instead of a woman with slender wrists who bruised easily. So she was up on the roof, pacing the tennis court, second time around, from the flag of Spain to the flag of Japan. Her mind clamped onto thoughts best discarded, like a newspaper-hoarding packrat unable to toss the yellowing headlines.

It was hard to unleash fury for a husband who was dead; death diluted fury, as in: may he rest in peace.

But Sophie? What could soften her betrayal?

Nothing.

Nothing at all.

Except—she told herself on her third pace around the court—Sophie and Michael couldn't stand one another. She knew this. And she knew:

The need to be desired.

Knew the power of that need. Power that could push you off a cliff, have you appreciating the velocity at which you were traveling.

Desire. Betrayal. Cliffs.

Words with picture definitions circled her mind like she was circling the dark tennis court: without destination.

Her cell rang, volume on low, but jarring her. She picked up the phone from the court, trying to shift emotional gears in four rings, her voice only partially cooperating.

"Hi, Mom."

"Did I wake you, Jeanette?"

"Not even close."

"I couldn't wait to call."

"Everything okay in Argentina?"

"Nothing was okay in Argentina. I'm calling from my apartment."

"You're back in Paris?"

"Massimo got food poisoning."

"From what?"

"He blamed it on the branzino his sister-in-law cooked. Then she broke out in hives, blamed it on stress from Massimo. So his brother threw a plate of panna cotta at him. That's when we got the hell out of there. Can you imagine throwing panna cotta at someone who has food poisoning?"

"Jesus."

"Since you brought him up, do you have plans for Christmas?"

"*A* plan. To *ignore* it."

"How would you like to ignore Christmas on an airplane? Perfect day to fly...airport will be empty," her mother said, in that appealing, teasing way she had of heightening the anticipation of good news. "You can be the first to sleep on my new futon."

"What happened to your tenants?"

"I arranged for them to stay in another apartment right here in the building. Come to Paris—I want to bring in the New Year with my daughter."

"No way I can get a plane ticket to Paris for Christmas, not at this late date."

"I want to buy you a ticket."

"Too expensive, now."

"That's why God created SkyMiles."

"I would love to, Mom. *Love* to be with you in Paris."

"Then that's where you'll be—in Paris with me. Mother and daughter starting the New Year, together, feeling *très très français!*"

"But there's a problem, my dog."

"Al? Bring him."

"He needs a new rabies shot. And even if he didn't, it's too long a flight for him just to—"

"So board him."

"You do realize it's the day before Christmas Eve already, in Paris?"

"You're not in Paris. Use your nine extra hours to figure it out."

Jeanette stopped pacing. She looked up at the flag that she was standing beneath—*France.* "Amazing."

"What's amazing about a mother wanting to bring in the New Year with her daughter in Paris?"

"I wasn't talking to you, Mom."

"Who were you talking to?"

"Myself."

"You don't want to do too much of that over the holidays, dear. Too much pressure holding up your end of the conversation."

A smile sneaked past Jeanette's frustration. "I'll try," she said. "Try to figure out someplace for Al. But I doubt that I can make it happen."

"My darling Jeanette. Anything you want in life that's difficult to get, large or small...has to start with you believing you can make it happen."

A sudden gust of wind kicked up, slapping Jeanette's face with her hair; wind that rolled a plastic cup of wasabi-coated peas across the court. She reminded herself: She didn't believe in signs. But the flag of France was flapping above her—demanding her attention.

***

She'd lost track of how many places she'd called that boarded dogs. Rates ranged from thirty-five a night to ninety-five; the priciest places (providing the dog passed the pre-acceptance interview) touted their perks: bone-shaped swimming pools, private "cottages," TV and radio for each dog ("we don't presume every dog's taste in entertainment to be identical"), designer dog beds, daily report cards; webcams. She'd phoned veterinary offices (doggie jail: cage, food, water), followed up recommendations of women who made ends meet by boarding dogs in their backyards. Overpriced or almost reasonable, the answer was always a variation of: "Do you know how far in advance we book for the holidays?"

So that was that.

Au revoir, Paris.

She wished her mother had never extended the invitation. Then she wouldn't be feeling the disappointment of not going. Wouldn't have the strong sense—she needed to be there.

Her cell rang as she walked down the hallway to the restaurant.

Please be someone from a dog-loving kennel with an opening.

But it was the Realtor, saying Jeanette's tenants would be moving out in thirty-one days. What were her plans for the house? Would she be moving back? Or was she interested in renting it out again? If so, short term or long? Or had she considered selling?

Jeanette answered without hesitation, "I can't deal with this now. Let's talk after the holidays."

No one was in the restaurant, except Angie and Oscar. Jeanette didn't feel like eating alone, tonight, in an empty restaurant. She started to leave, but Angie said, "One of our guests... he's on the TV."

"Right there," Oscar said, pointing up at the TV above the bar. "Mr. Millburn!"

How could she have forgotten it was debuting tonight?—the Rigidyne spot.

"Oh, my God, Mr. Millburn's hand," Angie said. "It's under the woman's dress."

"Al*right*, Mr. Millburn!" Oscar said.

"Look, look...look where he's taking her," Angie said, delighted. "A hotel!"

"He can't wait to get there," Oscar said. "I never seen Mr. Millburn move fast."

"He looks kinda sexy," Angie said to Jeanette.

"He does look kinda sexy," Jeanette said, thinking, *because I shot him exactly right.*

"Not all achy looking," Angie said. "Like when I bring him room service."

"There they go...down the hall to their room," Oscar said. "I never seen Mr. Millburn with *anyone* in his room."

"Look, look. Look what it says. It's a pill...makes his *thing* hard," Angie said, with a giggle. "That's why he all of a sudden was wearing a coat."

"Rigidyne," Oscar said, as the word appeared on TV across an elevator door. "He *got* it!"

A voice-over recited the side effects (an argument Jeanette had lost; she'd wanted a visual scroll), the man's voice sounding upbeat...like a possible seven-hour erection might be a perk of the product.

"Seven hours?" Angie said, bringing her palms to her blushing cheeks.

"Could be worth it," Oscar said with a wink.

"Beautifully directed commercial," Jeanette said, heading toward the corridor.

"Before you go," Angie said, pouring champagne into a flute, "take this with you." She handed Jeanette the flute.

"We're celebrating," Oscar said. "New chef, *gone* chef." Oscar thrust his right thumb over his right shoulder. "Outta here."

"Fired," Angie said. "Girlfriend too."

"Congratulations," Jeanette said.

"Every new chef comes in here tries to change what's working," Oscar said. "Things go back the way they were...till a new one comes along."

"So where's *your* champagne?" Jeanette said.

"In the kitchen," Oscar said. "Don't tell nobody."

"Nobody," Jeanette said.

"You spending Christmas with family?" Angie said.

"No. I'm not. What about you?"

"I'll be right here," Angie said.

"Me too," Oscar said.

"That makes three of us."

Jeanette walked down the corridor, swigging champagne like it was soda.

38

LOATHING ME LOVING YOU

From: Sophie
Subject: FORGIVENESS

Jeanette stared at the unopened email on her computer screen. Not now. She'd read it after dinner. She required protein before dealing with Subject: FORGIVENESS.

Jeanette glossed her lips, grabbed her purse, kissed Al on the head. She opened the door, realizing she'd left the key on the table beside her laptop. She picked up the key, unable to avoid the computer screen.

From: Sophie
Subject: FORGIVENESS

She instructed her finger not to open the email. Her digit disobeyed. She read the note.

Dear Jeanette,

Up all last night. Worrying about our friendship. How I don't want to lose it. Scared that I already have. A new word should be invented for how sorry I am. A word that combines I'm sorry with regret (I'm *regrorry*)? Or I'm sorry with regret and despicable (I'm *despicregrorry*)? Been eating like a pig. Double-fudge brownie. Gelato too. Macaroni and cheese. Many little chocolates filled with coffee vodka, disgusting myself. I want our friendship to survive but I know it's not up to me. Only you can make it happen, Jeanette.

Please find it in your heart to forgive me.

> Loathing me. Loving you.
> Sophie

Jeanette read the note again. Five words jumped out at her— *you can make it happen.*

✱✱✱

Sophie sounded fragile when she answered the phone:
"Hello."
"Sophie?"
"Jeanette?" Sophie's voice perked up. "I'm so glad it's you. You don't know how glad."
"I have a favor to ask."
"Anything, anything at all."
"I need you to take care of Al."
"You want me to take care of your dog?"
"It's the only way I can visit my mother in Paris. I'd leave on Christmas. Be back the week after New Year's."
"I want to do this for you."

"Good."
"But Howie's allergic to dogs."
"Put Howie out in the backyard."
"I don't know if you're kidding or not."
"You said you two needed to take separate vacations."
"But on Christmas? New Year's too?"
"So is that a no?"
"I want to do this for you."
"Then you'll do it?"
"Howie just walked in the door. I'll call you back."

39

A PERFECT DAY TO FLY

The flight attendant for Air France was wearing a Santa hat.

"*Joyeux Noël*! Merry Christmas," she said, beaming like she'd just had a tryst with Santa in *le toilette*.

"*Joyeux Noël*," Jeanette said as she boarded the plane.

The woman in the aisle seat looked up from her *Le Monde* as Jeanette placed her carry-on inside the overhead compartment. "*Joyeux Noël*," the woman said.

"*Joyeux Noël*," Jeanette said, stepping over the woman's red leather pumps (perfectly accessorizing her red leather skirt), taking the window seat beside her.

"Since you are by the window," the woman said, her French accent a rhythmic lilt, "you must promise to tell me if you see Santa and his reindeer."

"*Je promets,*" Jeanette said as she remembered her mother's words:

How would you like to ignore Christmas on an airplane?

40

C'EST RARE

Tess sat beside an early nineteenth-century English Cornhill organ, her still-great legs scissor crossed, the toe of one suede high heel grazing her stockinged ankle while the other toe tapped the floor in time to an oboe, of all things. She gazed out the window of *Andre Sonnet's Instruments Musicaux Anciens* through the red, white, and black strings of an eighteenth-century Irish harp, beyond the graceful curves of a one-hundred-year-old mute violin; her attention divided between the passersby on rue du Pas de la Mule and Andre, who was in his rear cave of a workroom, playing a nineteenth-century oboe for an oboist who taught at the conservatory in Holland.

Tess liked counting the instruments that were housed and nourished in the tiny shop, the number in constant flux. Today, she'd counted: ten hurdy-gurdys, nineteen mandolins, eight guitars, three banjos, two coronets, two trombones, two trumpets, a sax, a tuba, a French horn...and that was just in the workroom, hanging above Andre's tools. Four French horns hung beside eight violins near the front door—just before you got to the 1886 Ronisch upright grand (complete with attached candelabras) and the 1870 monochord (a one-string instrument played with a bow as well as a keyboard) hidden in the corner. But Tess's latest favorite was the *serinette*: an eighteenth-century barrel organ, designed to teach tunes to canaries.

Tess had wandered into the Marais shop, across the street from Place des Vosges, ten years ago, days after moving to Paris; instantly comfortable, not only with Andre (he'd played every instrument she'd shown the slightest interest in), but the steady flow of musicians, from all over the world, had her feeling like Tess the Tailor, again—minus the sewing machine.

She didn't know Andre's age; didn't care. Plumpish, gray-haired, eyes watching through spectacles, ready to be delighted; the contagious pleasure in his work obscured the fact: He was a shrewd businessman. Like this very moment, he was whetting the oboist's interest in an oboe he'd yet to obtain, as Tess gazed at the couture shop across the street...a solitary, bejeweled, white gown in the window—and imagined her daughter in that elegant gown.

These past few days, walking around Paris, together, Tess had sensed a distracted sadness in Jeanette. And when Tess broached the subject: men/sex/love; Jeanette simply said, "Stop worrying about me."

Tess *was* worried about Jeanette. Her social connections in California seemed to be work related, work that brought little satisfaction. Certainly, no elevation of the spirit. And Tess knew: if her daughter's energy wasn't channeled into passion and discovery, it diffused into restless dissatisfaction.

The last time Tess saw Jeanette, other than at the memorial, was in San Francisco, two weeks before Michael's death. Tess had declined the invite to stay with them at their house in Bernal Heights for the weekend, opting for a hotel; the tension between Jeanette and Michael—palpable. Like the smell of cigarettes settles into the fabric of a shirt that hasn't been worn in months, their disharmony lingered, thickening the air: husband and wife inhaling and exhaling each other's frustration.

Mother (or mother-in-law, depending on who might be doing the blaming) refused to provide an excuse for their marital boredom and/or resentment.

It was on a walk up Esmeralda Street that Jeanette confided to Tess, "I don't think I can do it anymore...live with him." She had finally faced the inevitable—a good thing—but Tess tempered her response, knowing Jeanette would defend Michael out of loyalty. So, she merely asked in a tone impartial to the answer, "Are you leaving him?" Jeanette's response touched her:

"If I didn't love him so much...I would have left him years ago."

Would Jeanette's life be different now—if she hadn't told Michael she wanted a divorce the day before the accident? Was guilt monitoring her daughter's intake of happiness? Her daughter deserved joy, to give and receive it. Would Jeanette have met some man by now...at least have had an affair?

These were Tess's thoughts as she stepped outside Andre's, craving an espresso. She was meeting Jeanette in an hour at Mariage Frères for tea, but a quick espresso at Café Hugo could hit the spot.

A man stood at the end of the shop, staring at the fanned display of twenty-two wooden flutes in the window. "It's not enough he has *you*?" he said into his cellphone.

Tess made three instant observations:

Good face. American. Musician.

"You want him to have my blood too?" the man said.

Tess was right about all three: good face, American, musician.

The American musician with the good face was Evan, sounding more bewildered than angry, "If I do it, I'm not doing it for *him*. I'd be doing it for *you*. Let me, let...let me call you back. I need"—he shook his head as if he couldn't believe what was being said to him—"I need to, I'll call you later." He clicked off the phone, suddenly aware of Tess standing by the door.

"*Êtes-vous français?*" he said.

"No. American."

Tess thought he looked disappointed, as if he realized: She not only overheard his conversation, she understood it. "I haven't been standing here long," she said.

"My wife," Evan said, walking toward Tess, feeling the need to explain. "She fell in love with a man who has the same rare blood type as me."

"She was a vampire in another life maybe?"

Evan's face warmed, and Tess detected a kindness in his eyes. "May*be*," he said, running his fingers through his hair, Tess thinking: musician's hair for sure...relaxed, longish waves free to do their thing.

"He needs an operation in two weeks," Evan said, gazing down at a discarded metro ticket on the sidewalk. He looked at Tess. "She wants me to donate my blood to him."

Tess shook her head in amazement. "And will you?"

"If I were in the same...I don't know." He opened the door to the shop. "Their baby deserves to have a father."

***

Tess returned from Café Hugo, pleased, although not knowing why, that the man with the rare blood type was still in the shop, examining a rare cello.

Andre's voice was low-key, hushed, like talking about price in front of the cello was an insult to the instrument. "14,500 euros."

"*Trop cher pour moi, Monsieur,*" Evan said.

"*Dommage,*" Andre said. "*Un instrument rare.*"

"*Oui,*" Evan said. "Rare."

"So you're a cellist," Tess said, stepping around the stringless frame of an eighteenth-century harp carved with red and pink roses.

Evan nodded, unable to take his eyes off the cello.

"Playing here in Paris?" Tess said, as she sat on a stool at the ancient upright.

"Played last night, Palais des Congrès."

"I ran out of invitations," Tess said, removing a card from her purse. "I'm having a party at this restaurant." She handed him the restaurant card. "Great food, great people...Andre will be there. New Year's Eve."

"Thanks, but I'll be playing in Italy. Flying to Germany to-night," he said, returning the card.

"Keep it," Tess said. "Next time you're in Paris, wonderful place for dinner."

"*Vous voulez jouer le violoncelle*? Andre said, offering Evan a bow.

"Go ahead," Tess said, sliding the stool over to him. "How often do you get to play an 1870 cello?"

Evan accepted the bow from Andre. He sat on the stool, positioned the cello between his knees. He wiped his left hand on the thigh of his jeans, placed his fingers on the neck of the cello. Then he introduced the bow to the strings.

Evan played for two minutes and nine seconds: Benjamin Britten's Cello Suite No. 1, Opus 72. It was as if the instrument had finally, after one hundred and forty-nine years—met some-one who understood it. Someone it could talk to...sing to.

Nothing short of glorious.

Tess and Andre gave him a standing ovation.

"*Superbe*," Andre said, glowing, the pace of his words quick-ening with enthusiasm. "*Il faut un musicien extraordinaire pour jouer d'un instrument extraordinarie...c'est seulement alors quils peuvent être tous deux veritablement heureux.*"

"I can get by in French," Evan said to Tess, "long as some-one speaks slowly. Otherwise, I'm lost. What did he say?"

Tess translated Andre's words: "An extraordinary instru-ment needs to be played by an extraordinary musician...only then can they both be truly happy."

"Andre is right." Evan ran his hand along the curve of the

cello. "But 14,500 euros," he said, smiling, "is *still* too expensive for me."

Tess glanced at her watch. She wished Jeanette were meeting her here, instead of Mariage Frères.

41

TINY DANCER

"Anytime I want it, it's there—pussy on a platter." That's what a married percussionist told Evan on a bus headed to a gig in Kansas City. Perk of the road, he'd said; the week Evan married Nancy.

Evan had always passed on the platter. Resisted temptation. Always. Except that one night. One night with Jeanette.

"I'm married...I have certain boundaries." His words. His rules. From mind to voice with no lag time, having given zero thought to what they were before he'd needed them. A line not to cross—*partial* pleasure—as if he and his rules, alone, controlled the stability of his marriage. It never occurred to him: His wife had been receiving pleasure from another man—with *no* boundaries. How could he have assumed, all those days, months, *years* on the road...his wife had no desires at home, begging to be satisfied?

He wished he were already in Italy on stage playing, lost in rhythm and tone; not on the plane, lost in unsettling self-analysis, his mind booked to maximum capacity. He should have taken Lou Reed's advice, years ago, when they were touring together: learned Chen Tai Chi. Then he could be practicing Chen Tai Chi moves in his head, now, like Lou used to do on the plane;

still the turmoil of his thoughts.

Across the aisle, Tom Waits was writing. Maybe if he wrote his thoughts down, his mind wouldn't have to store them. Evan scribbled on the back of a receipt from the brasserie La Closerie des Lilas. He crumpled the receipt and shut his eyes.

Four months it had taken his wife to tell him. And when she did, she'd picked a public place: The Getty. After the Minimalism concert—in keeping with the theme—her revelation delivered in few words: stark. They were waiting for the tram, Nancy staring at a baby in a carriage, the mother smiling at Evan. "Adorable," Evan told the mother, although he didn't think the baby was the least bit adorable, sensing a compliment was expected from him. The first time Nancy tried to tell him was on the heels of his phony compliment:

"It's not easy to say..."

He thought Nancy was talking about the baby he'd pretended to find adorable, so he laughed, said into his wife's ear, "That's for sure."

Nancy looked uncomfortable. She patted her belly. "The baby..."

"Kicking again?" Evan said. "She's going to be a dancer, you know."

The tram arrived as Nancy said, "I'm so sorry, Evan." She held her belly with both hands; her words escaped her mouth sudden as a sneeze, "This baby isn't yours."

The door to the tram opened; Nancy stepped inside. Evan followed his wife into the packed car. She took the last seat.

Evan stood while the tram descended. He caught a glimpse of his face reflected in the window—a stunned man, lips clenched...a man afraid of what he would say if he allowed his mouth to open.

Tom Waits was fighting a cold, saving his voice, speaking so softly, Evan leaned across the aisle of the plane so he could hear him. "You drop this?" Tom said, holding Evan's crumpled receipt from La Closerie des Lilas.

"Guess so," Evan said.

"The words on the back," Tom said, "you write them?"

"They kind of wrote themselves," Evan said.

The plane shuddered from turbulence. Tom spoke barely above a whisper. Evan couldn't hear him.

"Don't strain your voice, Tom," Evan said.

Tom wrote on the receipt. He handed it to Evan.

Evan read Tom's words: I've got the perfect verse for this.

Then Evan read his own words—*My blood. His baby*—a distilled expression of pain that would find its way into a Tom Waits song.

42

LA NOUVELLE ANNÉE

Jeanette never liked New Year's Eve. Pick a year, pick an age, she'd been uneasy with the forced cheer the occasion demanded. Especially while watching TV in California, passive witness to the disappearance of time; the year's final ten seconds—the ball dropping in Times Square, the frenzied crowd—Jeanette quelling anxiety during The Countdown, the insidious pressure to feel exactly *happy* at exactly midnight, unable to forget: The televised merrymaking had already expired.

But tonight was different. Tonight, she was in Paris. Amid a swirl of excitement, independent of the holiday—was it three or four languages she was hearing?—feast of dialect; feast of food: breads, cheeses; vegetables (plump and juicy), heaping bowls of couscous; beef, chicken, lamb, soaked in exotic sauces (prune, honey-almond-sesame, tomato-rose-petal). Jeanette declined the pigeon cooked with twenty-seven spices. (*"Merci, mais je ne mange pas de pigeon, Monsieur."*) But said yes to wine, more than once. Champagne too. And pastries, drenched in honey and nuts (flaky Baklava-esque cylinders...her favorite), that made her fingers sticky.

Une célébration de la Nouvelle Année—the words on the

embossed invitation—in a Moroccan restaurant in the 11th arrondissement, nearest metro: Faidherbe-Chaligny, where few tourists ascended the stairs to the street.

The restaurant's size was deceptive: large yet intimate. A maître d' stand/wine counter divided the right side from the left, each half sectioned into two smaller rooms, seating twenty-five to sixty. Which is why Tess liked throwing parties here. You could forget there were people in the other rooms, think you had the place to yourself. And you could imagine you were in Morocco, what with the intricate mosaics painted on wood, the brocade sofas gathered around ornately carved tables, the Moroccan servers; and the Moroccan music (the staff's personal CDs).

Jeanette sipped champagne on a green brocade sofa, wearing a belated birthday present from—and made by—Tess the Tailor: a long-sleeved, black silk dress, dramatically slit on both sides from waist to ankles, adorned with a violet silk panel, from mandarin collar to hem, featuring a black calla lily centered perfectly on Jeanette's abdomen. (Tess didn't make the sheer, black silk slacks. She bought them in a shop frequented by locals in the 15th.)

Jeanette studied Tess, framed in the archway of the adjacent room, a red, green and gold, floor-to-ceiling mosaic behind her, like a set designer had placed it there to enhance her natural glow. Her vibrant mother—she always walked it like she talked it ("don't let anyone make you older than you feel, darling")— held hands with Massimo who was one inch shorter than Tess, eleven years younger. The lines on Massimo's handsome face accentuated each smile, laugh and frown. Testimony: The man had never been afraid to express himself. Like right now, he was laughing with Andre Sonnet who was tuning a lotar, a Moroccan version of a guitar.

Tess glanced over at Jeanette—the dress she'd made for her daughter fit her curves perfectly—a painting of a radiant woman come to life. Yet, tonight, Jeanette seemed more observer of the party than participant, Tess thought, as she blew a kiss to her.

Jeanette blew a kiss to Tess in return, thinking the party

was her mother's style: sumptuous, everyone having a grand time.

"*Voulez-vous danser, Madame?*"

A French environmental inspector invited Jeanette to dance, oblivious to the couscous speckling his handlebar mustache.

"*Merci,*" Jeanette said. "*Mais no, Monsieur.*"

"*S'il vous plaît, Madame.*" The inspector refused to accept no for an answer. He took Jeanette's hand, escorted her from the mound of green and gold pillows to a small circle of floor... where a Belgian woman, flaunting a great ass, danced with a Spaniard who twirled her so he could admire it.

Jeanette and the inspector danced without touching, the Frenchman dancing as if in class, learning steps from the couple beside him. Jeanette heard Andre playing the lotar, in harmony with some Moroccan CD. She closed her eyes, focused on the sensual pulse of the music. And wished she were dancing with a man she wanted to touch.

✳✳✳

Two hundred and ninety-nine couples danced inside the glass-enclosed *bateau mouche,* its lights illuminating the Seine and the splendidly ornate Pont Alexandre III above it. A renegade couple danced on the deck of the boat, waving to a man on the bridge.

Evan waved back at the couple.

Yesterday morning, the cold that Tom Waits had been fighting delivered a knockout punch: Tom had lost his voice completely—no sound at all. Laryngitis, compounded by a throat infection and a plugged ear, had forced him to cancel concerts in Italy and Spain. Or, as the botched American translation of an Italian music blog put it:

"Although, one does not visit a Tom Waits concert desiring the voice of a accomplished singer, the writer of songs darkly realist sentimental had not voice to even speak his writings, resulting in a cancelled concert disappointment much his loyal fans Italiano."

Tom, musicians, and crew flew back to Paris, this afternoon, so they could fly to New York from Charles de Gaulle, tomorrow. And tonight, Evan was alone on a bridge, watching three hundred couples dancing along the Seine as if the boat were transporting them to the New Year.

He'd wanted to walk, needed to walk; a walk that should have taken forty-five minutes, tops, had turned into two hours and sometime during that two hours, he'd stopped caring that he was lost. It didn't matter if he got to where he'd been heading: a brasserie to eat and drink with the same guys he'd been on the road with for a month.

Evan's hands were cold as he waved to the dancing couple. (He'd left his gloves in his hotel room in Italy.) The *bateau mouche* glided under the bridge beneath him. He cupped his hands, blew into them, rubbed his palms together. He warmed his fingers inside the pockets of his coat, felt a card inside his left pocket. He held the card up to the light of the Art Nouveau lamps that aligned the bridge: a restaurant card.

He noticed a sculpture in front of him. Part woman/part sea creature—*une nymphe de la Seine*—spending New Year's Eve like he was, alone, gazing at the river. He remembered who gave him the card; the woman at the antique instrument shop. The woman with the remarkable energy and remarkable legs.

43

'ROUND MIDNIGHT

"All is full," said the cousin of the owner of the restaurant. He gestured toward the room on the right, the sound of celebration spilling to the maître d' stand/wine counter that separated the raucous side from the tranquil side.

"*Dommage,*" Evan said. "Next time I'm in Paris, *peut-être.*" He headed toward the door.

"*Monsieur!*" the cousin said. "You *welcome* here."

The cousin escorted Evan to a room on the left. Half-filled (half-empty?) with guests who'd been turned away from the happening side.

An hour later, both sides were happening. Evan struggled to identify the Moroccan instruments on a CD, he could barely hear, above the surge of international chatter. Here he was at a New Year's Eve party—invited by a woman he didn't know, surrounded by people he didn't know, in an arrondissement he didn't know, craving air.

"*Pardon,*" he said (accentuating the second syllable with a hard *o*, like the French do), weaving his way through the revelers, making slow progress.

Finally. Within grasping distance...a door to the courtyard. He reached for the glass doorknob just as a woman, playing metal castanets, danced between him and the door, her French too rapid, too wine-drenched, for Evan to understand. A Portuguese woman joined her. They danced around him like he was a maypole wearing corduroys.

A server poured Moroccan tea *a la menthe* from a silver pot, lengthening the stream of tea, raising the spout high above the narrow, gold-rimmed glass.

"*Merci Monsieur,*" Jeanette said.

"*Je vous en prie, Madame.*"

Jeanette inhaled the scent of honey and mint. She gazed across the room, out the window, wondering if the champagne she drank (before, during, and after dinner) just sneaked up on her. Because a man in the courtyard was standing with his hands in his pockets, staring at a rosebush as if willing it to bloom in winter—what she could see of him: just his profile beneath the light of a half-moon and a solitary lantern. But still, it was uncanny how much the man resembled Evan. She squinted for a better view, adjusted the focus on her lens of reality.

He turned toward the door as if he knew someone was staring at him. The man did not resemble Evan. The man *was* Evan.

Her heart sped.

No warm-up.

Sudden sprint.

Pounding.

Strangely in time with the beat of the Moroccan music.

Her mind raced, trying to catch up with the beat of her heart, as he smiled...at whomever opened the door to the courtyard.

Her mother.

Her mother rushing across the courtyard to Evan?

A wall between two windows momentarily blocked Jeanette's view of Tess. When she reappeared through the window—Tess was greeting Evan with a kiss on each cheek.

Jeanette watched them: Evan and her mother *talking*.

Tess gestured toward the restaurant. Evan shook his head

"no." He pointed to the moon, said something that had Tess smiling, nodding in agreement. She headed into the restaurant, leaving Evan alone. Alone with a flowerless rosebush and half a moon.

Oh...

Mon...

Dieu!

Jeanette plowed through the partying crowd. She brushed against bare shoulders that smelled of expensive perfume; narrowly avoided the ember of a cigarette in the hand of a British anchorwoman; sidestepped a splash of Bordeaux from the glass of a gregariously smashed French poet.

"*Excusez-moi.*" One room. "*Pardon.*" Then another.

No! A knot of champagne drinkers at the maître d' stand/wine counter blocked her path. She could not get to the other side.

"*Je dois parler à ma fille.*" Her mother's voice.

Jeanette couldn't see her mother, but she sure could hear her:

"I need to speak with my daughter, pardon."

Tess pushed her guests aside with a fond touch, so as not to offend, speaking authoritatively, now, in Italian, "*Devo parlare con mia figlia,*" until she was beside Jeanette.

"Sweetheart," Tess said. "There's someone I want you to meet."

She took her daughter's hand—like she used to, in Laurel Canyon, when she'd walk Jeanette to kindergarten—Tess leading Jeanette through the restaurant, her voice fading in and out of the din of music and chatter, speaking to guests, switching languages with ease, Jeanette hearing scattered words, all the while following her mother from one room to another. But the words Jeanette did make out, clearly, were important ones:

"He's a cellist, dear. I have a feeling you'll like him."

Tess did not let go of her daughter's hand until she opened the door that led to the courtyard...and the man she wanted Jeanette to meet.

If this were a movie would I be walking in slow motion? Jeanette thought. *Would everything be out of focus but—him?*

That's how she felt, like she was moving in slo-mo. Thinking in slo-mo. Seeing nothing but Evan. Nothing but his back, actually.

He was staring at the moon as Tess said:

"I want you to meet my daughter."

Evan took his time turning from the moon.

Then he took his time—staring at Jeanette.

His amazement eased as his lips slowly committed to a smile. "This is your daughter?" he said to Tess, still staring at Jeanette.

"My one and only," Tess answered. "Jeanette dear," she said, to her one and only. "This is Evan."

Jeanette waited for Evan to speak.

Evan waited for Jeanette to speak.

They shook hands.

And there they were again...his fingers. On her skin.

"Your hand is warm," Evan said.

"Tea," Jeanette said.

"Your hand is sticky," he said.

"Honey," she said.

"Well, I must mingle," Tess said. "I'll let you two get acquainted."

Tess didn't wait for a response. She entered the restaurant, congratulating herself: She knew her daughter so well, she'd introduced her to a man she was attracted to.

"You have no idea..." Evan said, "how many things had to happen..." He wanted to hold her. "For me to be on this exact spot of the universe..." He wanted to inhale her scent. "With you." He wanted to feel the fullness of her breasts beneath that black-and-violet silk against his chest. He ran his finger down the strip of violet and said, "The color of a good night."

"You remember."

He held her; inhaled her: her hair, her skin; her scent...*her*— feeling the fullness of her breasts beneath that black-and-violet silk against his chest, like he'd wanted to.

She asked a question; a question she hadn't known she would

ask until she was asking it:

"But what about your wife?"

He stepped back. Stared at the black calla lily centered perfectly on Jeanette's abdomen. He placed his hand below the flower, on her belly, smoothed the violet silk which was rumpled from his embrace.

"We're getting a—"

A sudden, collective shout of celebration spilled from the restaurant:

"*Bonne Année!*"

The New Year.

It had arrived.

No countdown. No forced cheer. No expired revelry.

Just Evan saying, "Divorce."

The door opened as a champagne cork flew across the courtyard...followed by the gregariously smashed French poet and two equally smashed French chefs, whose glasses he filled with champagne.

But Evan spoke softly, "*Bonne Année*, Jeanette."

"*Bonne Année*, Evan," Jeanette said even softer.

"Let's get out of here," he said.

"Where?" she said. "Where should we go?"

He kissed the palm of her hand. He tasted honey.

✳✳✳

The hotel was in the 17th arrondissement. Evan closed the door to his room. Jeanette switched off the ceiling light. Evan unbuttoned her coat as she unbuttoned his coat. Like it was a race to see whose coat could fall to the floor the fastest.

He kissed her.

A wee-small-hours-of-the-morning kiss.

A kiss that infused her with want.

A kiss that started out tender...lingered enough to build.

A kiss that took its cue from the soul as well as the loins; from imagination, not intellect—a kiss that in a breath turned ferocious and invaded her.

He unzipped her dress. Slid it off her—they hadn't even moved from the door yet. She took his hand, led him toward the bed. She could see, through the window, the vertical sign that spelled HOTEL...same color as the half-moon. Only, she couldn't see all the letters. Just the first three: HOT—as Evan unclasped her violet lace bra. Threw it toward a chair.

Her bra landed on his cello case as she whispered his name.

✳✳✳

They left the room at 9:00 A.M. with a bliss hangover—Evan in a hurry to make the bus that would take him (and the other musicians in Tom Wait's band) to the airport—feeling the reverberations of sex and little sleep.

"I think I'm going to invent a new instrument," Evan said. "Call it the Jeanetto."

"I think you already did," she said.

Jeanette watched the bus pull away. She walked in the Paris chill of the first morning of the New Year. A breeze kicked up. She smelled the faint sexual scent of last night's passion on her body.

44

HOME

"Did you enjoy yourself in Paris?" the Graveyard Guy said.

"I did, yes," Jeanette said. "Very much."

"Glad to hear it," he said, stapling her credit card imprint to her guest folio. "A complimentary fruit basket should be waiting for you in 144."

"Well, thanks. I appreciate it."

"Our pleasure, Ms. Coles." He handed her a keycard along with a key to the minibar. "Welcome home."

"Home," she mused, as she wheeled her suitcase across the lobby.

"Just let us know," the Graveyard Guy called after her, "when you have a departure date."

LYRIC HOTEL

GUEST FOLIO

MS. JEANETTE COLES   ARRIVAL: January 8, 2020

DEPARTURE: OPEN

The Santa Anas had welcomed Jeanette back to L.A. with wind-gusto—blowing spinach leaves off her plate onto the rooftop-patio, during lunch. Now, she sat on the terrace of room 144, brushing Al, listening to the wail of sirens in the distance—and Helena Lutz, on her cell, in full-blown rep-mode, "What's so bad about a pill that gets rid of your period *and* your appetite?"

"I'm not the director for the product, Helena."

"Jet lag takes one day of recuperation for every time zone crossed. What's Paris? Nine time zones? Let's revisit this conversation when you're up to full speed, back to your normal sleep pattern."

"I'll sleep easier knowing we've already had this conversation."

"Look, I'm not saying this because I'm your rep…I just want you to be sure you're making a wise decision."

"*Je suis absolument certain que je fais une sage décision.*"

"What?"

"It's French."

"What's it mean?"

"It means—I'm not giving a sexy flair to the deprivation of a woman's appetite *and* menstrual cycle."

"You decline their—"

"Talk later. Gotta go, call waiting."

Her call waiting really was beeping.

Helena's words fled her mouth like it was on fire, "You decline their offer I worry about down-the-line repercussions."

"Side effects may include a sense of who I actually am." Jeanette clicked on the other call and said, "You've reached your favorite daughter."

"Guess who I'm sitting with in Café de Flore," Tess said.

"Who?"

"Dee Dwight."

Jeanette heard the raspy, abused voice, in the background, of a British blues guitarist. (Tess used to make shirts for him in Laurel Canyon.)

"Dee says hello," Tess told Jeanette.

"I can't believe he's still alive," Jeanette said.

"My darling daughter says hello too," Tess told Dee. Then she said to her darling daughter, "Dee asked me to make him a shirt for old times' sake—hold on."

Jeanette heard her mother speaking French to the waiter, ordering a second Armagnac, punctuating the request with a happy *merci beaucoup*. "It'll be fun, Jeanette...being Tess the Tailor for a few days."

"Unlike you, Mom, I just turned down a job—directing a commercial for a pill that curbs women's appetites *and* their periods."

"Good for you!" Tess said. "Hold on, I'm sorry. The waiter is talking to me."

Al shook himself, hurling dog hair and dust onto the geraniums as Jeanette heard Tess telling the waiter, "Ah, *oui, et Gâteau au Chocolat Opéra*."

"Midnight," Jeanette said to Al, "and my mother's ordering chocolate cake."

Tess came back to the phone. "In the United States, people live to work. In France, people work to live."

"As in chocolate cake at midnight?"

"Exactly as in chocolate cake at midnight," Tess said. "Work to *live*, Jeanette."

"I want to. I want to do that very thing."

"I'm having trouble hearing you. I have to get a new phone, but buying a phone in Paris is like..."

"Now I'm having trouble hearing you," Jeanette said.

"Can you hear me now?"

"Yes."

"I do love chocolate cake and good Armagnac."

"I'm going to take your advice, Mom."

"Which advice is that?"

"The advice you gave me before the Armagnac derailed your crystalline thought process."

"There you go again, sounding like my daughter." Tess laughed.

"Of course, I know what I told you. I just wanted you to hear *you* say it again."

"You said—I should work to **live**."

The wind blew Al's scattered hair from the terrace toward the Hollywood Hills. Jeanette couldn't see the hills behind the smog. She assumed they were still there.

LYRIC HOTEL

GUEST FOLIO

MS. JEANETTE COLES   ARRIVAL: January 8, 2020

DEPARTURE: February 1, 2020

45

MY FUNNY VALENTINE

The sun glittered off the Seine like a procession of cloned Tinker Bells. A busker played "My Funny Valentine" on the Pont Neuf, a trumpet player with so-so chops blowing (the Miles Davis arrangement) to a rhythm track; his so-so notes elevated to evocative by the beauty of the Seine...a valentine drifting across the river toward Notre-Dame, in the distance.

Valentine's Day in Paris!

Jeanette stood on the opposite side of the bridge, facing the Eiffel Tower, as Al wolfed down croissant crumbs at her feet. But she wasn't looking at *La Tour Eiffel*. She was studying the intrigued and amused faces of the tourists who were perusing the paintings displayed against the wall of the bridge—*her* paintings: portraits of men and women—captioned in French, subtitled in English.

A tourist, carrying a tote bag patterned with baguettes and cheese, scrutinized a portrait of a man, painted on a 25" by 25" piece of an old, maple wood headboard.

"You the artist?" the tourist said to Jeanette, her voice a nasal—maybe Texas—twang.

"I am," Jeanette said.

"Quite an expression he's got on him," Ms. Maybe Texas said, squatting at eye level with the eyes of the man in the painting. "Like he's tryin' to look all innocent...but might not be."

Jeanette laughed. "Everybody sees something different."

The woman read the caption: "*'I NEVER EVEN THOUGHT ABOUT CHEATING ON MY WIFE UNTIL TONIGHT.'* Well, I sincerely doubt that," she told the man in the painting.

She studied the other portraits, read the subtitled captions aloud:

"*'I WAS NAUGHTY BUT MY WIFE TOOK ME BACK.' 'MY LEGS ARE LONELY.'*"

"There's another one over there," Jeanette said, gesturing to the painting displayed on the curve of a stone bench. She felt a sudden, familiar caress on her shoulder.

"Hey, Madame," Evan said.

"Hey, Monsieur," Jeanette said. "How was the sound check?"

"No tantrums. Not even one."

"None here either," she said. "I got nibbles on three paintings."

"Probably more nibbles than Van Gogh got in an afternoon."

Jeanette laughed. "Plus I have both my ears."

"You're a walking and talking miracle."

"I'm a woman. A woman who believes in possibilities."

"You make it hard to leave," he said. "I wish I wasn't leaving tomorrow."

"Playing...it's what you do."

He nodded.

"It's what you love."

"I love what we did this morning in your bed."

"And in April, you'll love it all over again...when I visit you in *your* bed in Brooklyn."

"A small apartment in Brooklyn will never be a small apartment in Paris."

"But I will be me, and you will be you," she said. "And April is right around the corner."

"He's kinda half-smilin'," Ms. Maybe Texas said, eyeing the portrait of a man, painted on a section of headboard, propped against the stone bench. She read the caption in French, mispronouncing the words but enjoying herself. She read the English subtitle: "*'I'M MARRIED...I HAVE CERTAIN BOUNDARIES.'* I'm leanin' toward this guy, here," she said. She turned to Jeanette.

Jeanette was looking at Evan, touching his restless hair, which flowed to his neck from beneath his hat—black threaded with gold—the hat he lost and she found.

"You're not *him*...are you?" Ms. Maybe Texas said to Evan. She pointed to the man in the painting. "You're not the man with the boundaries?"

"No," Evan said. "I'm a different man."

"In *some* ways," Jeanette said to him.

Evan kind of half-smiled.

The busker segued into another tune, "You Go to My Head."

Evan sang to Jeanette: "*'You go to my head and you linger like a haunting refrain.'* You are the woman in the lyric," he said. Just before he kissed her.

A Pont Neuf Kiss.

The kind of kiss tourists photograph to bring home as a souvenir of Paris.

That's what Ms. Maybe Texas was doing, capturing The Pont Neuf Kiss on her camera.

The Pont Neuf Kiss with a power to send Jeanette slumping to the pavement—like Fanny Ardant in the arms of Gérard Depardieu (back when Gérard Depardieu used to be Gérard Depardieu). Except Fanny hadn't been kissed by Gérard for ten years. And Jeanette had received a kiss of equal passion from Evan, just this morning in the apartment: the reason she was still on her feet.

✳✳✳

Ms. Maybe Texas didn't buy Jeanette's painting. Not that day. She bought it two days later. On the bridge in front of the marble plaque that said:

PONT NEUF
COMMENCE
SOUS HENRI III
ACHEVE
SOUS HENRI IV
LE GRAND
1578-1607

A lone seagull soared above the Seine, wings flapping determinedly toward the Eiffel Tower, in a hurry; maybe to meet a friend. Or a lover.

And Jeanette thought: If it took twenty-nine years to build the Pont Neuf...what's forty-nine years to build a life?

ACKNOWLEDGEMENTS

I met a man at the hotel, where I lived (longer than Jeanette lived at the Lyric), who told me: "I will always think of you as a woman of mystery with a sense of purpose." I want to thank this man, whose name I don't remember, but whose words helped fuel my determination to write the book, and to feel worthy of his description.

I am giddy with gratefulness to Stephen Tobolowsky, a human divining rod for emotional truth in character and story, no matter how hidden the treasure. His untiring encouragement, generosity, and insight improved the book, as well as my spirits.

Thanks to Amy Alkon for her support and belief in the book, during an early draft, which she made time to read even while working on her own book. I remember, with fondness, our afternoons spent writing at 18th Street Coffee House.

Melodious thank-yous to Tom Hensley and Richard Bennett for the early reads and upbeat feedback.

I appreciate Wendy Hammers, for her support. And for connecting simpatico writers like a jeweler strings a necklace of gemstones.

Audrey Franks has cheered me on, since reading an early draft. It means a lot to me that her enthusiasm for the book has never wavered.

Thanks to Bill Dolinksy, for his support, decency, and voice of reason during chaos.

Much appreciation for artist, Chris Bonno. His beautiful painting, which is on the wall in front of my writing table, nourishes my imagination.

Merci Beaucoup to my Paris writing enablers:

Gloria Montenegro and Bernard, for their friendship, coffee, and view of the Seine through the window of Cafeoteque, as I wrote.

ACKNOWLEDGEMENTS

Café de Flore, for the *allongés*, the "secret" chocolates, the corner table, and the chilly late afternoons spent writing in the room where Simone de Beauvoir used to write, imagine, and (probably) hope.

La Closerie des Lilas, for granting me permission to write in the "private" room, upstairs, because of my promise: no computer, *seulement stylo et papier*. I intend to take the manager up on his offer: to display my novel in the cabinet beside Hemingway's books.

Corinne Moreau, for her encouragement, sparkly friendship, womanly sensibilities, and vast collection of scarves and brooches.

Natalie Fynn, for listening to my stories, sharing profiteroles with champagne...and for outbidding a man for a letter written by Josephine Baker.

Violaine Roussel, for making it possible for me to write on the glorious street where Matisse used to paint.

The music of Bang on a Can and Terry Riley ("In C") helped propel me through my rough first draft like a mantra. Ethel's music gave me an early push that I needed as well.

From time to time, I think of the joy of meeting Neil Innes in the lobby of the hotel, which resulted in a gleefully spontaneous trip to a movie theater. And Peter Fonda, who arrived at the hotel on his motorcycle, and made me feel as if he were glad to see me, every time we ran into each other, with a kindness undiminished by celebrity.

ACKNOWLEDGEMENTS

***

Love and gratitude, always, for Les Carter: my late husband. He was unique. A wonderful writer who had so many stories yet to tell, in a way that only he could tell them. Les once said to me, "Writing fits you like a glove." But he didn't know that the glove would be made in France, and that it would sit beside my notebook on the table of a Paris café, as I wrote scenes that would find their way into my first novel.

Café de la Paix
BONNO
13

ABOUT THE AUTHOR

SUSAN SISKO CARTER has written teleplays for some of the major producers in television, and she is on the Writers Guild of America's list of 101 best written TV series. Her essays have been published in *Shondaland*, *LA Weekly* and *HuffPost*. An internationally acclaimed singer/songwriter, her recordings include albums for Verve and Epic. And she is working on a new album. Susan lives in Los Angeles. But spends as much time as possible in Paris.